DUBLIN ROGUE

STEPHANIE HARTE

B

Boldwood

First published in Great Britain in 2025 by Boldwood Books Ltd.

Copyright © Stephanie Harte, 2025

Cover Design by Colin Thomas

Cover Images: Colin Thomas

A CIP catalogue record for this book is available from the British Library.

Paperback ISBN 978-1-83533-210-8

Large Print ISBN 978-1-83533-211-5

Hardback ISBN 978-1-83533-209-2

Trade Paperback ISBN 978-1-80656-066-0

Ebook ISBN 978-1-83533-213-9

Kindle ISBN 978-1-83533-212-2

Audio CD ISBN 978-1-83533-204-7

MP3 CD ISBN 978-1-83533-205-4

Digital audio download ISBN 978-1-83533-208-5

This book is printed on certified sustainable paper. Boldwood Books is dedicated to putting sustainability at the heart of our business. For more information please visit https://www.boldwoodbooks.com/about-us/sustainability/

Boldwood Books Ltd, 23 Bowerdean Street, London, SW6 3TN

www.boldwoodbooks.com

To my Irish family and friends from Cobh and beyond.
This one's for you!

1

SEAN

London, October 1975

The rain lashed against my back as it washed the narrow side street in Mayfair. I pulled my flat cap lower down on my head and tucked my chin into the collar of my coat as I glanced over my shoulder. There wasn't a soul around, so I stopped outside the unassuming black door of the glazed brick building and pulled out the crowbar I had concealed inside my donkey jacket. As I tried to force open the only entrance to the ghost station, which had seen no passengers since 1932, muffled footsteps in the distance caught my attention. Flattening myself against the wet, ox-blood-red tiles, I waited to see who would emerge from the shadows.

'Sorry I'm late,' Niall said.

A dim amber glow illuminated my younger brother as he closed the gap between us. He'd just scared the shit out of me, but I'd never admit that to him. The sooner we got inside Down Street station and away from prying eyes, the better.

'What took you so long?' I asked.

The only way to get to the platform level was via the dusty spiral staircase. The lift had been out of service for a long time, so I switched on my torch to light the way down the hundred and twenty-plus steps.

'Philomena was acting up. She wasn't impressed that I was working on a Saturday night. She wanted me to take her to the pictures, so we had words over it,' Niall replied.

I stopped mid-step and turned around to glare at him while gripping the pitted metal handrail.

'That woman needs to be put in her place.'

Niall's girlfriend was a constant thorn in my side. An absolute pain in the arse. She had far too much control over him for my liking.

'She's got a point, though. Who wants to turn out to work when everyone else is getting drunk down the pub?' Niall questioned.

His penetrating eyes were black as coal.

'Enough of your whining. Everyone's replaceable, you know!' I barked.

Niall took heed of my warning and shuffled along in silence beside me as we paced along the walkway which led to the platform's entrance. Out of the corner of my eye, I could see his dark brown, collar-length curly hair take on a life of its own, bobbing up and down as he strode along, hands shoved into the front pockets of his flared jeans.

A labyrinth of disused tunnels lay buried beneath London's streets, which served as a secret meeting point for me and my associates. The underground economy that paid my bills was thriving, thanks to the financial struggles faced by working-class people in these uncertain times. One man's misfortune was another man's gain.

The faint rumble of traffic far above was a reminder that the city churned on, oblivious to what was happening below as Niall and I stood in silence, waiting for my shipment of whiskey smuggled from Ireland to arrive. Damp, musty air mixed with the metallic tang of rust. There was a strange atmosphere hovering around us tonight. A shiver ran down my spine, so I adjusted the collar of my coat. The chill from the tunnels was seeping into my bones. But it was more than the low temperature that made me feel uneasy. My wife's warning echoed in my head as the dim emergency lights flickered, casting eerie shadows on the mouldy tiles.

'Ducking and diving is a young man's game. Give it up before your luck runs out,' had been Josie's parting words as I'd left the house tonight.

The way Josie had been talking, anyone would think I was about to draw my pension. I was forty-two years old. In the prime of my life. At the top of the tree. Josie had done me a disservice talking that way. I had a huge advantage over my rivals. They were barely out of their teens. I had maturity on my side. With age comes wisdom. And I had it by the bucketload.

I'd like to say the way I made a living was easy money, but that wasn't true. My line of work carried risks. Big risks. Risks Josie wanted me to stop taking. But I wasn't about to listen to the little woman in-doors. I wouldn't work for a pittance like every other Tom, Dick or Harry. It was my destiny to keep the family business alive.

The drip of water from a leaking pipe was a form of torture as the minutes dragged by. We were in an open space, but I felt claustrophobic. My heart was hammering in my chest.

'Where the fuck are they?'

I glanced at my watch before peering into the sooty mouth of the tunnel. It was ten past midnight. Something was wrong. We usually carried out these operations with military precision.

'Is there any sign of them?' Niall asked, his voice bouncing off the tiled walls.

I was standing a few steps away from him, so he could see as well as I could, but I shook my head all the same before resting my right hand on the hilt of the crowbar tucked into my belt.

'They should've been here ten minutes ago.'

Niall crossed his arms around himself as his eyes scanned the shadows.

'Do you think the Kellys got wind of the shipment? Maybe we should...'

Before he could finish his sentence, the faintest sound of footsteps began to echo through the tunnel. I straightened my posture, my hand tightening again on the crowbar, ready to spring into action at a moment's notice. I could just make out a lantern bobbing in the distance, its light growing brighter. A short while later, a group of figures emerged from the darkness, pushing heavy trolleys laden with crates marked with faded Irish distillery logos. The squeaking of the wheels echoed in the cavernous space.

'About bloody time,' I muttered, stepping forward.

Paddy, a wiry man with a lopsided grin, led the group.

'Sorry, lads,' he said, his chest heaving from the exertion. 'Kelly's men were sniffing around the docks, so we had to take a bit of a detour to make the trail go cold.'

'Are you sure they didn't follow you?'

My eyes narrowed, but Paddy began shaking his head.

'No. I'm certain we lost them.'

'Let's hope you're right,' I said, stepping towards him. 'We've wasted enough time. I want to get out of here. Get the crates onto the truck as fast as you can.' My tone was sharp.

As Paddy's crew began transferring the whiskey from the trolleys to a concealed van parked near the service access point, the sound of heavy footsteps echoed again, this time from the opposite end of the tunnel. I froze; my heart was pounding. We might have given the Kellys the slip, but it looked like DCI Hargrove and the boys in blue had got wind of the handover. I'd had to grease that greedy bastard's palms countless times to get him to look the other way. Paying him off would put a big dent in my profit.

I moved quickly, positioning myself between Niall

and the sound. Being an overprotective older brother came naturally to me. We'd already lost Rory, our younger brother, to violence, so I wasn't about to let that happen twice.

From the shadows, several men emerged, their faces partially obscured by scarves. They weren't bobbies. They had to be Declan Kelly's men. The leader of the group, a broad-shouldered thug, stood grinning at me.

'Evenin', Sean. Fancy running into you down here.'

I took a step forward, adjusting my grip on the crowbar.

'You're trespassing,' I said.

I managed to keep my voice steady even though my pulse was racing.

The man laughed in my face before pulling a revolver from his coat.

'I'm doing no such thing. This is Kelly territory. Everything down here belongs to us—'

I didn't wait for the man to finish his threat. In one swift motion, I swung the crowbar, catching the guy's wrist, which sent the revolver clattering to the ground. Years of practice had made my movements precise. Chaos erupted as fists started to fly. Mainly mine. My bare-knuckle fighting days might be behind me, but I was still a handful. Thanks to my long reach and my six-foot-four, heavy-set frame, I had a height and weight advantage over Kelly's crew.

Out of the corner of my eye, I saw Niall grab a wooden plank discarded on the platform. He swung it with force, knocking one of Kelly's men off his feet.

While the commotion went on around them, Paddy's crew managed to load the last of the crates onto the truck.

'Go!' I shouted to Paddy as I felled the last attacker.

I turned around and faced my brother, who continued to grip the plank with all his might. He was breathless. Trembling from head to toe. Niall was as tall as a tree, but he hadn't yet filled out. A puff of wind would blow him over. He'd done the O'Connor name proud, though, and fought like a demon, which was to be expected as Celtic blood ran through his veins.

'You did well. Now let's get out of here.'

Niall threw down the plank and walked over to the truck, stepping over the pile of semi-conscious men lining the track. He climbed into the passenger seat, and his shoulders slumped as the adrenaline rush seeped out of him.

I jumped in beside my brother, resisting the urge

to boot the mouthy fucker with the revolver in the ribs as a parting gesture. As we emerged into the cold night air, I glanced at Niall, who seemed lost in his own world. The truck's engine rumbled low, a steady growl that matched the tension in my chest as I began easing it out of the alleyway behind the Mayfair townhouses.

'You OK?' I asked.

Niall turned towards me and nodded. 'What about you? You're bleeding,' he said, gesturing towards my knuckles.

'All in a day's work,' I replied.

'Do you think the Kellys will try and pull a stunt like that again?' Niall asked.

I smirked. 'Not if they know what's good for them, they won't.'

The words had barely left my mouth when the sound of gunfire echoed around us.

Dublin Rogue

2

JOSIE

The house was silent, save for the faint creak of the old wooden floors and the rhythmic ticking of the clock on the mantle. I sat by the window. The soft glow of a single lamp illuminated a small section of the room as I fingered my rosary beads. I'd had a bad feeling about tonight. Why hadn't Sean listened to me? Why was my husband so pig-headed? Only God knew.

I shook my head and let out a slow breath. That man would be the death of me! Sean could charm the birds from the trees. But his charm masked a darker side of his character. He was a natural-born fighter. He loved nothing more than beating other men to a pulp, but I shook that thought from my head. There was no point in dwelling on his past. It wasn't going to help.

'Hail Mary, full of grace...' I whispered, putting my all into the prayer as though the effort would influence the outcome.

The crystal beads clicked softly in my hands. The sound had become a comfort to me on nights like this. Nights when Sean was out in the shadows, risking everything for the family name. He'd say it was for our future. But we wouldn't have a future if he didn't come home. Why didn't he understand that?

I glanced at the clock. It was a quarter past two in the morning. He should have been back ages ago. My gaze shifted away from my rosary to the world outside my window. I got to my feet and pulled back the net curtains, craning my neck so my eyes could sweep up and down the street. It was quiet. No cars. No people. Only fog. It rolled along the pavement in thick waves, swallowing the glint of the street lamps, cloaking everything in its eerie mist. I could hear distant footfall carried on the wind, but it was too far away to be promising, so I let out a loud sigh and closed the heavy curtains to block out the view before I slumped back in my chair.

Sean, by his own admission, was a big lump. Six

foot four with hands like shovels. A force to be reckoned with. I'd give him that. My husband was tall, dark and handsome with the bluest eyes you've ever seen. He was more than a match for most men, but he wasn't indestructible. All it would take was one carefully aimed bullet or the slash of a knife against an artery, and it would be game over. Life was fragile.

After Rory had been killed in cold blood, I'd hoped Sean would rethink his ties to the family firm. I'd hoped his brother's sacrifice hadn't been in vain. I'd hoped I'd finally be able to convince him to walk away from all of it. Did he listen to a word I'd said? Of course not.

My nerves were shot to pieces. I couldn't take much more of this. Every faint murmur made my heart jump. I glanced down at the crucifix in my hand, ran my finger over the pale blue bead, and continued where I'd left off. Maybe by the time I'd finished another decade of the rosary, Sean would be sitting opposite me with a glass of Irish whiskey clutched in his hand, telling me I'd been worrying about nothing.

A faint knock at the door startled me. I froze, my fingers tightening on the rosary. It couldn't be Sean. He wouldn't knock; he had a key. The rapping came again louder this time. It was decisive. No longer hesitant. Uncertain. According to the clock on the mantlepiece, it was almost half past two. Nobody would be calling at this time for a social visit. My breath caught in my throat. I rose from my seat and reached for the iron poker resting by the fireplace as I moved towards the door.

'Who's there?' I called out.

My words appeared steady despite the pounding in my chest.

'It's me, Mrs O'Connor,' a familiar voice said.

I'd never been more delighted to hear Paddy's dulcet tones. I was petrified that the police were about to pay me a visit, but my relief was short-lived. What had brought Paddy here? And more importantly, why wasn't Sean with him? I opened the door just enough to get a glimpse of him, suddenly worried it might be a trap. He took off his cap and gave me a sheepish smile. His face was pale and drawn in the dim light, which made my stomach somersault.

'What's happened? Where's Sean?'

I fired the questions in quick succession, moving sideways to let him inside. Even at this unearthly hour of the morning, I didn't want to conduct private affairs on the doorstep. Paddy hesitated for a moment, his cap in his hands, before he accepted my invitation and stepped over the threshold.

'He's not back yet? I've just finished my shift at the

dockyard, so I thought I'd swing by and check he was OK,' Paddy replied.

'What's going on? What happened tonight? And don't leave anything out. I want the whole story.'

I threw Paddy a look. I could sense I wasn't going to like what he was going to say, but the sooner I knew the details, the better.

'It got messy at Down Street, missus. Kelly's men showed up. Sean told me to go...'

My heart sank. 'What do you mean it got messy?'

I narrowed my eyes. I had a feeling I already knew the answer to my question, but I asked it anyway while clinging to a tiny shred of hope.

Paddy shrugged.

'Sean seemed to be handling it. He's good with his fists. But they were outnumbered. At least one of Kelly's men had a revolver. I don't know if the others were armed...'

My wail cut Paddy off mid-flow. He looked startled and stared at me like a deer caught in the headlights. I could tell he felt awkward. Uncomfortable. He didn't want to be the bearer of bad news. But he had no reason to feel guilty. He was only doing what I'd asked.

'Sweet Jesus, have mercy on us!'

I clasped my hands together before looking up at the ceiling. The Lord worked in mysterious ways, and there couldn't be a better time for some divine intervention.

'Try not to worry. I'm sure the big fella's fine. He'll be home before you know it.'

Famous last words, I thought as I closed my eyes briefly, my grip tightening on the poker. Try not to worry. That was easy for Paddy to say. I'd like to think I knew my husband better than he did. When Sean was in the thick of it, fists swinging, adrenaline pumping, he was in his element. Something was wrong, or he'd have been home by now.

'Thanks for stopping by, Paddy,' I said, giving him his cue to leave.

'It's no bother,' Paddy replied, giving me a nod of the head.

'Get home safe,' I said as he walked down the garden path.

Paddy lifted his arm in acknowledgement.

'Will do, missus.'

I watched the fog swallow his silhouette before I closed and locked the door. Then I walked down the hall and planted myself back on the chair by the window. The rosary beads felt heavier in my hands as though they were laden with worry. I resumed my prayers. My voice was firmer now. Louder. As I willed my words to reach heaven faster. I felt lost. Hopeless. All I had were my prayers, my faith. But the gnawing fear that one day Sean wasn't going to come back was stronger than ever.

3

DECLAN

My South London headquarters were far from plush. The damp backroom above The Black Harp pub reeked of stale whiskey and cigarettes. But it served its purpose. Many a plan had been hatched within these walls.

I tore my eyes away from my men, leaned back in my chair and glanced up at the single bulb swaying slightly in the draught. The dim light cast long shadows across the scarred wooden table, which mirrored the battered faces of my trusted crew. That bastard, Sean O'Connor, had a lot to answer for.

The low hum of conversation from the bar below filtered through the floorboards as we prepared to debrief. My men were a sorry sight as they sat around the table, nursing drinks and licking their wounds from the skirmish in the tunnels.

'You've got some explaining to do. How come the ambush didn't go as planned?' My voice was cold.

Fergal, my right-hand man, squirmed in his seat as my eyes bore into his. His bottom lip was cut, and the right side of his face was bloodied and swollen. It was clear he'd taken a pasting on my behalf, but that didn't mean I'd cut him any slack. He was on company business, so getting into a scrap was par for the course. Giving me the silent treatment wasn't going to work. I wanted answers, and I wanted them now!

'Come on then. I'm still waiting to hear how Sean O'Connor walked out of the tunnel with the consignment of whiskey. You lot completely outnumbered him, and yet you let him get away...'

The men knew without me having to raise my voice that I was furious they'd ballsed everything up. Fergal flashed me a guilty look and then his gaze dropped from mine.

'Nothing went to plan. It was chaos, boss. All hell broke loose before we could stop it. Sean's a bloody animal. He disarmed me with a crowbar before I had a chance to use the revolver on him, and his brother started battering our lads. I managed to fire some shots at the truck when he was driving away...' Fergal blabbed before coming up for air.

My jaw tightened. I picked up my glass and swallowed down the contents. Then I put it down on the table.

'What was the point of firing at him when he was driving away?' I said, shoving my chair away from the table and getting up in Fergal's face.

The sound of the legs scraping the floor silenced the murmurs that had been circulating the room.

'I was hoping to hit Sean or Niall,' Fergal replied as he nursed his injured hand.

'You were hoping you were going to hit one of the O'Connors, were you?' I mocked. 'You're pathetic! If you weren't going to shoot him while he was standing six feet away from you, there was no point bothering to aim at a moving target, was there?'

'I definitely hit the truck, boss. More than once. Didn't I, lads?'

Fergal cast his eyes around the room, hoping one of my men would back him up, but none of them wanted to get involved, so he went back to fighting his own battle.

'Who's to say Sean and Niall aren't lying dead in pools of blood as we speak?'

Fergal was riled up, but I didn't appreciate him using an angry tone with me.

'I can tell you now that won't be the case. You had one job to do, intercept the shipment, and you cocked it up. Now O'Connor's sitting on a small fortune, and we've got nothing to show for tonight's work but bruises and bloodstains.'

My mood had darkened. I turned to my younger brother, Aidan, who was leaning casually against the wall, a smirk playing on his lips.

'What are you so happy about? Got anything useful to add?'

Aidan shrugged and pushed himself away from the wall.

'Maybe next time, you shouldn't put lads on the team who can't handle a fight. O'Connor's a tough bastard. You know what he's like,' my brother replied, attempting to lay the blame for the fiasco at my feet.

'Excuses. That's all I ever hear from you lot.'

I pointed at each of my battered men in turn.

'Sean's tough all right, but he's not invincible. He's just as vulnerable as the rest of us.'

'If you think you could have done any better, why don't you lead the next ambush and show us how it's done?' Aidan smirked.

The cheeky little fucker was trying to make me

look bad in front of my crew. I had nothing to prove. I was the brains of the operation; I didn't get my hands dirty.

'If you know what's good for you, you'll shut your trap before I shut it for you,' I said before turning my attention back to Fergal. 'What's going on at the docks? Any sign of their next move?'

Fergal shook his head.

'No, boss. The O'Connors are keeping their cards close to their chests. But I've got blokes asking around. I'm confident that when another shipment's about to come in from Ireland, we'll hear about it.'

I slowly nodded. My anger was starting to wane, but it would be a while before it stopped simmering beneath the surface.

'Good. Because this isn't over. I'm not letting this slide. The O'Connors will think they've got the upper hand now, but they've just made the biggest mistake of their lives. We're going to hit them where it hurts, hard and fast. And the next time we strike, we won't miss. We'll make sure it's the last time they ever cross us. I won't tolerate failure like this again.'

I paused, letting the words hang in the air. My authority was absolute, but the shadow of tonight's cock up lingered heavily. My gaze swept across the room, piercing each man in turn. My men exchanged uneasy glances, but none of them dared to question me. My word was law, and they knew better than to challenge it.

'Fergal, get that hand sorted. I need you fighting fit,' I said.

He smiled, grateful for the reprieve.

'Will do, boss.'

I stepped away from the table, my shoes thudding against the worn wooden floorboards as I moved towards the window. The muffled noise of the pub below carried on, oblivious to the plans brewing above. I stared out at the city lights, my reflection faint in the glass.

'Sean O'Connor thinks he's won,' I murmured, more to myself than the room. But he'd just given me the motivation I needed to bring him to his knees. I turned to Aidan, my expression hardening once more.

'O'Connor's not getting the better of us again. Get it sorted. I want every angle covered and plans drawn up by morning so we're ready when his next shipment arrives.'

Aidan gave a sharp nod, the fire of anticipation glinting in his eyes.

'Consider it done.'

The men around the table were lost in thought, each absorbing the weight of what lay ahead.

'Fergal, make sure we've got enough muscle for the job. No screw-ups this time.'

I threw him a look, and Fergal grimaced.

'Understood, boss.'

'I'll give Sean and Niall a night to celebrate before we show them what real trouble looks like. From now on, it's war!'

Eyes darted from left to right, but no one dared voice their concerns aloud. They all knew the next encounter had to be flawless.

'The O'Connors have got too comfortable. They think they're untouchable. We'll show them just how wrong they are. No more games. When we strike, it'll be final. Aidan, Fergal, be ready. This isn't ending until all the smuggling routes belong to us and we're the only ones left standing.'

The room fell silent as I picked up the bottle of Irish whiskey and topped up my glass, raising it slightly, the amber liquid glinting in the dim light.

'To the Kellys. To victory. And to finishing this once and for all.'

My voice was steely and resolute.

My men raised their glasses to echo my toast, but the tension in the air was palpable. I had a reputation for being a hard bastard. My wrath was as much a motivator as it was a warning. I didn't need to spell it out to the crew. They knew failure was not an option a second time.

The backroom was shrouded in smoke as I dropped back in my seat and leaned over the table. My fingers traced the worn map of London laid out before me. The O'Connors were celebrating their win. But in the not-too-distant future, they'd have no reason to celebrate at all. Imagining the chaos my lads would unleash made me grin. Sean and Niall might have won this round, but the war was far from over.

4

SEAN

That was another close call. I'd had to boot it along the narrow lane behind the station, tyres screeching as the truck sped away from the access point. I gripped the wheel tightly, glancing in the rearview mirror every thirty seconds to check we weren't being followed. Much to my relief, the alleyway was empty, except for the faint yellow glow of street lamps casting jagged shadows across the cobblestones. The shooter had disappeared back inside the tunnels, having spent the ammunition in his gun. Luckily for us, he was a terrible shot and couldn't hit a cow's arse with a banjo!

The crates of whiskey hidden beneath a tarp in

the back rattled as I turned onto the main road. Mayfair was quiet at this hour. The symmetrical Georgian terraces looked regal in the muted light. This wasn't the sort of place for chaos. Not openly, anyway. But I knew the truth. Behind those immaculate front doors where wealthy people lived, deals were struck, alliances were forged, and secrets were hidden.

I adjusted my flat cap so the brim shaded my eyes as we passed a lone constable on the street corner. Despite the early hour, we needed to look like delivery men on a routine job. The bobby barely glanced our way, but that didn't stop my heart from thudding harder in my chest. If he'd pulled the truck over, he'd have discovered the cargo I was carrying.

The streets widened as we moved towards Marble Arch. The truck's tyres clattered over the uneven paving, which knocked the bottles together. The lights of the West End gleaming faintly in the distance drew my eyes towards them, but I stayed focused and kept my speed steady. I didn't want to give the cops any excuse to stop me before I reached Kilburn. It wasn't far, but disaster could still strike. A sudden checkpoint or a wandering drunk stumbling into the road could unravel everything.

I turned onto the Edgware Road, which was still bustling even at this hour. I'd chosen this route on purpose. The activity made it easier to blend in, but it also meant there were more eyes. Too many eyes for my liking.

A flash of headlights in my side mirror made me tense. A black car pulled out of a side street and drove a short distance behind us. Was it following us? My grip on the wheel tightened again, and my pulse quickened.

'Don't let ideas get inside your head and run away with themselves, or you'll lose control of your common sense,' I muttered to myself.

I eased my foot onto the brake as I approached a set of traffic lights. Glancing into the rearview mirror, I could see the black car slowing, keeping its distance but matching my pace. My jaw clenched. Were Kelly's men tailing us? If they were, I'd have to give them the slip before reaching Kilburn. I couldn't afford to lead trouble to the drop-off point.

As the light turned green, I veered left onto a side street without indicating. The truck's tyres screeched on the slick asphalt. The road was narrow, flanked by rows of terraced houses, mainly in darkness; some had hazy glows at the windows. I thought the car had gone straight on, but its headlights reappeared as it rounded the corner.

'For fuck's sake!' I shouted, slamming my hand down on the steering wheel.

Niall's head snapped towards me.

'What's wrong?' he asked with fear in his young eyes.

'I think the Kellys are following us.'

My mind raced. I could try to outrun them, but the truck wasn't built for speed. Besides, the whiskey bottles in the back needed careful handling. So I'd have to find a different solution.

'What are you going to do?'

Niall fidgeted in his seat while he waited for me to reply.

'I'll take a detour and see if I shake them off.'

At the next junction, I took a sharp right, then turned into a narrower lane barely wide enough for the truck. It was a gamble; if the car followed us, it would confirm my suspicions. I stole a glance in the mirror as we emerged onto a wider street; no sign of the black car. Relief washed over me, but I knew better than to relax. I'd been in this game long enough to know that danger had a way of lurking where you least expected it.

I kept my speed steady as I drew closer. I'd memorised the drop-off point and rehearsed the handover in my head a dozen times, but plans had a funny way of falling apart when it mattered most. I'd not sold whiskey to this contact before, and I was beginning to wonder if this was a set-up. There was only one way to find out.

The rendezvous was an unassuming yard behind a row of shops, shielded from view by a high wooden gate down a side street in Maida Vale. I killed the engine and stepped outside. The place was deserted. Everything was quiet. Had the opportunity to shift some of the booze passed me by? Time and tide wait for no man. I was just about to get back in the truck when a figure emerged from the shadows, his silhouette sharp against the faint light leaking from a nearby window.

'You're late,' he said. His accent was thick with a northern lilt.

'I ran into a bit of trouble,' I replied.

Then I walked around to the back of the truck and pulled back the tarp. The liquid amber gleamed under the street lamp's glow. The man stepped closer to inspect the cargo, lifting a bottle of whiskey from one of the crates. He nodded and grunted in approval.

'This looks good. Real good,' he said.

I allowed myself a brief smile, but the tension in

my shoulders didn't ease. I wouldn't relax until the truck was empty and I had a glass of the latest batch in my hand.

'Only the finest Killarney grain goes into making it,' I said, beaming with pride.

The deal wasn't done yet. No money had changed hands, but it was close enough that I could imagine the weight of the reward in my pocket.

'It's all there,' the man said, handing me a wad of rolled-up notes secured with an elastic band.

I knew I should count it properly. But I was still rattled by the Kellys' ambush. I wanted to get back on my turf sooner rather than later and unload the rest of the shipment. I quickly thumbed through the cash while he loaded two crates into his van. It looked about right, so I shook the man by the hand.

'Nice doing business with you,' I said.

'Likewise,' he replied.

I jumped back into my truck and fired up the engine. We were on the home stretch. By the time we crossed into Kilburn a short while later, the streets had taken on a different character. The polished homes of Mayfair and Marylebone were long behind us, replaced by rows of brick buildings, their exteriors worn but alive with the buzz of working-class life.

* * *

I leaned against the bar in the dimly lit speakeasy, a smile playing on my lips as I surveyed my domain. We'd had a close call tonight, so we needed to let off some steam before heading to our respective homes.

The hidden room in Kilburn was alive with energy. The air was thick with smoke, celebratory chatter, clinking of glasses and bursts of laughter, which was a tonic to the senses. Watching people enjoying the finest whiskey and poitín Ireland had to offer reminded me why I risked life and limb to bring it to these shores. It was plain to see the men in County Kilburn appreciated the effort Sean O'Connor was making. There was nothing quite like the taste of home.

My speakeasy was tucked beneath an unassuming butcher's shop, its entrance hidden behind a steel door. Entry to my establishment required a specific knock. Inside, the space blended grit and charm. A mahogany bar stretched along one wall, polished to a shine despite its age. Flickering lanterns illuminated the large selection of whiskey and poitín which lined the shelves behind it. Mismatched tables and chairs filled the room, their scratches and dents holding secrets of countless nights like this one.

The mood in the speakeasy was mellow, but as the hours ticked by, I couldn't shake the unease gnawing at the edges of my mind. Declan Kelly wouldn't let tonight's humiliation go unanswered. He wasn't going to let this slide. This wasn't the time to dwell on it, so I pushed the thought from my head and raised my glass.

'To the O'Connors! To victory and the finest whiskey in London!' I said, my voice cutting through the din.

A cheer erupted from the crowd. Niall came to stand beside me, his face flushed with drink and pride.

'You did it again, Sean,' he said, clapping me on the back. 'The Kellys didn't know what hit them when you tore into them.'

I turned to face my brother and grinned, my bruised knuckles sore as I gripped the glass.

'I couldn't have done it without you, Niall.'

He smiled back, buoyed up by the compliment.

'I don't know about that, but one thing's certain – the Kellys will be licking their wounds for a while yet.'

'You're right about that, but don't think they won't strike back. Let's not worry about that now, though. Tonight is for celebrating!'

I raised my glass again, and Niall clinked his

against the tumbler. For now, surrounded by the warmth of my people and the taste of hard-won success, I'd allow myself to enjoy the moment. The fight was far from over, but we'd reclaimed our place as London's kings of the underground, so we should enjoy it while it lasted.

5

JOSIE

The clock on the mantlepiece struck four. The chimes echoed through the silent house, reminding me of how long I'd been waiting. I sat rigid in the chair by the dimly lit fireplace, my rosary beads slipping between my fingers, my whispered prayers barely louder than the faint crackle of the dying embers. A feeling of dread swirled inside me. Worry had wrapped itself around me like a creeping vine and was suffocating the life out of me.

'Hail Mary, full of grace...' I murmured, though my mind struggled to focus on the words.

Where was Sean? What was keeping him? Either something had gone wrong, or he was with one of his whores. Tears threatened to fall, but I sniffed them back. Crying would solve nothing. A lump formed in my throat, but I swallowed it down and closed my eyes.

The wind suddenly rattled the windowpanes, startling me. I got to my feet, pulled back the net curtain and peered out. The street light outside the house flickered weakly against the thick London fog. Every distant footstep made my heart lurch, but just as I got my hopes up, the sound faded into nothing, leaving me in agonising uncertainty again. I clutched the rosary tighter as anxiety gripped me.

I tore myself from the window and sat back in the chair. The warmth of the fire was fading, but the glow from the almost spent coals was hypnotic. I'd spent nights like this before and it never got easier. The fear never lessened. Every time Sean walked out that door, there was a chance he might not come back.

Just as the tension became unbearable, a noise from the street sent my heart galloping. A heavy set of footsteps, steady and familiar, made me bolt upright. I held my breath and listened. There were boots on the steps outside, the sound of a key scraping against the lock. I shot to my feet just as the front door swung open.

Sean stood in the dim light, his broad frame filling the doorway. His coat was damp. His knuckles were raw and bloodied, but his smile was intact. The scent of whiskey, smoke and danger clung to him like a second skin. I exhaled sharply, pressing a hand to my chest as relief warred with fury.

'Lord in heaven, preserve us!' I blew out a breath and rushed towards him. 'Do you know what time it is? I thought you were de—' I stopped myself from saying the word. 'I've been so worried. I thought this was the night you weren't going to come home.' My voice cracked with emotion.

'Ah, Josie, I'm sorry. I didn't mean to worry you, love,' Sean replied, and the smile slipped from his face.

Sean turned away from me, shut the front door and locked it before facing me again. He took a step closer and brushed a calloused hand over my cheek.

'Don't be angry with me,' he said quietly. 'I know it's late, but I got caught up...'

I scoffed, stepping back from my husband and folding my arms tightly against my chest.

'Caught up,' I repeated. 'I'm not stupid, Sean. It's clear you've been brawling, and you stink of booze and fags, and all you've got to say for yourself is you got caught up?'

My anger manifested in a half-laugh, half-sob.

Sean sighed and ran a hand through his damp hair. His usual smirk was absent.

'We had a rough time tonight. Kelly's lads showed up at the tunnels. We handled it, but there was an almighty scrap,' he said by way of explanation.

My stomach flipped.

'You handled it? It doesn't look like you handled it! This is what happens when you smuggle whiskey under the Kellys' noses.'

'It's just a few bruises, nothing serious.'

Sean attempted to reassure me, but the cut on his lip and the dried blood on his knuckles told a different story.

'For the love of God, why don't you get a different job? A safe job. Talk to the brewery about taking on The Bald Faced Stag. The publican's retiring, and you'd be a great replacement. You have a nice way about you.'

'Ahh, now, stop with the flattery. It'll get you nowhere. Smuggling is all I know. It's in my blood and my family's done it for generations. You can't ask me to give it up.' Sean flashed me a smile.

I closed my eyes and gripped my rosary so tightly I thought the crystal beads might snap.

'One day, Sean, it won't just be bruises. Mark my words.'

Sean reached for me again. I scowled at him, but he took no notice and pulled me into his arms. At first, I resisted, but his warmth and the solid weight of his presence soon broke my resolve. I rested my head against his chest and felt the steady thrum of his heartbeat beneath my cheek. His arms tightened around me. I should be grateful for small mercies. He was home. He was alive, for now.

Sean had a gift. He always managed to talk me around. Always managed to gloss over situations. Always managed to play down close calls. But ever since the Kellys had killed Rory over a turf war, I'd had a bad feeling about the way my husband made a living.

I wriggled out of Sean's embrace and stared up at his handsome face as he towered over me.

'You're an idiot for taking on the Kellys, you know that, don't you?' I said. I couldn't hide the tremble in my voice.

'But I'm your idiot,' Sean replied.

His voice was playful and he had a twinkle in his blue eyes. I put my hands on my hips and glared at him.

'I know what you're doing. You're playing things down so you can get off the subject.'

Sean let out a loud sigh.

'I don't want you to worry, Josie. I'm always going to come home to you.'

My eyes narrowed.

'One of these days, I'm scared you won't.'

'That day'll never come.'

'And if it does, what am I supposed to do? How am I meant to raise Orla on my own? If you won't do it for me, do it for your daughter. I'm begging you, Sean.'

My husband pulled me back into his arms and tilted my chin up. His gaze was intense.

'I'll have no more talk of this. I promise you, Josie, nothing's going to happen to me,' he murmured.

He kissed the side of my neck, sending tingles through my body, and then he buried his face into my hair. I tightened my arms around him.

'Don't make promises you can't keep.'

'I won't, swear to God,' Sean replied.

As much as I wanted to believe him, the fear lingering in my chest wouldn't let me.

We stayed wrapped in each other's arms for the longest moment. I let the comfort his hug brought me take my worries away, if only for a little while. The world outside was momentarily forgotten. But deep in my bones, I sensed that this war with the Kellys would bring more heartache our way. My faith was strong, but I was terrified my prayers wouldn't be enough to keep Sean safe in the long run.

6

REGGIE

I hammered on the weather-worn door with my sizable fist, then immediately flipped the letterbox. I was a busy man. I didn't have all day to hang about.

'Mrs O'Hara! How long are you going to make me stand out here? You'd better open the door right now if you know what's good for you!' I bellowed at the top of my voice.

I saw the curtain to the left of the entrance twitch, and a beady eye met mine. The figure jumped back in alarm, letting the once-white nets fall back into place. I glanced behind me and nodded to Freddie, one of my men, a brute of a man with a crooked nose and a mean glint in his eye. A moment later, I heard footsteps approaching.

'Hello, Mr Bennett,' Mary O'Hara said.

She swept a few unruly strands of dark hair, which had escaped from a loose bun, away from her sharp, high-cheekboned face as she stood to one side, allowing me to pass.

It was obvious the woman was skint. She was wearing a well-worn cardigan and dress with a stained pinafore tied around her middle, but that wouldn't stop me from laying the law down. I was known for my brutal tactics and disdain for outsiders.

I gestured to Freddie to follow before I stepped inside. My heavy boots left muddy imprints on the ageing lino as I led the way to the front room. I cast my eyes around the dingy place. It was plain to see it was in a bad state of repair, but it was still too good for the likes of the Irish scum residing here. The damp walls of the small Kilburn flat had paper peeling from them, the floral pattern faded from years of neglect. The air was thick with the scent of boiled cabbage and half-dried garments hanging on a wooden clothes horse in the corner of the room.

'Timmy, Erin, keep out of the way while I speak to Mr Bennett,' Mary said with an undertone of panic in her voice.

The two scrawny-looking children scurried off to the other side of the room and flattened themselves against the wall like they were lining up for the firing squad. Now there was an idea!

'So have you got my money, Mrs O'Hara?' I asked, getting straight to the point.

Mary exchanged a glance with Timmy, who couldn't have been more than twelve but already understood too much of the world. His slight frame was tensed like a coiled wire as he glared at me. Brazen little fucker.

'I'm sorry, Mr Bennett, I just need a little more time.' Mary straightened her back and clasped her hands in front of her, no doubt to keep them from shaking.

I shook my head as I surveyed the cramped living space.

'Mary, Mary, Mary. Time's a luxury, and you've had more than enough of it.'

My gaze flicked to Timmy and his little sister Erin, who stood in silence, staring at me, freckled-faced and wide-eyed.

'Please, Mr Bennett...'

I lifted my hand to cut her off mid-flow.

'You owe rent, so you either need to pay or get out.'

Mary folded her arms across her chest in a show of resistance.

'But where would we go? This is our home. My husband—'

'Is dead,' I interrupted, then I stepped closer, grabbed hold of the front of her dress and got up in her face. 'Plenty of families would be grateful for a roof over their heads. So, this is your last chance. You get hold of the money I'm owed, or you leave. Simple as that.' My voice had a menacing edge to it.

I could see Mary's bottom lip trembling, but she kept her chin up. Defiant. So I gave her a clatter around the face to teach her a lesson. Her kids wailed as her cheek blew up instantly. I could practically see it throbbing in time with her heartbeat, but she didn't waver. She stared at me with her green cats' eyes. Unblinking. Focused. She was trying to put on a brave face, but Mary was no match for me. She needed reminding of that. I reached into my coat pocket and pulled out a small silver Zippo lighter. With a flick of the spark wheel, the tiny flame danced in the dim room. My eyes met hers, cold and unforgiving.

'You know, Mary, accidents happen in old buildings like this. Gas leaks. Fires. People get hurt...' I let my sentence trail off as I snapped the lighter shut with a metallic click and tucked it away. 'We wouldn't want anything to happen to you or your lovely children, would we?'

Erin whimpered, burying her face into Timmy's side. The boy glared at me, his bony hands balled into tiny fists.

'You leave us alone,' he spat.

I let out a laugh, walked over to where he was making his stand and ruffled his hair in mock affection.

'He's a feisty little bastard, ain't he?' Then I turned my attention back to Mary. 'You've got until next week. After that... well, let's just say I'd hate to see this place go up in smoke.'

Mary's legs nearly gave out, but she managed to hold herself up by gripping the edge of the table. Erin sniffled and buried her head further into her brother's side. They were a sorry sight, but I was short on sympathy. Scenes like this were all too familiar in my line of work.

I smirked at Mary, and then I strolled out of the shithole, my brute of a companion following me like a well-trained dog. When the front door clicked shut, it left behind shocked faces and a silence thick with fear.

7

JOSIE

My spirits lifted as I climbed the stone steps leading to the Catholic church in Kilburn. I wasted no time pushing open the heavy oak door and dipping my fingers into the holy water, crossing myself before I went inside. Rows of flickering candles on either side of the altar beckoned me towards them.

I slid into a worn wooden pew near the front and glanced up at the stained-glass windows casting fractured light onto the walls. The tranquillity calmed my nerves instantly. St Jude's was my haven.

I lowered myself onto the padded kneeler, closed my eyes and bowed my head in prayer while letting my rosary beads slip through my fingers. The week's stress pressed down on me like the lace headscarf covering my hair. I needed a moment of peace. A moment where I wasn't worrying about Sean's bruised knuckles and bloodied face.

As I prayed, I felt somebody kneel on the cushion next to me. But I paid no attention to their presence until a soft voice interrupted my thoughts.

'Josie? Josie?'

I opened my eyes and turned my head. Mary O'Hara was in the pew next to me, wrapped in a threadbare wool coat with her hands clasped tightly before her. Her face, framed by the lace of her mantilla, was pale and lined with worry. She looked smaller than usual as if the weight of her troubles had shrunk her thin frame.

'Oh, hello, Mary.'

Sensing she wanted to talk, I got off my knees and sat on the wooden bench. Mary hesitated for a moment before she followed my lead. She wrung her hands together as they lay in her lap. But instead of speaking, she sat in silence for a long moment, the murmurs of the other parishioners in the background filling the space between us.

'Is everything all right?' I asked when I noticed the purple bruise on her cheek.

'He's been back again, Josie.' Mary's voice was barely above a whisper.

'Reggie Bennett?'

Mary nodded, her fingers tightening over each other until her knuckles went white. I put my hand on top of hers in a show of compassion.

'I'm guessing he did that?' I gently moved the lace away from Mary's face so that I could inspect her injury.

'He stopped by again yesterday,' Mary replied, avoiding answering my question. 'He told me I'd be out by the month's end if I didn't pay him what was due. How am I meant to find the money? He's doubled the rent since last year.' Mary's breath hitched. 'Me and the kids have got nowhere to go...'

My jaw clenched. I knew how men like Reggie operated. They squeezed every last penny out of those who had nothing, using fear like a hammer to break them down. Mary O'Hara was a proud woman in her late thirties, with the weary grace of someone who'd spent a lifetime fighting battles she'd never asked for. She'd been left widowed after her husband died in a factory accident. Raising two young children alone was tough. God love her. She was an easy target. No man in the household meant no protection. And that was exactly what Reggie Bennett was counting on.

'There must be something we can do. He can't just

put you out on the street...' My lips pressed into a thin line.

Mary's wide, tear-filled eyes met mine.

'What can I do, Josie? I don't have the money to pay him off. I barely make enough to feed Timmy and Erin as it is.' She swallowed hard, her voice thick with shame. 'I asked the parish for help, but when I mentioned it to Father Riley, he said the church can't interfere in such matters.'

Silent tears rolled down Mary's gaunt face. My heart bled for her. God forgive me for thinking this, but it was typical that the church wouldn't get involved. They'd offer prayers and pity, but when it came to men like Reggie Bennett, prayers weren't enough.

'Now you listen to me.' My voice was steady. Firm. 'You're not alone in this. I won't let that man make you and the children homeless.'

Mary's lips parted, and her eyes darted around as if she was scared someone would overhear us.

'I don't want no trouble—'

'There won't be any trouble,' I interrupted. 'Not for you anyway.'

Mary studied me for a long moment, her expression hovering between fear and hope.

'I don't know what I'd do without you, Josie.'

I squeezed her hands before releasing them and gave her a reassuring smile before turning away and staring ahead at the flickering candles near the Virgin Mary's statue. My mind was already working over-time. Reggie Bennett had made a mistake thinking Mary had no one to stand up for her.

8

SEAN

The stench of sweat, beer and blood lingered in the air of the smoky, dimly lit basement beneath an old East London pub. The crowd were rowdy, packed shoulder to shoulder, shouting over one another as they threw down bets. In the centre of the cellar, a crude pit had been marked out with chicken wire.

I stood near the edge of the makeshift ring. My fists curled in my coat pockets as my eyes flicked across the room, taking in the gamblers, the bookies and the drunks. This was the kind of place where a man could get into trouble if he wasn't careful. They were a rough crowd. I wasn't worried, though. I'd keep my wits about me. I'd scrapped in worse places.

Reggie Bennett lounged against a post, smirking

through a thick plume of cigar smoke on the other side of the pit. He was a stocky, broad-shouldered man with the swagger of someone who thought he owned the world, or at least a good chunk of Kilburn. Gold rings flashed on his stubby fingers. He was in his mid-forties, but he wasn't in good shape. His ruddy face was lined from years of smoking and drinking, and his three-piece suit couldn't hide the belly beneath it.

Bennett was a mean bastard. The kind who'd built his empire by squeezing the last drop from the desperate and kicking the needy who were already on the ground. He thrived in the cracks of society, where power was taken, not earned. He made up the terms as he went along. His business dealings never made it onto official records.

Reggie caught my eye and grinned, then raised his drink in a mock salute.

'Didn't think this was your scene, O'Connor,' he called over the noise in his heavy East End accent. 'Are you here to lose some money? I'll happily empty your pockets.'

I moved through the crowd, my presence cutting a path without effort. I stopped short of Reggie, but I was close enough to smell the alcohol on his breath.

'I don't bet on fights I know are fixed.'

Reggie chuckled, swirling the last of his drink around in the glass.

'Fixed? That's a serious accusation, Sean. Are you saying I'm a cheat?'

'I'm saying you're a greedy bastard, and there's no way you'd let a fight go ahead unless you knew who was going to win.'

Reggie exhaled a large cloud of smoke. The grin never left his face.

'That's business! There's no point rolling the dice if you don't load them first.' He jerked his head towards the two battered gamecocks, sizing each other up. Their beady eyes were sharp with aggression. 'Some of the mugs in here will bet their last quid on a dream. It's not my fault if they wake up broke.'

'You do more than just rig fights, though. Don't you, Bennett?'

Reggie abruptly lost my attention when I heard the crowd roar. One of the birds had lunged; its beak tore through its opponent's flesh. Feathers scattered. Blood spurted. Coins and notes exchanged hands.

'Jesus, Mary and Joseph,' an old man cursed, picturing his bet going up in smoke.

I turned to face Reggie and kept my gaze locked on his.

'I know you've been leaning on Mary O'Hara.'

I looked daggers at him. My temper had spiked.

Reggie let out a sharp laugh.

'So that's what this is about.' He leaned in and lowered his voice. 'That bitch owes me a lot of money, Sean. She's got no husband, and no way of paying me back any time soon on the pittance she earns scrubbing people's floors. Do you think I'm running a charity?'

My jaw tightened. I was one step away from swinging for the bloke.

'You stay away from her. You hear me?'

Reggie clicked his tongue.

'Or what? Are you going to start something in here? In my domain?' He looked around at his oversized goons lining the perimeter of the basement and spread his arms wide, inviting the challenge. 'Come on then, Sean. I dare you to throw the first punch. And let's see if you make it out of that door.'

Reggie eyeballed me, but I didn't bite. I simply smiled.

'The problem with you is that you always bet on a sure thing. That's your weakness.'

Reggie narrowed his eyes.

'What's that supposed to mean?'

I turned away from him and walked back towards

the crowd. As I passed the pit, I flicked a glance at the bookie.

'Put me down for a grand on the underdog.'

Reggie's face darkened. He turned back to the ring just as the smaller, weaker bird, his supposed loser, found its fighting spirit and lashed out in desperate fury. There was some frantic crowing followed by a final screech. Then silence descended over the onlookers.

The crowd erupted. Their outrage was palpable. I didn't stop to watch. I was already on my way to collect my winnings. Then I headed for the door, leaving Reggie to stew in the loss. Some fights were won with fists. Others with patience. And some with a simple, well-placed bet. I'd walked away from the cock fight with four grand more in my pocket than I'd had at the start of the day.

* * *

The stairwell smelled of mildew and piss. This was the kind of place where people learned to keep their heads down and their business to themselves. It was depressing. Not a good location to raise a family.

I rapped my knuckles against the door, glancing over my shoulder out of habit. Then my fingers traced the outline of the envelope in my pocket, pressing against my ribs. A shuffling sound came from inside.

'Who is it?' a soft voice called out.

'Sean O'Connor,' I replied before the door creaked open a fraction.

Wide, wary eyes peered up at me.

'Hello, Mr O'Connor?'

Timmy O'Hara had the slenderness that youth afforded. His cheeks were hollow with hunger, and a mop of dark hair fell into his eyes.

I gave him a small smile.

'Hello, son. Is your ma home?'

Timmy hesitated before he replied. 'She's making dinner.' He pulled the door open a little wider. 'Mr O'Connor's at the door,' he shouted down the hall.

A moment later, Mary O'Hara appeared in the kitchen doorway, a faded cardigan wrapped tightly around her frail frame. The lines of worry etched deep into her face eased slightly when she saw me. Erin, no older than six, peeked at me from behind her mother's skirt, her big, round blue eyes full of quiet curiosity. She was small, delicate-looking, with dark brown curls framing a heart-shaped face.

'Sean.' Mary smiled. 'What brings you here? Come in, come in.'

Mary wiped her hands down the front of her

pinny before beckoning me into the hall. I stepped inside. The conditions in the flat weren't that different to the damp outside.

Mary led the way into the front room. It wasn't much, a small space with mismatched furniture, a threadbare rug barely covering the splintered floorboards. The wind rattled the windowpanes, making the thin curtains flap. They were doing a bad job of blocking out the chill. A single lamp flickered in the corner, casting long shadows against the peeling wallpaper.

'I'm sorry to call unannounced,' I said, pulling off my flat cap and rubbing the back of my neck. 'I don't want to keep you from your dinner.'

'It's nothing much. Just some mince and spuds, but you're welcome to join us,' Mary offered, happy to share what little she had with an uninvited guest.

'That's very kind of you, but I have to get back. Josie will be wondering what's keeping me.'

'Fair enough,' Mary replied, no doubt relieved she didn't have another mouth to feed.

'Josie told me about your trouble with Bennett...'

Mary cast her eyes to the floor. I hadn't come here to embarrass the woman, so I'd get straight to the point.

'I have something for you.'

Mary looked up at me and frowned.

I reached into my donkey jacket and pulled out an envelope thick with banknotes.

'This is for you. Next time Reggie comes knocking at your door demanding cash, you'll be able to give him what you owe,' I said, holding it out to her.

Mary's breath hitched. She didn't reach for the envelope.

'Sean, I can't take that.'

'You can, and you will. I insist,' I cut in, my voice gentle but firm. 'He's been leaning on you long enough. This'll cover what he's asking and then some.'

I took a step towards Mary. Her hands trembled as she inched closer to the envelope. Her movement was hesitant, as though touching the money might make it disappear. She stared at the packet for the longest moment. When she finally opened it, her eyes widened at the sight of the cash inside.

'This is too much. I don't know what to say, Sean,' Mary whispered, shaking her head. 'I'll pay you back every penny.'

I shook my head. 'There's no need.' I glanced at Timmy and Erin. The way they watched me with quiet, hungry eyes tugged at my heartstrings. 'I've got no use for it sitting in my pocket. Better that it helps keep a roof over your head.'

Mary pressed a hand to her mouth, blinking rapidly. When she looked back up at me, there were tears in her eyes and something raw in her expression: gratitude, relief, maybe even disbelief.

'Did Josie put you up to this?' she asked, a small, wry smile breaking through as she waved the envelope at me.

I chuckled. 'She doesn't know yet. But she'll tell me I did the right thing when she finds out. She was worried sick about you and the little ones.'

'I've been so scared, Sean. I didn't tell Josie the half of it. But before Reggie left, he threatened to burn down the flat.'

'He did what?'

'I know, I could barely believe what I was hearing.' Mary shook her head.

'Jesus. That man is pure evil. Taking advantage of a family in a vulnerable position would be a step too far in most people's books. But not Reggie's. Never be too proud to accept help when it's offered to you,' I said, staring into Mary's green eyes.

'You're good people, you and Josie. Salt of the earth.' Mary let out a watery laugh, swiping at her eyes before looking down at Erin. 'What do you say to Mr O'Connor?'

Erin glanced up at me, clutching a well-worn stuffed rabbit in her small hand while clinging onto her mother's skirt with the other.

'Thank you,' she murmured in a tiny voice barely above a whisper.

I crouched down, resting my forearms on my knees, and stared into her freckled face.

'No need to thank me, sweetheart. Just make sure you're a good girl for your ma.'

Erin nodded solemnly. The poor little mite wore the worry of a child who'd spent too much time watching the world instead of playing in it. I straightened myself and slipped my cap back on.

'Thanks for your generosity, Mr O'Connor,' Timmy said without being prompted.

'Not a bother,' I replied, ruffling his unruly dark brown hair.

Life had forced him to grow up fast. Too fast. As the eldest and only son, I could sense he felt the weight of responsibility pressing down on his small shoulders. With his father gone, he saw himself as the man of the house, even though he was still just a boy.

'You'll be all right now, won't you, Mary?'

'We'll be grand. Thanks for everything, Sean. And tell Josie I was asking about her.'

'I will,' I replied as I made my way to the front door. I paused in the hallway and let my gaze sweep over the family who were living through such hardship. 'Promise me this – if Bennett so much as looks at you crooked, I want to hear about it. OK?'

Mary swallowed hard, then reached out and squeezed my arm in a rare display of affection.

'You'll be the first to know. You've got a good heart, Sean O'Connor.'

'Don't be telling people that! I've got a reputation to keep.'

I smirked as I pulled the door open and stepped back into the cold night air. As the door clicked shut behind me, pride swelled inside my chest, knowing that I'd helped the O'Haras in their hour of need.

Mary was a grafter and worked her fingers to the bone, trying to make ends meet, and yet she still fell short every month. She'd moved to London from a small village in County Mayo with her husband in search of a better life. But fate had dealt them a cruel blow when his life had ended prematurely, and now she was swimming against the tide. There were a thousand ways to make money in this city, but nothing seemed to stop the rich from getting richer and the poor from getting poorer.

Josie hated it when I gambled. She reckoned a person would end up worse off than when they started if they went down that route. There was some truth in that. But tonight, at least, something good had come from me having a little flutter. When she found out what I'd done, hopefully, she wouldn't read me the riot act. My winnings had saved her friend's skin. That should be enough to stop her from chewing my ear off, shouldn't it? Well, a man could dream, couldn't he?

9

JOSIE

The clock on the mantelpiece ticked out the passing minutes, slow and deliberate, like a metronome marking my rising frustration. I sat by the window, rosary beads slipping between my fingers, my murmured prayers drowned by the quiet hum of the world beyond the glass.

'What's keeping Sean? He should have been home by now,' I said.

I spoke out loud even though I was alone in the room. I'd tucked Orla in hours ago. It had been another night where she'd gone to bed without a kiss from her father. She hadn't seen him for days. Orla was growing up fast. If Sean wasn't careful, her childhood would pass him by before he noticed.

I loved my husband with every bone in my body. I married him ten years ago when I was twenty. He'd been thirty-two. I thought he was older and wiser. He was older, full stop. Only a fool would put themselves in danger like Sean did in order to make a living. There were plenty of other ways to put food on the table, but my husband was a proud man. He called the shots. He pulled the strings.

Sean answered to nobody. He did as he pleased, often coming home late, stinking of whiskey. Stinking of women. Why did I stay? He had my heart. My loyalty. I'd be lying if I said it hadn't crossed my mind, but I knew how hard it would be to raise Orla alone. I only had to look at Mary if I needed reminding of the hardship that would surely come our way. But waiting by the window like this wasn't good for the soul. I told myself I wasn't worried, only angry. But that wasn't true.

My mind turned over the possibilities like cards in a dealer's hand. Had Sean had a run-in with Reggie Bennett? The Kellys? The police? No. I'd have heard by now if he was in trouble. Someone would have sent word. Something else was keeping my husband from coming home. The first time the thought crossed my mind all those years ago, I pushed it away. But it kept creeping back, unwelcome and insistent. I never wanted to be the type of woman who pretended to be clueless when it was blatantly obvious that her husband was messing around behind her back, and yet here I was.

I stood abruptly, making the chair scrape against the wooden floor. If Sean wouldn't come home, I'd find him myself. I walked over to the stairs and listened. All was quiet. All was well. Orla would be fine if I popped out for a couple of minutes. I wouldn't be long. She wouldn't even know I was missing. She was five years old and slept through the night. It wasn't as though she was a tiny baby. I reached for my coat before I talked myself out of it and pulled the front door behind me.

The cold night air bit at my cheeks as I stormed down the street with anger burning in my chest. I checked The Crown first. It was virtually empty. So I tried The Queen's Head. Nothing. No sign of Sean. But I knew him well enough to know where he'd be if he didn't want to be found – O'Rourke's.

The pub sat on the corner of a narrow, dimly lit street, its crooked sign swaying and creaking in the wind. Its windows were glowing amber, beckoning me towards them, so I quickened my pace. I couldn't wait to get out of the cold. I hesitated for just a second before I pushed the door open. The smell of tobacco and alcohol hit me like a slap when I stepped inside.

I didn't have to search for Sean. I spotted him as soon as I walked in. He was too busy to notice me, so I slipped into an empty booth to watch how things would unfold. He was leaning against the worn mahogany bar with a cigarette dangling from his fingers. His broad frame was relaxed. It struck me that he was never like this at home.

'Do you want another?'

The barmaid leaned in close. Her bright smile was teasing as she held the bottle of whiskey in front of him.

She was young, dark-haired, and her manner was warm and easy. A stab of jealousy hit me in the gut as tears pricked my eyes.

'Ahh, go on, then,' Sean said, his voice husky.

My anger spiked, suffocating my envy. I'd been worried sick about Sean, and here he was, larger than life, drinking and smoking as though he didn't have a care in the world. It took all my strength not to storm up to him and demand an explanation. But my curiosity kept my feet firmly planted on the ground.

The barmaid slid the glass towards him, her fingers brushing his as she did. It wasn't an accident. He didn't pull away. I knew what was coming before it happened. I wanted to run from the pub. I wasn't sure I could bear the humiliation. But I needed to see his betrayal for myself.

My eyes were on stalks when the barmaid walked around the counter in the shortest skirt I'd ever seen and stopped in front of my husband. They looked comfortable in each other's company. Familiar. Her fingers brushed the collar of his coat as she whispered something in his ear. Sean laughed, low and rough, before turning his head towards her. He gazed into her eyes, and then his lips met hers. The kiss was slow. Easy. Well-practised. It shocked me how easily I'd slipped from his thoughts.

For a moment, everything around me disappeared. The clink of glasses, drunken shouts and the roaring fire in the corner all faded into a dull, meaningless hum. All I could see was him and that girl. It was like I was watching them from outside my body. It was surreal.

They pulled away from each other, and she placed her hands on his waist. Sean didn't stop her. He was smirking, delighted with himself, while my heart was breaking. How could he do this to me? He'd made his vows before a priest, promised to be faithful to me and forsake all others for the rest of his life when he placed a ring on my finger. He'd made a mockery of his commitment to fidelity. I couldn't believe I meant so little to him. I sniffed back a sob and steeled myself for what was still to come.

Sean couldn't take his eyes off the girl. He was mesmerised by her beauty. And she knew it. He was putty in her hands. I stared open-mouthed as she pushed her ample chest towards him, flaunting her goods for all to see, giving him an open invitation. Sean pulled back slightly, but she continued to jiggle her large breasts, barely contained in a semi-sheer cheesecloth peasant blouse, at him.

Something inside me cracked. I couldn't stand another minute of watching her seduce him. I knew he didn't have the willpower to resist, so it was time to take matters into my own hands. I didn't deserve to be treated like this.

Sean was still smirking when he finally noticed the movement in his peripheral vision. He turned just enough to see me heading his way with a face like thunder. His blue eyes locked on mine, and his smirk fell away.

Unaware of my presence, the barmaid ran her hands up Sean's sides to refocus his attention, but his mind had drifted away from being unfaithful. His shoulders had tensed, and his whole body had stiffened as though he was bracing himself for what was coming his way.

The girl glanced in my direction to see what Sean was looking at, confusion flickering across her face, and then a moment later, the penny dropped, and she sprang back from my husband and scurried away. I had no interest in having a showdown with her. This was about him.

'You bastard!' I shouted as I stormed up to him.

The words came out low and controlled but carried across the room like a gunshot. Heads turned in our direction. Conversations slowed then ceased until silence hung heavy in the space between us. My eyes were blazing, nostrils flaring as I waited for a response.

Sean exhaled sharply, then straightened his posture, forcing me to look up at him. His movements were slow. Deliberate.

'For God's sake, Josie, get a grip of yourself,' he said in his heavy Dublin drawl as though I was the one making a show of myself.

I reached forward and grabbed the glass sitting in front of him. In one swift motion, I threw the contents straight into his face. The whiskey hit him hard, running down his cheeks and soaking into the collar of his coat and shirt.

Gasps and peals of laughter rippled through the pub, but I didn't give a damn if I'd embarrassed Sean. What he'd done to me was far worse. There was no undoing what I'd seen.

Sean wiped his face with the sleeve of his coat, but before he could open his mouth, I stood on my tiptoes and leaned into him, close enough that only he could hear what I had to say.

'I've been worried sick. I thought something terrible had happened to you,' I whispered, my voice shaking, not with sadness, but with fury. 'And all the while you were here, with her.'

Sean swallowed hard.

'It's not what you think, love.'

I let out a sharp, humourless laugh.

'Not what I think?' I turned to face the girl who'd reappeared behind the bar. My gaze was sharp enough to cut glass. 'Did he tell you he was married? That he's got a wife and daughter at home?'

The girl paled. I didn't wait for her to answer before I turned back to Sean.

'I'm disgusted at you. I trusted you, and you've thrown everything back in my face. You know how much loyalty matters to me. Without it, we have nothing,' I said, lowering my voice again to a whisper.

Sean reached for my wrist, but I jerked away before he could touch me. I didn't want him to lay his hands on me, not after he'd been messing around behind my back. I was a lot of things, but I was nobody's fool. I was small in stature, but I had an iron will. Growing up in County Kerry, Ireland, in a poor farming family had been tough, and I'd learned from a young age that strength wasn't only measured by muscle. I had bucketloads of cunning and resilience, too.

'You can all get back to your drinks now. The show's over. And don't bother coming home, Sean O'Connor. You're not welcome. First thing in the morning, I'll be changing the locks,' I said, loud enough for the whole pub to hear.

'You'll do no such thing. Don't talk nonsense, Josie,' Sean replied for the benefit of the onlookers.

I could tell by the expression on his face that he knew I wasn't bluffing.

Then, without another word, I turned on my heel and walked out, shoulders back, head held high. I might only be five foot two, but I felt like a giant as I strode out of O'Rourke's.

'Josie, wait!'

There was an urgency in Sean's voice. But I didn't look back. Not once. I kept putting one foot in front of the other until I reached the door. As soon as I stepped outside, I felt the fight leave my body, but I wouldn't give in to tears. Not in public, anyway. I'd save those for my pillow.

I headed home alone. Dejected. Humiliated. I was furious with myself for not taking heed of the count-less warnings over the years. The whispers. The snig-gers. The curtain-twitching neighbours. The gossip mongers of Kilburn had had a field day at my ex-pense. It was well-known that Sean had a roving eye and couldn't keep his John Thomas in his trousers, but I'd ignored it until now. I'd turned a blind eye to the evidence because I'd wanted to avoid facing the painful truth – something I bitterly regretted.

10

SEAN

When I'd arrived at O'Rourke's with three grand more in my pocket than I'd had at the start of the day, I'd been as happy as a pig in shit. It should have been a night for celebration. But instead, my whole world had come crashing down around me. Josie and Orla were my life. I couldn't face a future without them in it.

'Jesus, Sean, what are you going to do? You're welcome to stay at mine,' Martina, the barmaid, said.

I didn't reply. My thoughts were elsewhere. My mind was on other things. I was in no mood to have a meaningless conversation. Martina was a lovely girl, but she was a bit on the side. I wasn't about to leave my wife and shack up with her. She was just the latest in a long line of infidelities. When a woman tempted me with her charms, I was powerless to stop myself.

Worry clawed at me, deep in my gut. Why did I have that last drink? I should have gone home. I knew Josie would be waiting. Worrying. Tiny fingers clutching tightly to her rosary beads. And yet, I hadn't. I'd stayed where I was. I had nobody else to blame. I'd brought this on myself. Staying here would only make matters worse. I needed to see Josie. Talk some sense into her before it was too late.

I pushed my shoulders back and marched towards the door, ignoring the whispered conversations going on around me. I knew the whole pub was talking about me. Talking about Josie. The rumour mill was going into overdrive. The events of tonight would be all over Kilburn by daybreak, but not one of the bastards who'd witnessed first-hand what had happened would have the balls to say anything to me. They'd prefer to talk behind my back.

'Sean, wait! Where are you going?' Martina called as I disappeared out the door.

Josie's face flickered in my mind as I paced back to our house. Her olive-green eyes had been haunted when she'd stared up into my face. The hurt she'd worn cut me deep like she'd plunged a knife into me.

She was small and slight, but there wasn't an ounce of fragility in her when she'd confronted me.

Josie must have moved like the wind. I'd expected to catch her up along the way, but she'd already made it home by the time I pushed open the front gate. The house was noiseless, bathed in the dim glow of the street lamp outside until the distant rumble of an engine shattered the silence. I glanced behind me. A black car was disappearing down the street, its tyres hissing against the damp road. Something felt off. The road was too quiet. Too still.

I went to walk up the front steps, and that was when I saw it: glass glinting on the crazy paving. My stomach twisted. I rushed to the front door, key in hand. As soon as I opened it, the smell of petrol hit me in the face. My senses were on high alert. The floor was slippery where it had been poured through the letterbox, so I stood rooted to the spot, taking stock of things.

'Josie,' I called. My voice was sharp. Urgent.

My eyes darted around. I was frantic for reassurance that she was OK. Relief swept through me when I zoned in on her. She was standing frozen with fear at the bottom of the staircase. I stepped over the puddle of petrol and paced over to her. The cold hit me before I had a chance to speak. A draught that shouldn't have been there was coming from upstairs. My heart started pounding in my chest. As I flew up the steps two at a time, only one thing was on my mind. Orla.

'Stay here,' I said over my shoulder. Whoever had done this might still be in the house.

I pulled my flick-knife out of my back pocket and raced forward. When I reached the landing, I saw my daughter's bedroom door swaying in the breeze. I stepped into the room, eyes scanning left and right, looking for danger lurking in the shadows. My gaze fell on the lightweight curtains dancing at the gaping hole in the window. Glass was scattered across the end of Orla's bed and the floor surrounding it. I rushed across the room. The broken window was letting in the chill of the night. The jagged edges glistened like tiny knives under the dim glow of the street lamp. I peered outside. There wasn't a soul to be seen. Whoever had done the damage was long gone. They'd delivered the message and then vanished into the night.

I turned to look behind me when I heard Josie gasp. Her hands flew to her mouth as she took in the scene. There was a brick lying inches from where our daughter lay, sound asleep with her Womble clutched to her chest. She looked so small, so innocent, tucked beneath the thick blankets. Josie rushed over to the bed. She ran her hands over Orla's face. She didn't stir.

Her chest continued to rise and fall steadily. She was unharmed. Unaware of the drama going on around her. Thank God.

I crouched down and picked up the brick lying ominously on the covers. A sheet of paper was wrapped around it, secured with a piece of twine. Stepping away from the bed and turning my back on my wife and child, I pulled it loose and unfolded the note. My eyes narrowed as I held it out in front of me and read the words written in a red marker.

GET OUT OF KILBURN. THIS IS YOUR LAST WARNING O'CONNOR.

There was no signature. I clenched my jaw. My knuckles were white from gripping the paper.

'Who do you think it's from?'

I looked up at the sound of Josie's voice and cast my eyes to the side. She was staring at the note in my hand. I hadn't heard her move away from the bed, but she was right next to me.

I shrugged. I'd made a lot of enemies over the years.

My gaze flicked to Orla, still sleeping soundly, oblivious to the danger that had been inches from her tiny body. The brick had landed right next to her angelic face. She'd had a lucky escape. We'd had a lucky escape. If anything had happened to her, I'd never have been able to live with the guilt. My daughter was so precious to me. She was my whole world.

Josie's breath became unsteady, so I led her from the room. She needed a stiff whiskey after what she'd been through tonight. We both did, but that would have to wait.

'Go and turn down the covers, and I'll bring Orla through,' I said, gesturing to our bedroom.

'You're not suggesting we stay here tonight, are you?' Josie looked alarmed.

'Where else can we go at this time of night?'

'Couldn't we stay with Niall?' Josie's eyes were pleading.

I shook my head.

'But I don't feel safe here. What about the petrol? What if they come back and finish the job?'

'I won't be hunted from my house...'

'But Sean...'

'Enough,' I said, putting an end to her protest. 'If we leave, whoever did this has won. Now do as I asked.'

I pointed to our room. Josie threw me a look, but she didn't reply before she headed across the landing.

I went back into Orla's room, untucked her from

the blankets and scooped her into my arms. She stirred a little, letting out a soft murmur, but didn't wake. Orla slept on as I carried her across the landing and into our room. I placed her in the centre of the bed. Josie began fussing over her before covering her up and kissing her forehead. I stood rooted to the spot, gazing at my girl.

'I'll put the kettle on,' Josie said, already heading for the stairs.

I dropped onto my knees and stroked my daughter's mass of wavy deep auburn hair. She looked peaceful. I shouldn't disturb her. But I was scared to leave her unattended after what had just happened, which brought the broken window to the forefront of my mind. It needed boarding up before I turned in for the night. It wouldn't do that itself, so I reluctantly tore myself away from my sleeping child.

The kettle had just come to a boil when I walked into the kitchen. Josie had the tea caddy out and two mugs lined up on the counter while she warmed the pot. That wouldn't hit the spot, so I reached into the cupboard and took out a bottle of whiskey and two glasses. I didn't wait for Josie to respond before I poured large measures into them and handed her one. My wife stared at me wide-eyed. She rarely drank. I knew that. But she'd been put through the wringer tonight, so it would help to settle her nerves.

'Thanks,' Josie said when she finally took the drink from my hand.

At least she didn't throw it in my face this time. There was no mention of the business with Martina, and I wasn't about to bring it up. If Josie wanted to brush my indiscretion under the carpet, she'd hear no complaints from me.

'Whoever did this means business. What are we going to do, Sean?' Josie asked before taking the tiniest sip of her whiskey.

She'd said 'we', so hopefully, she wasn't going to carry out her threat and show me the door. I had to stop a smirk from spreading over my face.

'We're going to stand our ground. If it's a war they want, a war they'll get!'

11

DECLAN

The fog hung low over the Thames, swallowing the distant city lights and masking the illicit dealings. I stood on the slick wooden planks, the scent of oil thick in the air. My breath came in steady streams. My eyes swept the murky waters where a cargo boat silently slipped into the dock.

Aboard, a handful of my men worked swiftly, pulling up crates of whiskey from the hull and stacking them onto waiting trucks. My gaze was trained on Fergal as he led the operation.

'Keep 'em moving, lads, we've got ten minutes before the tide shifts,' he said, wiping sweat from his brow with his grimy sleeve.

'We've got eyes on us,' Aidan muttered.

My younger brother gestured to a nearby ware-house. I glanced over and clenched my jaw when I saw a dark figure standing at the edge of the building.

'Fuck,' I said under my breath.

A whistle cut through the air. Seconds later, all hell broke loose. Blue lights flooded the scene, sig-nalling the cops' arrival.

'This is the Metropolitan Police!' a voice bellowed over a megaphone, as if they needed any introduction.

'For fuck's sake, Hargrove must have sold us out!' I said, pulling a pistol from my waistband.

The corrupt detective had ties to us and the O'-Connors. He played both sides, feeding information to the highest bidder while pretending to enforce the law. His greed and shifting loyalties made him a dan-gerous wildcard.

'Keep loading the trucks!' I barked, holding my weapon low. I didn't want to provoke a Bonnie and Clyde shootout.

Half my men scrambled to shove the last crates into the lorries while the others grabbed their weapons, unsure whether I would ask them to fight or run.

Before I'd made up my mind, a shot rang out. Then another.

'Go! Get out of here!' I called, and the engines roared to life.

I hadn't come here for a battle, so I sprinted towards the nearest truck, but before I reached it, a pair of coppers emerged from the shadows, one of them swinging a baton. He aimed straight for my ribs. I dodged to the left and caught the second officer with an elbow to the nose when he tried to apprehend me. He stopped in his tracks when blood started pouring from his nostrils. The distraction cost me valuable time, allowing the first bobby to come at me again, but I had no intention of ending up in the slammer. My breath was ragged. My heart was hammering, but I grabbed hold of the man and drove him headfirst into a stack of crates lined up on the quayside as bullets whizzed past my head. Behind me, Aidan fired back at them before we both dived into the cab of one of the trucks.

'Jesus, we're boxed in,' Fergal shouted, looking for a gap through the squad cars.

Officers were flooding the dockside like a swarm of ants. One of them was aiming a shotgun at the tyres.

'Put your foot down and drive at him,' I ordered, grabbing hold of the crowbar in the footwell.

Fergal didn't hesitate. He gunned the truck's engine, and it lurched forward. He drove at speed, which sent the police scattering in all directions. Once I was close enough, I wound the window down, leant out and swung the crowbar at the shotgun-wielding officer, knocking the weapon from his hands.

Fergal scoured the scene for an exit route. He was skilled behind the wheel, so he led the convoy of trucks through the docks, smashing past cargo before slipping through a gap in the blockade. The sound of scraping metal filled the cab as he barrelled between two panda cars. He'd done what he had to do. Paintwork could be repaired. Lives not so easily.

As we sped into the night, swerving all over the road, sirens wailed in pursuit. It wasn't the clean getaway I'd planned, but we were alive and the shipment was intact. Things could have turned out a whole lot worse.

The convoy of trucks roared away from West India Docks and through the backstreets of London. The city's underworld shifted in the darkness and slunk into the shadows to avoid the cops on our tail. But they wouldn't be in pursuit for much longer. We were on the verge of outmanoeuvring them. We'd had a head start, and we had a plan in place. We were going to splinter off in different directions using the network of roads surrounding Bow, Bethnal Green and

Whitechapel. We'd only venture back to my premises in Southwark when we were sure the coast was clear.

I sat back in the seat while Fergal did a tour of the backstreets. I was exhausted from the exertion and adrenaline. Hargrove had put me through hell; what I wouldn't give to cut that bastard down to size.

12

JOSIE

I pushed open the door of St Jude's and was glad to see it was empty except for the flickering glow of votive candles. I hurried down the aisle and knelt at my usual pew, fingers tight around my crystal rosary, whispering silent prayers into the vast, hollow space of the church. My heart was heavy, weighed down by anger. Confusion gnawed at my soul.

I'd never doubted my faith before – far from it; I was a devout Catholic – but as I knelt beneath the watchful gaze of Jesus on the cross, I wasn't sure what I was praying for. Strength? Courage? A sign? Sean's betrayal burned in my chest. It had cut me like a knife. I wasn't sure the wound would ever close, and yet, despite all the suffering he'd caused me, I still loved him.

I couldn't just switch off my feelings in an instant, no matter how much I wanted to.

We hadn't discussed his infidelity. The moment had passed before we'd had a chance to, and now it was hard to bring it up. What had happened to our house while Orla was there alone had given me nightmares and shocked me to the core. I was worried that if I confronted Sean, we'd row and he'd walk out the door. I felt vulnerable. I was scared to be without him in case our enemy came back.

Sean was probably hoping that maybe, just maybe, I'd forget. But I couldn't just pretend it hadn't happened. I couldn't unsee my husband kissing that girl. The vision of them together was stamped in my memory. I'd lain awake all night mulling things over while snuggling beside my daughter. Sean had slept in her room. To protect the house from being broken into, he'd said. To prevent the showdown with me, more like.

I didn't know what to do for the best. Should I continue with my threat and throw him out, or should I give him a second chance? My internal battle between pride and devotion was the worst part of this. I felt humiliated. Disrespected. Distraught that my husband could do something so awful to me. But I was scared of being alone.

The soft creak of the church doors echoed through the quiet space. I didn't turn. I didn't need to. I recognised the sound of the footsteps on the tiled floor. A moment later, Mary O'Hara slid into the pew beside me.

'I thought I'd find you in here,' Mary began.

I could sense she wanted to talk, so I got off my knees and sat next to her.

'I just wanted to say thanks a million for the money.'

A smile lit up Mary's face as confusion clouded my thoughts.

'What money?'

Mary studied me before she spoke again.

'The money Sean gave me. Didn't he tell you he gave me a thousand pounds so I can pay Reggie off?'

My breath caught in my chest. My eyes sprang open and locked onto Mary's. She read the look on my face, and her smile slid.

'He did what?'

Mary looked panicked when she realised she'd put her foot in it.

'I'm sorry, Josie, I thought you knew. I thought you'd put him up to it after our chat the other day...'

The weight of Mary's words pressed down on me. I wasn't angry that Sean had given her the money. I was glad he'd helped her. But I was furious he hadn't told me about it. Keeping secrets from one another did a marriage no good. What else hadn't he told me?

'I didn't want to take it, but he insisted. I'm going to pay you back every penny...' Mary said.

Guilt wormed its way into me when I saw tears spring to her eyes. I shouldn't be making her feel bad. She'd done nothing wrong. I placed my hand on her arm in a show of comfort. I considered confiding in her for the briefest moment, but I was a proud woman. Being the laughing stock would fill me with shame.

'Pay no mind to me. I'm not angry with you. It's just a bit of a shock, that's all. I wish Sean had told me,' I replied, attempting to gloss over the way I was really feeling.

'I presumed he had. I didn't mean to drop him in it. I'm not out to cause trouble between you. I just wanted to thank you in person.'

Even though I'd tried to reassure her, Mary still looked awkward.

'I'm glad he was able to help you.'

I smiled. It was genuine. Damn Sean. He was generous to a fault. The first to help those in need. This was the kind of thing he did. The kind of thing that made walking away so bloody hard.

'He's a lifesaver. I'll be eternally grateful to him for keeping Reggie Bennett off my back. You're a lucky woman. You've got a good one there, Josephine O'-Connor,' Mary said before stepping out of the pew and leaving me to my thoughts.

A lump formed in my throat as my eyes filled with tears. I blinked them away, turned back to the altar and focused on the candles. They blurred before me, wavering in the dim light. I didn't know what to do. I tightened my grip on the rosary, hoping for some divine intervention, but no answers came.

13

SEAN

The low hum of conversation came to an abrupt halt when I shoved open the door of the dingy Cricklewood pub Reggie Bennett sometimes frequented when he wasn't lording it up in Soho. The place was thick with smoke and the stench of stale beer. Heads turned, eyes darted away. Even the most hardened men shrank into the shadows as I stood, filling the doorway, silhouetted against the glow of the street lights.

I didn't speak. I didn't need to. The atmosphere shifted. The air was thick with something primal. Everyone knew a predator had entered the room. They knew trouble when they saw it. They sensed the danger before anything had kicked off.

Reggie sat in a corner booth, laughing with a pair of his cronies: his sidekick, Freddie, and another mad bastard who worked for him, Pistol Pete. A thick roll of notes lay on the table beside his half-empty pint. His cockney drawl rang out across the silence as he turned and greeted me.

'Evenin', Sean,' Reggie said, flashing his usual smirk. Then he picked up his drink with one hand while a fat cigar rested between the fingers of the other. 'I didn't expect to see you out and about. I thought you'd be at home with your wife and kid after what happened. Nasty business that.'

His words fuelled my suspicions. The cowardly act had his name written all over it. I didn't reply. I paced forward and loomed over Reggie. Grabbing the pint glass from his hand, I slammed it against the table, shattering it into jagged shards. The barmaid gasped, but no one dared to intervene.

'Do you seriously think you can throw a brick through my daughter's window and walk away without any consequences?' My voice was low. Menacing.

Reggie licked his lips and sat back in his seat, trying to play it cool.

'I don't know what you're on about. I ain't responsible for every bit of mischief in this town.'

It was no surprise that he was denying his involvement, but I was more convinced than ever that I'd found the culprit. I moved fast before he realised what was about to happen. The element of surprise startled him. He looked shocked when I suddenly reached forward, grabbed him by the front of his shirt and dragged him out of his chair.

'Get your grubby mits off me,' Reggie protested.

I responded by slamming him against the wooden table. Glasses tumbled and beer spilt as his arms and legs flailed wildly. He was like a beetle on its back. Reggie's men tensed and froze. Not even trigger-happy Pete, who had a habit of shooting first and asking questions later, moved a muscle.

'My little girl was asleep in her bed when you left your calling card,' I growled, my eyes burning with fury. 'You could've killed her or scarred her for life. The brick you hurled through the window landed inches from her face, and there was broken glass everywhere, all over her covers.'

Reggie's hands scrabbled at my wrists. His breath was coming in panicked bursts. His blue eyes were sharp. They were always assessing, always looking for a weakness to exploit. He was out of luck tonight.

'Get your facts right before you start throwing

your weight around. I had nothing to do with what happened.'

I knew the spineless git was lying, so I drove a fist into his gut, which knocked the wind out of him but skinned my knuckles at the same time. He coughed and wheezed for air as I towered over him, fists clenched. I could barely hold myself back from finishing the job then and there.

'I don't care if it wasn't your hand that delivered the threat,' I snarled. 'You sent the message. What kind of man bricks a child's window and pours petrol through a family's letterbox?' I leaned in closer and dropped my voice to a venomous whisper. 'You're a coward. Consider this my reply.'

I reached for Reggie and gripped his wrist in an iron vice. Before he had time to react, I pinned his hand down onto the table and drove a shard of broken glass through the skin between his fingers. He let out a blood-curdling scream. His body jerked in pain, but I didn't let go. Everyone in the pub held their breaths and waited to see what I would do.

'If you so much as look at my family again, I'll make what's just happened feel like nothing,' I said, my voice cold as steel. 'Do you understand me?'

Reggie's face was slick with sweat and contorted in agony.

'Y-yeah, yeah, I understand,' he babbled as he nodded frantically.

Reggie Bennett had made it personal when he'd vandalised my house. My victory over him had been short-lived, which was a pity as it had tasted all the sweeter when I'd given Mary his money so she could pay him what she owed, but now part of me wished I'd never got involved.

I released my grip on him and wiped my bloodied hand on his grey suit jacket. He clutched his injured hand to his chest and closed his eyes momentarily. When he opened them, they were blazing with pain and hatred as he glared into my face. The war between us wasn't over. I knew that for a fact.

As I strode towards the door, the pub remained deathly silent. Nobody was brave enough to make eye contact with me. I stood outside the entrance, clenching and unclenching my fists as my nostrils flared. Fury was bubbling inside me. I couldn't go straight home even though I was worried that Josie and Orla could be in danger. I'd made a fool of Reggie in a crowded pub. He wasn't going to let that slide. Would he take advantage of my absence and retaliate in the heat of the moment? I hoped not.

My chest felt tight. My mind was at war with itself, so I decided to swing by my brother's house.

'What are you doing here?' Niall asked, surprised by my unexpected visit.

'I've just had a run-in with Reggie.'

'Are you hurt?' Niall's eyes roamed over me.

'Nah. I need you to do me a favour. I heard a whisper that there's a fight in the tunnels tonight. Will you corner for me?'

Niall didn't hesitate to do as I'd asked or question my motives.

'Just a second,' he replied, grabbing his coat from the stand in the hall, and then he followed me down the garden path.

* * *

Brompton Road station was a ghost of its former self, buried beneath the streets of London. Forgotten to the outside world, frozen in time. Its tiled walls were cracked and blackened with age. A single flickering bulb dangled from an exposed wire, casting long shadows across the makeshift ring, a rough square of ropes strung between steel poles, where the night's blood sport would unfold. The air was thick with the electric anticipation of violence.

I ducked beneath a rusted sign, Niall at my heels, our footsteps echoing off the damp walls. A crowd of gamblers, gangsters and lowlifes pressed in around the ring, shifting like a pack of wolves, their eyes gleaming with the thrill of what lay ahead. Money changed hands in murmured bets, the scent of cheap whiskey and unfiltered cigarettes wrapped around us like a fog.

Niall leaned in close, his voice barely audible above the noise of the crowd.

'Are you sure about this? You're still bleeding from that scrap with Reggie.'

I stood at the edge of the ring, my gaze fixed on the hulking brute across from me. The jostling chaos in the tunnel was underpinned by the dull thud of his fists meeting his opponent's flesh.

'That's as may be, but I need to do this.'

Rage still burned in my gut, a pulsing, untamed force demanding release. I was hungry for a fight. I couldn't take my fury out on Reggie without bringing more heat down on myself, but I could unleash it all in here and walk away with money in my pocket.

The formidable legend Crusher Doyle was in the ring, towering over an almost beaten opponent who barely had the strength to stand. With one last, devastating right hook, Crusher sent the man sprawling to the dirt, unconscious before he even hit the ground. A roar erupted from the crowd. Money changed hands as the announcer, a wiry fella with a bent nose and a rat-like grin acting as the referee, stepped into the ring. He lifted Crusher's arm in victory, and the baying mob went wild.

Doyle was the reigning bare-knuckle fighting champion in the underground circuits of London. A huge man in his late thirties, he was built like a wrecking ball, thick-necked, barrel-chested and covered in old scars from previous fights. Judging by the shape of his nose, it had been broken countless times.

'Who's next?' Crusher sneered, his voice like gravel.

He looked unfazed, rolling his neck as he turned towards the crowd, and lapped up the glory. The ref raised his arms to hush the restless mob, then turned to the fighters waiting in the shadows.

'You heard the man. Who's got the balls to take on our reigning champ tonight?'

I stepped forward, peeling off my jacket and shirt and handing them to Niall. The crowd muttered; some looked perplexed, some nodded in recognition, and others exchanged knowing glances.

Crusher eyed me up and down as I stood in front of the ropes, bare-chested, hands wrapped tightly in tape. He was a massive brute, barely a man, more like a slab of muscle carved from rock. He glared at me, cracking his neck with a deliberate motion. His knuckles were already split from his earlier victories.

'You sure you wanna do this, old man?' He smirked.

Cheeky fucker! I couldn't be more than five or six years his senior. He'd underestimated me at his own peril. I was already tasting his defeat. I grinned back at him. My eyes were as cold and sharp as a blade.

'Old man, you say. We'll see about that.'

I rolled my shoulders as I exhaled slowly and steadily. Then I spat on the floor. The crowd roared as I stepped into the circle and faced the towering beast.

'All right, lads! You know the rules. Two men enter, and one man walks out. No weapons, no tapping out, no backing down. You fight until one of you can't stand. Plain and simple,' the ref said.

He looked like a midget as he stood between us. Crusher cracked his knuckles with an audible pop. Then a bell rang, a harsh clang of metal on metal, and the fight began. The announcer barely had time to step back before the champ lunged, fists flying in a flurry of raw aggression.

'You're going down. Sleep tight,' Crusher jeered.

I ducked the first swing and sidestepped the second. Moving quickly, I darted in and landed a punishing right hook into Crusher's ribs. The impact sent a dull thud through the cavernous station, a sound more felt than heard. The crowd roared, but Doyle barely flinched.

'Is that all you've got?' he mocked.

Then he swung a massive fist in retaliation. I only narrowly dodged it. Out of the corner of my eye, I saw the crowd surge forward, their cheers deafening as we exchanged blows. Crusher lashed out with a strike that I had trouble blocking. I staggered slightly, recovering quickly. My forearm screamed in protest, but I ignored the pain. Stepping inside Doyle's reach, I delivered an uppercut that snapped his head back, followed by a brutal shot to the gut that sent him crashing to his knees. He wheezed and clutched his stomach.

'Still think I'm an old man?' I taunted.

Crusher dragged himself back to standing, and we stood toe to toe, eyeballing each other for a second. He jabbed me with a sly punch while I graciously allowed him time to catch his breath. Blood trickled from my lip, but I didn't falter. I danced around Crusher, landing quick, precise strikes that started to wear the big man down. My knuckles were like granite from years of brawling. The fight would soon be over, but the rage inside me hadn't burned out yet.

I continued to toy with Doyle and humiliate him

in front of his fans. Frustrated that he hadn't been able to annihilate me, he lunged wildly, leaving himself open. I seized the opportunity and drove a final blow to the side of his head that sent him crashing to the ground.

Silence hung in the musty air for a split second before the station erupted. Shouts and cheers rang out as money exchanged hands. I barely registered any of it. I stood over Crusher with my fists still clenched. Blood was seeping through my wraps, but my breathing was steady and controlled. I crouched down next to him as he lay sprawled in the dirt. He was conscious, but his eyes were glassy with pain.

'This is what happens when you think you're indestructible,' I growled, my voice cutting through the noise.

Then I got to my feet and stepped over his body as the announcer held up my arm and declared me, the 'old man', the new champion.

Niall clapped a hand on my back. He was grinning from ear to ear as I left the ring.

'Are you feeling any better?'

I exhaled, flexing my bruised hands.

'I'm getting there.'

14

REGGIE

I stepped inside my casino, nestled in the heart of Soho. Smoke hung thick in the air and curled lazily around the huge chandelier in the centre of the room. A heady mix of expensive cigars and perfume clung to the damask curtains and soft furnishings.

I headed to my private booth, half-hidden by a damask curtain, and surveyed my domain. The Velvet Ace pulsed with the low hum of conversation, painting an illusion of civility, but a motley crew were at the poker table. Gang figures sat with wealthy businessmen who had no qualms about rubbing shoulders with London's criminal elite.

I was in a foul mood, so even the quiet clatter of chips, the rattle of dice on felt and the occasional burst of laughter from drunken gamblers who'd yet to realise the house always won couldn't lift my spirits. My eyes flicked to the floor, where punters handed over their hard-earned cash, oblivious to the storm brewing behind my steely gaze.

Freddie leaned his enormous bulk towards me, and his booming voice rang out above the din.

'A little birdie told me O'Connor's been bare-knuckle fighting down Brompton Road station. Rumour has it he obliterated Doyle and walked away with the purse.'

My nostrils flared as I swirled the brandy in my glass. Then my knuckles whitened as my grip on the tumbler tightened, as I imagined it was Sean's throat I was squeezing. Freddie was more of an idiot than I'd given him credit for if he thought news like that would be welcome at this moment in time, given the fact that I was nursing a fresh injury from my encounter with the Irish thug a few hours ago.

How could anyone have beaten Crusher Doyle? He'd been undefeated for as long as I could remember. The man had superhuman strength. He was a former dockworker who'd turned his hand to underground enforcement, which was the perfect job for a man who thrived on violence and intimidation. It was an obvious move when he'd branched out into illegal fights, as he made a living from muscle work and collecting debts for London's crime syndicates.

O'Connor was a bigger threat than I cared to admit. Doyle should have made mincemeat of him. I'd have put money on that fight. This was a disastrous outcome. The victory over Crusher would only fuel Sean's enormous ego. The Dubliner would consider himself invincible. He had to be stopped before he got out of hand.

My jaw tensed as I set the glass down with a sharp clink.

'That bastard's getting too big for his boots. He humiliated me in the middle of a crowded pub, but he's not getting away with it. I won't have people thinking I've gone soft.'

Pistol Pete sat in the booth across from me. He was a weird guy with a twitchy disposition. His unpredictability made him a liability, but he had his uses. Emptying his gun was his favourite hobby, so he was a handy bloke to have around.

Pete drummed his fingers against the mahogany table. Then he swivelled around in his chair and looked over his shoulder. His eyes darted left and right, taking in the casino floor to check if anybody was earwigging before he spoke.

'Doing away with Sean won't be as simple as that.

He's got a crew behind him, Reg. Niall's a beanpole, but he's not a pushover. If we escalate things with the O'Connors, we'll start a war. Those Paddies stick together, so their extended network will come crawling out of the gutters like vermin.'

I let out a low chuckle, my lips curling into something that wasn't quite a smile.

'You lot always think too bloody small. I had no intention of going after Sean directly. I was thinking of starting closer to home. His missus. His little girl. Shame he hasn't got a dog...'

Freddie's cheeks reddened, and he shifted uncomfortably.

'People don't like it when animals get hurt, Reg. They get proper riled up.'

'Do me a favour and shut the fuck up, Fred!'

'What are you suggesting? Are you gonna do something to his wife and kid?'

I gave Freddie a death stare and leaned forward.

'I'm going to make him feel powerless. A man like Sean is built like a brick wall with the power to match. He's as strong as an ox, so he can take a beating. His business is thriving, so he can take on a financial loss. That's why we have to think smart, which is why I'm the boss and the brains of the operation. There'd be no point in leaving the finer details to you pair of knuckle-heads, would there?'

Neither Freddie nor Pete replied. They stared at me blankly as though nothing was going on behind their eyes.

'Sean's weakness is his family, so that's put them on my radar. If we target them, we'll hit the bastard where it hurts the most, and he'll come undone.'

My lips stretched into an ear-to-ear smile. I was so delighted with my plan as it began to hatch that for a brief moment, I almost forgot the throbbing in my hand.

Freddie swallowed hard and rubbed his palms on his trousers, sensing the shift in the air. Something dark, something inevitable, was about to happen.

'This time, we won't just send a message, we'll carve the warning into his bloody soul. We'll harm something that matters to him, and make it personal.'

Pistol Pete nodded slowly, a sinister smirk creeping onto his face.

'I know some lads who'd be perfect for the job. Nasty fuckers, they are.'

I narrowed my eyes as my fingers tapped against the glass in a slow, deliberate rhythm.

'They sound ideal, but make sure they understand this ain't a quick job. I'm gonna tear Sean's world apart before he sees us coming. I'll torment the Irish bastard and really make him suffer. Break him from the inside and send him back to Dublin with his tail between his legs.'

Pete grinned. He was already reaching for his phone. I raised my glass and swirled the brandy around before taking a sip. Sean was going to be sorry he'd started this. I was a man who was used to getting what I wanted, whether through persuasion, intimidation or the act of calculated violence. Despite that, I considered myself above common thugs. The O'Connors and the Kellys were a different breed. I manipulated others to do the deed on my behalf rather than getting my hands dirty. But I wasn't afraid to remind people who stepped out of line that accidents happened, especially to those who crossed me.

15

DECLAN

The Black Harp wasn't just a pub. It was my fortress, my command centre. I ran my bootlegging empire from the premises with ruthless efficiency having carved out a name for myself over the years. I was feared over the whole of London, thanks to the brutal tactics I used.

The air was thick with cigarette smoke and the lingering aroma of stale beer that had soaked into the floorboards. The pub's backroom was the real heart of the operation, away from the prying eyes of punters and the ever-watchful coppers who were forever hanging around, making a nuisance of themselves. Hargrove had been keeping a low profile since the fiasco at the docks. Just as well. It would stick in my throat to line his greasy palm after what happened.

I sat at the head of the battered oak table with a cigarette smouldering between my fingers and a near-full tumbler of neat whiskey, scanning the men gathered before me. Aidan was perched on the edge of his seat, restless, fidgety, fingers tapping against his bouncing knee.

In contrast, Fergal leaned back in his chair, arms crossed, waiting for me to speak with the calm of somebody with maturity on his side. Aidan could learn a thing or two from Fergal. A man who was a master of patience was a master of everything else.

Sean O'Connor considered himself a rival because he was also involved in the trade, but he couldn't compete with me. He'd resorted to forming an uneasy alliance with Hargrove to try and take me out of the game, but his plan had backfired spectacularly. His betrayal was about to come back and bite him on the arse.

I exhaled a long stream of smoke, tapping ash into a chipped ashtray, as I prepared to put Aidan out of his misery.

'O'Connor and Hargrove think they've got one over on me. It doesn't sit well that they're meddling in my business. Trying to make a show of me. Sean is going to pay dearly for setting me up.'

My voice was calm, steady, but carried the weight of barely restrained fury. My words hung heavily in the room as the dim light cast jagged shadows across my men's faces.

'They made a mistake messing with us, Dec. We should go in heavy. Do away with O'Connor and Hargrove before they see it coming,' Aidan said.

Fergal raised an eyebrow. He seemed unimpressed with my brother's suggestion. I couldn't agree more. We were on the same page. We shared blood, but our temperaments couldn't be more different. I was calculated and methodical. He was impulsive and hotheaded, always eager for action and prone to violent outbursts. He was fiercely loyal to the Kelly name, but he could be reckless, which made him both an asset and a liability in our war against our enemies.

'Jesus, Aidan, pulling a stunt like that would bring the heat straight down on us. A plan like that will get us all killed. We need to be smarter than that,' Fergal said, giving my brother a dressing-down before turning his attention to me.

I flicked my cigarette into the ashtray and downed the large drink in a few swallows. My expression was unreadable as my fingers drummed against the table.

The best plans were hatched over a drop of the good stuff.

'Don't you worry, I've got an idea in mind. I'm not going to let this slide. I fully intend to dismantle O'-Connor's crew piece by piece. His operation relies on loyalty, on fear. If we break that, we can turn his men against him.'

Determined nods and murmurs of agreement rippled through the group, but each of my men carried the unspoken weight of knowing what failure might cost us.

'That's all very well, but what about Hargrove?' Aidan questioned.

By the look on his face, I could see he wasn't sold on my idea.

'Nobody touches Hargrove!'

I narrowed my eyes and glared at my brother, challenging him to defy me. Then, I drained the last of my whiskey and slammed the glass down with a finality that echoed through the room.

Hargrove wasn't just any copper. He was a detective chief inspector with significant control over major investigations, including those into organised crime. He dictated what cases took priority and which quietly disappeared. He knew every major player in London's underworld. His access to confidential information made him invaluable to criminals but allowed him to manipulate both sides of the law.

Hargrove wasn't in this alone. He'd built an entire network within the Met, including a sea of other officers, solicitors and even judges who ensured that any case against him or his allies fell apart before it reached trial. Evidence vanished, witnesses recanted statements, and cases got dismissed on technicalities. He was too big a player to take out of the game. Much as I hated to admit it, our operation needed him on-board to remain successful.

'I'm not convinced Sean's men will turn on him just like that,' Aidan scoffed, then he leaned forward, intrigued to hear what I'd have to say.

My expression darkened. My brother could be a cocky little shit at times.

'O'Connor's got a family. A wife. A daughter. He can't afford to go to war with us, but we'll make sure he knows it's coming. We'll find the weak links in his team and start pulling threads until the whole outfit unravels. We won't just hurt them. We'll ruin them.'

Fergal smirked, a slow, satisfied smile. The room fell silent. My men knew that I always followed through when I set out to do something.

16

SEAN

The moment I stepped inside the house, I could feel the tension. Josie stood in the hallway with her arms crossed tightly over her flat chest. Her face was pale, but her olive-green eyes were burning with fury.

Orla was asleep upstairs, but the walls were thin, and noises carried, so Josie kept her voice low, although the venom in her tone was unmistakable.

'When are you going to stop lying to me? Do you really think you can waltz in here after everything you've done and pretend nothing's wrong?'

I didn't reply but pushed past Josie as she tried to block my path with her tiny frame. My jaw tightened as I pulled off my jacket and tossed it onto the kitchen chair, wincing as the fabric grazed my fists, still bruised and swollen from the night's fight. It had been a long, stressful day, and the last thing I wanted was to get into an argument with my wife.

'What do you want me to say, Josie?' I muttered.

'Why were you carrying on with that barmaid? Aren't I enough for you?'

Most women would scream and roar, but Josie didn't raise her voice. She didn't need to. Her words were enough to cut me down to size. The hurt etched on her face was plain to see. Guilt rose inside me. I felt terrible for putting her through this much pain. But that didn't mean I wouldn't fight my corner. Rolling over and submitting wasn't in my nature.

'Give it a rest. You don't know what you're talking about, woman,' I said, asserting my dominance.

Josie would do well to remember I was the man of the house. Her response took me by surprise when she let out a hollow laugh, which made my temper spike.

'Don't try to deny it, Sean. I saw you with my own two eyes. You had your hands all over her and your tongue down her throat!'

My shoulders tensed as my hands curled into fists.

'You don't know what you saw.'

Never admit to anything, was my rule of thumb. It had always served me well in the past.

'I beg your pardon? I know exactly what I saw!'

Josie's voice went up a notch before it wavered. Her fury was warring with something more profound. She was hurt. Devastated. Loyalty mattered to my wife. Most people wouldn't get a second chance if they crossed her. I seemed to be the exception to the rule.

'You can't keep doing this to me.'

Tears rolled down Josie's face, so I took a step towards her, but as I went to wrap my arms around her, she pushed me away.

'I love you more than you'll ever know, but I won't tolerate your infidelity. I'm not going to turn a blind eye to you and your whores any longer.'

Josie put her hands on her tiny hips and stared up at me with a determined look on her face. She knew I wouldn't get drawn into a conversation about this, but she paused all the same, allowing me time to respond.

'And your recklessness has got to stop. Orla could have been killed or seriously injured because of your war with your enemies.'

'Don't you dare blame me for that! You're the one who left our daughter alone in the house,' I roared.

'Keep your voice down. Orla's asleep upstairs, and we don't want the whole road listening to our affairs,' Josie scolded, intensifying my rage.

'What kind of mother leaves a five-year-old asleep

in the house alone? Forget about my enemies. Anything could have happened. And you're accusing me of making reckless moves.'

I shook my head as I scowled at Josie with a black look on my face.

'You know why I left Orla. I came looking for you. I was worried something terrible had happened. You should have been home hours earlier—'

'Stop with the sob story. You're not my keeper, Josie. If I want to stay out half the night, I will. I don't have a curfew,' I shouted, cutting her off mid-flow.

'Sean, keep your voice down. The neighbours...'

Josie's eyes darted from side to side.

'Fuck the neighbours. I won't be told what to do in my own house!' I said, towering over my wife.

Josie's face darkened.

'I was beside myself because I thought you might be in trouble, but I found you in the arms of another woman. I won't let you make a fool out of me again.' Josie's voice hitched.

'I don't need you to fight my battles, Josie. Your job is to look after our daughter,' I replied, sweeping her concerns under the carpet.

I hadn't intended to make a fool out of her, but she had no business spying on me. If she'd stayed home like she should have done, she'd have been none the wiser.

'And your job is to keep us safe.' Josie took a step closer and jabbed a finger into my chest. 'But it's crystal clear we're not your priorities. I tell you something, blood comes first in my book.'

I knew Josie was fiercely protective of those close to her. I was, too. We shared that trait.

'And in mine. Despite what you think, my family means everything to me,' I replied.

Josie shook her head.

'That's rubbish. Fighting is your one true love. It comes first for you. Always has. Always will. Look at the state of your hands, Sean.'

I tore my eyes away from Josie and glanced at my weeping knuckles, around which bruises had begun blooming on my skin. I exhaled loudly and ran a battle-scarred hand through my dark brown hair.

'Do you think I like doing this? Do you think I want to be out there risking my neck? It's called survival, Josie.'

'Survival? So you weren't bare-knuckle fighting down Brompton Road? With money riding on you after you told me you'd given it up?'

When Josie narrowed her eyes, I felt the heat from her scrutiny as they swept over me, making a mental note of my injuries. She'd have noticed there was no blood on my clothes the way there would have been if I'd been in a fight defending my territory. She didn't challenge me on that, but she probably couldn't take another disappointment. Another broken promise.

'You can't help yourself, can you? You need the fight, the rush, the blood. It's part of you. No matter what you say, it'll always come first!'

My chest heaved, my fury mixing with something raw, something I struggled to admit. I was ashamed of myself. My tiny wife had cut me down to size with her words.

'You think I don't love you? That I don't love Orla?'

Josie swallowed hard as she tried to hold back her tears.

'Love isn't enough, Sean. Not when we're living in fear because of the choices you make.'

Silence stretched out between us, heavy and suffocating. I tore my eyes away from hers and gripped the edge of the table. Nobody had forced me to face Crusher Doyle in the ring. I'd put myself forward to let off some steam. Let off some aggression. My wife knew that I'd lied to her again. But she knew she wouldn't get anywhere probing me on this, so after a long pause, she steamrolled on to the next item on her agenda.

'I bumped into Mary today...'

Josie broke off her sentence, leaving it open. I could guess where this was heading, but I wouldn't take the prompt.

'I would have thought it was common courtesy to mention to me that you were giving her a thousand pounds before you threw the money in her direction.'

'Jesus Christ, I can't win, can I? She's your friend, Josie. I thought you'd be glad I helped her. I gave Mary that money to keep her safe!' I fumed.

'I am glad you helped her, but why the big secret? Why didn't you just tell me?' Josie shook her head. Her eyes were glistening now.

'Stop fucking nagging me, woman. I sorted the problem, didn't I?'

Josie let out a breath and studied me for a long moment, while shaking her head. Then she played me at my own game and didn't bother replying. Instead, she turned on her heel and walked out of the room, leaving me standing in the kitchen, fists clenched, jaw tight, a storm raging inside me that no bare-knuckle fight could ever settle.

17

REGGIE

London, November 1975

My knock on the door was sharp, impatient. It carried the weight of trouble. Mary O'Hara should have been expecting it, but I saw her hands shaking when she pulled the door open. I stepped forward, filling the threshold like a storm cloud. Freddie loomed over my shoulder as an ominous figure.

'Evenin', Mary,' I drawled, my lips curling into something that wasn't quite a smile. 'Hope I'm not disturbing you.'

Mary swallowed. Her eyes were as wide as saucers.

'I have the money I owe you, Mr Bennett.'

Mary thrust the small envelope she was gripping in her hand towards me.

'Every penny's there,' she insisted.

My mood darkened as she stood in front of me, grinning from ear to ear. I stared at her for a long moment, my eyes narrowing, my expression shifting from amusement to rage.

'Is that so?' I questioned.

Mary nodded as she held my gaze.

'It's all there. You can count it if you like.'

A loud chuckle rumbled from my throat. Then Freddie and I stepped inside without waiting to be asked and closed the door behind us. Mary looked alarmed. She was clearly hoping to keep us on the doorstep before sending us on our way.

'See, the thing is, Mary. I wasn't expecting you to come up with the money...'

Mary straightened her posture, then smoothed back an unruly strand of dark hair that had escaped from her bun.

'But you said—'

I cut Mary off with a wave of my hand.

'I said I wanted you out. Handing over a wad of notes doesn't change that.'

Mary looked horrified. She was blindsided by what I'd just said. Unable to understand what was going on, she took a step back. Her breath was shallow, and her eyes were brimming with tears.

'But that's not fair. You can't put us out on the street. I've paid you what I owe.'

Mary was doing her best to stand tall, but an edge of desperation had crept into her voice as tears sprang into her eyes.

If she was hoping to appeal to my better nature, she was wasting her time. I didn't have a sympathetic bone in my body.

'Where did you get this from?'

My eyes narrowed as I snatched the envelope from her hands.

'Umm... Umm...' Mary muttered, trying to buy herself some time.

I was bored of her stalling, so I waved the packet in her face before tearing it open in a fit of rage. I flicked through the banknotes like they were scraps of paper. Then I threw them to the floor.

Mary's eyes darted around the room. Her mouth opened and closed, but no words came out. She was agitated. Startled by my response. She didn't know how to react.

'So come on then, where did you get it? Did you rob a bank?' I laughed, looking over at Freddie. 'What d'you think, Fred? D'you reckon Mary held up the Nat West?'

'Spread her legs, more like,' Freddie replied, and his lips stretched into a grin.

'I borrowed it, Mr Bennett,' Mary blurted out, suddenly finding her voice.

'Oh, you borrowed it?' I mocked.

Mary's head started bobbing up and down.

'Who from?' I felt my expression darken. 'Who in their right mind would lend you a big pile of cash?'

But I had my suspicions. I was pretty sure I already knew the answer to the question.

'A-a f-fr-friend.' Mary spluttered and her cheeks reddened.

'What friend?' I quizzed.

'Somebody I know from the church,' she replied.

'Ah, that's nice. Well, your so-called friend has wasted their time. This ain't enough to keep a roof over your head,' I snarled.

With a sudden, violent movement, my hand shot out. I grabbed Mary by the throat and slammed her against the wall before she had time to react. She gasped, clawing at my grip, her feet struggling to find the floor.

'It's too late to buy your way out of this,' I growled,

my face inches from hers. 'You should have left when I told you to.'

Menace was etched into my features. Mary stared back at me with terror written all over her face.

Her fingers continued to scrabble at my wrist, but my grip was like iron. I had no intention of letting go. Listening to her breath rasping in her throat and watching her vision begin to swim gave me immense pleasure. The kind of pleasure money couldn't buy.

'P-please, d-don't do this,' Mary croaked.

'Mummy,' Erin called from behind me.

Her high-pitched, panicked voice cut through the air, startling me.

I loosened my grip, just slightly, just enough for Mary to suck in a breath. But the moment was lost, so I released her with a shove, sending her stumbling to the floor. She coughed and spluttered while pressing a hand to her throat. The little girl rushed to her mother's side, oblivious to the danger she might face. Mary battled to focus on her child as she clung to her with tiny hands. She blinked repeatedly, perhaps hoping the rapid movement would stop her vision from dancing. Judging by the way she was swaying, she was losing the fight.

I clicked my tongue as I glared down at her pathetic, crumpled form. I could see she was terrified of me. She was trembling from head to toe.

'I've got plans for this place, so don't get too comfortable. This ain't over by a long shot.'

I kicked some of the scattered banknotes across the floor as I looked down my nose at Mary.

'Pick those up. I'll meet you back at the car,' I said to Freddie.

'Yes, boss,' he replied.

I stepped out into the cool night air, slamming the door behind me as the sound of Erin's crying filled the silence.

18

SEAN

I could see the lights were on as I walked up the garden path, but when I reached the front door, I noticed it was ajar, swaying slightly in the draft. The moment I stepped inside, my stomach twisted. The house was quiet. Too quiet. Something was off. Something was wrong.

'Josie? Orla?' There was an urgency in my voice.

My heart galloped as I waited for a response. Nothing came. Nobody answered.

My fists clenched as I moved further down the hall. The living room was a mess. Somebody had wrecked the place. Chairs were overturned, a lamp was smashed on the floor, and the coffee table was shattered. Broken glass glinted under the dim light.

My breathing was heavy, my pulse hammering against my skull. My gut started to spasm when I saw the blood on the floorboards. My eyes followed the trail back out to the hallway. There was a smear on the wall at the bottom of the stairs. I listened for sounds of movement. Silence. Then I heard the faintest whimper.

A trembling breath left me before I charged up the stairs two at a time, pulling my flick-knife out of my back pocket and opening the blade as I moved. My heart slammed into my ribs as I followed the sound. The bedroom door was hanging off one hinge. Splinters littered the floor. The sight inside stopped me in my tracks.

'Oh my God!' I said, then rushed over to my wife.

Josie was on the floor, curled in on herself. Her dress was torn, and one strap hung loose over her shoulder. Her lip was split, and blood was dribbling down her chin. One of her eyes was nearly swollen shut. The bruising was already blooming across her cheekbone. Her fingers trembled as she clutched her stomach.

I dropped to my knees beside her, my hands hovering over her. I was afraid to touch her. Afraid to hurt her. My whole body was vibrating, like I was on the edge of something uncontainable.

'Jesus Christ, Josie, what happened?'

She coughed, her breath ragged, as she tried to push herself up. Her eyes were dazed, barely focusing.

'Th-th-they took Orla.'

A shiver ran down my spine. My body went cold like someone had walked over my grave.

'They took Orla?' I echoed, unable to believe what I was hearing.

'Yes,' Josie replied in the tiniest voice.

She was a protective mother, so she'd had the fight beaten out of her. She was battered. Broken. Distraught.

My breath caught in my chest, and my heart felt like it had stopped momentarily. It couldn't be true. I needed to see for myself. I scrambled to my feet and raced into my daughter's bedroom. I looked over at the bed. It was empty. The sheets were ripped, and the mattress was half hanging off the frame. Everything around me narrowed to a pinpoint as my thoughts homed in on the singular, horrifying realisation. My little girl was gone. Kidnapped.

For the life of me, I couldn't fathom why somebody would force their way into a person's home, where they should have been safe, and attack a defenceless woman before snatching her child. Josie being beaten to a pulp was bad enough. But the fact that Orla was missing on top of that was messing with my brain.

I raced back to my wife and dropped down beside her.

'Who did this?'

Josie tried to rally as fresh tears rolled down her battered face. The pain in her haunted eyes made my heart break.

'Reggie Bennett.'

Her voice was hoarse, raw with the kind of fear that made her shake.

I'd suspected as much, but my entire body went rigid at the mention of his name.

'Reggie was here? Inside my house?'

Josie nodded.

So he'd taken no heed of my warning.

'And he had two of his men with him. I fought them, Sean. I fought them with everything I had, but they were too strong.'

Josie's voice broke. She gripped my arm with shaking fingers, and then she began to sob.

I pulled her close, cradling her as gently as I could so that I didn't cause her more pain while I let the enormity of the situation sink in. Despite the fury coiling inside me, I did my best to suppress it as I comforted my wife. She tilted her anguished face towards mine and began clawing at my shirt.

'I tried to stop them, but they took her, Sean. Reggie took her.'

Josie's tiny body shuddered as she cried her eyes out, all the while her fingers tightening in my shirt. My breath came out in ragged gasps, and my vision blurred, not with tears, but with pure, unfiltered rage. The kind of fury that settled deep in a person's bones. It wouldn't fade any time soon, so I forced myself to focus.

'Where did they take her?'

Josie buried her face into my chest. 'I don't know.' She pulled away and stared into my soul. Her face crumpled as fresh tears streaked down her bruised skin.

'Did Bennett do anything else to you?'

I didn't want to ask the question, but Josie's dress was ripped as though Reggie had tried to tear it from her. I might not like her answer, but I needed to know what I was dealing with.

Josie shook her head.

'He tried to,' she whispered, shame flickering in her eyes. 'But I managed to fight him off.'

My entire body stiffened. My hands flexed, then curled into fists. A shuddering breath rattled through me before I swallowed the bile rising in my throat.

'I'm sorry, Sean.'

'You've nothing to be sorry about.'

I pulled Josie into my arms and wrapped them around her with a fierce protectiveness. She gripped me tightly as I rested my chin on her head.

'Orla was screaming when they dragged her out of the house. She was screaming for me to help her. There was nothing I could do. I let her down. I let you down. I'll never forgive myself if something happens to her.'

I felt rage crawl up my spine like a living thing as my last shred of control snapped. My hands shook, but not with fear. With the need for revenge. The need to kill.

'You didn't let anyone down. You fought like a demon to save her. This isn't your fault. I'll find her and I'll bring her home where she belongs. But I swear to God, Josie, I'm going to kill the man responsible.'

My voice was hard like steel.

Josie pulled away from me. She looked up at me. Her eyes were pleading.

'Please be careful, Sean.'

'I will.'

My voice was deadly calm. I was glad she hadn't tried to talk me out of it.

I curled my fingers into the floor as I pushed myself up, my muscles coiled like a predator about to strike as I stood towering over Josie. A storm of violence was about to break. I clenched my jaw so hard it ached. My fingers were twitching for blood. Reggie's blood. I was a hair's breadth from unleashing absolute carnage on Bennett. When I caught up with him, he'd wish he'd never started this.

19

SEAN

I pushed open the heavy oak door of The Velvet Ace and stood filling the entrance, surveying the scene. The place pulsed with life. Laughter and the clatter of poker chips filled the room. Gamblers clustered around the blackjack table, throwing small fortunes onto the felt. Smoke hovered over them in thick plumes. The scent of cigars hung like a dense fog. Waitresses weaved through the crowd, their miniskirts tight, their smiles well-practised, but the atmosphere shifted as soon as I stormed through the door. The air held an edge of something darker.

The room didn't go silent, but a ripple passed through the crowd. A pause in conversation. A sideways glance. A few men straightened in their seats instinctively, aware that something dangerous had entered their space. I wasn't a man who would go unnoticed. I was breathing like a bull ready to charge, my massive frame stiff with barely restrained fury. My eyes were wild as I scanned the place looking for the fucker who'd taken my child.

Partially hidden behind a damask curtain, Reggie lounged in his private booth with his legs stretched out. King of a rotten empire, he was flanked by his usual muscle. His ever-present fat cigar rested between his ring-adorned fingers as he swirled a glass of brandy like he hadn't got a care in the world. The cockney bastard had a smirk plastered across his ruddy face. I couldn't wait to wipe it off.

Reggie wore a tailored three-piece suit in dove grey. The lapels were wide and the waistcoat was snug. A gold chain from a pocket watch glinted against the fabric. His shirt was deep burgundy. He'd undone the top buttons to reveal a thick gold chain resting against his chest.

Bennett thought he was safe, so he hadn't looked over when I'd pulled back the curtain. As he clocked me, his smile faded. Niall was behind me, and the rest of my men were milling about close to my brother, but Reggie had barely noticed them. He was too busy staring at me.

The moment my eyes landed on him, the room may as well have emptied. This was between the two of us. It was personal. No words were spoken. No words were needed. I had murder on my mind.

Freddie was the first to react to my presence. He'd been sitting next to Reggie, but he suddenly moved like a storm rolling in, his broad shoulders tense, his fists clenched so hard his knuckles cracked. As the big lump swung for me, I didn't hesitate. I grabbed him by the lapel and slammed my forehead into Freddie's nose. The crunch echoed through the room, followed by an agonised cry as the man mountain crumpled, blood pouring down his face.

I glanced over my shoulder. The gamblers carried on, pretending they weren't watching, but the dealers had stiffened, and the bouncers were already shifting on their feet. Everyone felt it. The air in the room was charged.

Niall rushed past me like the wind and disarmed Pistol Pete as he aimed his gun at me. Pete didn't have time to move before Niall drove a fist into his gut, then he grabbed the back of Pete's neck and smashed his face into the edge of the table. His body hit the floor with a thud.

Reggie exhaled a slow breath, masking his nerves with a smirk.

'Now, now, Sean, that's no way to behave in my casino.'

I had to be quick. I didn't have a moment to lose. Time would soon run out for me. I needed answers before the bouncers showed me the door. I crossed the floor in long, heavy strides, then slammed my fists down on the table with enough force to make the glasses jump, catching Reggie by surprise. I grabbed him by the collar and wrenched him out of the booth. The brandy bottle tipped, spilling dark liquid across the wooden floor.

Reggie blinked rapidly when I slammed him against the wall with a force so hard the framed picture behind him crashed to the ground. The room held its breath. Reggie fixed his blue eyes on mine and grinned like this was a joke. But as sure as God was my witness, he wouldn't be smiling when I finished with him. My unspent violence was hard to contain.

I wrenched him upward until our faces were inches apart.

'Right, stop fucking about and tell me where she is. What have you done with my daughter?'

My voice came out as a growl. My breath was hot against Reggie's face. He let out a raspy chuckle to mask his fear. But I could see he was intimidated by the beads of sweat that had settled on his upper lip and the pounding of the pulse in his neck above his shirt collar.

'Come on, Sean. You know how this works. You fuck with me, I fuck with you,' Reggie said, his cockney accent thick and lazy.

That wasn't the response I was looking for. I hadn't come here to play games, so I punched him in the gut, a brutal, bone-cracking shot straight to the ribs. Reggie choked on the groan escaping from his lips. His knees buckled, but I didn't let him fall. I held him up by the lapels of his grey suit jacket as blood seeped between my fingers. My knuckles were still raw from my last fight.

'Let's try again, shall we? Where's my daughter?'

My voice took on a menacing, more lethal edge.

Reggie spat blood onto the aged wooden floorboards, then he laughed in my face in a show of bravado. I caught the stench of expensive cigars on his breath.

'Maybe you should've thought about the consequences before you stuck your nose into my business. Did you really think you could pay Mary's debt without facing any comeback?'

So that was what this was about. Reggie's reaction to my generosity was way over the top. I'd expected to tread on Bennett's toes when I got involved with the

O'Haras' threatened eviction. But he'd taken things to another level. If he wanted to up the stakes, I wouldn't disappoint him. I grabbed the cigar Reggie still had gripped in his hand and pressed the lit end against the soft skin of his neck. His scream ripped through the room. Then he started thrashing against my hold, but he was no match for me. There was no escape. The smell of burning flesh wafted into the air. It was putrefying, but I didn't flinch. Reggie panted as his whole body shook.

'Bring it on, but leave Orla out of this. She's just a little girl. This is between you and me, Bennett.'

My voice was calm. Although my fury still bubbled beneath the surface.

My words seemed to snap Reggie out of his pain. He suddenly stopped writhing, straightened his posture and exhaled slow, exaggerated breaths like the action inconvenienced him.

'You seem to have forgotten your manners, Sean. You barge into my place like a mad dog, barking threats, making a scene, trashing things...'

'Fuck my manners! Where's my daughter?' I raged, frustrated by Reggie's lack of cooperation.

Reggie's lips curled.

'That little girl of yours is a wild one. She gave my boys a load of trouble.'

My stomach turned to ice as a new kind of rage flooded my system.

'If you've harmed her in any way...' I clenched my jaw as I eyeballed Bennett.

'She's in one piece for now, but if you want that to continue, you need to settle down. All this stress ain't good for your blood pressure.'

My grip on him loosened. He smiled, then he patted my cheek like I was his pet. His grin was wolfish. His mouth was full of yellowed teeth. No wonder his breath stank.

'Do you really think I'd let you waltz in here, throw your weight around, and then tell you where she is? Christ, you Paddies are as thick as shit!' Reggie's eyes glinted with amusement.

I felt the presence of his men surrounding me. Closing in. Preparing to pounce. Hands in pockets, resting on the butts of pistols. Primed and ready for action. Reggie lifted a lazy hand to stop them.

'You're all heat and no brains, O'Connor.'

'You touch one hair on her head, Reggie... I swear to God, if you don't tell me where she is, I'll...'

'You'll what? You'll kill me? In my casino? With my men surrounding you?' Reggie hissed. His smirk widened, and suddenly the weight of the room shifted.

'Don't tempt me,' I replied through gritted teeth. My vision blurred at the edges with pure, undiluted rage.

Reggie leaned in, his voice dropping to a whisper. 'You think you're a big man, but you have no power here. If you want your little girl back, you need to play the game. My way.'

My jaw was clenched so tightly it ached. My muscles were coiled, ready to rain blows down on anyone who came into contact with me.

Reggie grinned wider and rubbed me on the chest like I was a dog. 'Now, do me a favour, get your grubby hands off me and fuck off out of my casino before my men make mincemeat of you and your bunch of hobos.'

By the time Reggie finished his sentence, the bouncers were on me. Before I could swing or move a muscle, two thick arms clamped around my shoulders and yanked me backwards. Pain ripped through my insides as a fist like a sledgehammer slammed into my gut, knocking the breath from my lungs. Gasps rippled through the casino as chairs scraped and people scrambled for cover.

They'd sensed I wasn't going to go down without a fight. They were right. I elbowed one of the bouncers in the face, the crunch of cartilage satisfying even through the haze of rage. One of the other men grabbed my arm in response, twisting it back, but I yanked it free with such force that it sent him crashing into a table. My crew and I inflicted damage, but being on Reggie's home turf, there were too many heavies to fend off. The odds were stacked against us.

A fist to my jaw sent white-hot pain bursting through the lower half of my face. I was still reeling from that when I felt the brutal blow to my ribs which knocked the wind out of me. Two men started pulling me towards the door, but I fought like a caged animal, throwing elbows, cracking skulls. Someone went down, clutching their nose. Then another strike hit me, this time to my temple, which rocked me further. The world spun. A hard boot to the back of my knee sent me crashing to the floor. More kicks to the ribs, back and stomach followed. Through the beating I endured, Reggie stood grinning, delight oozing from every pore in his slimy skin.

'You never learn, do you, Sean?' Reggie's voice was smooth and dripping with amusement.

I spat blood onto the wooden floor before crawling onto my hands and knees.

'You might have won this round, but you're a dead man, Bennett.'

Reggie laughed and fixed his blue gaze on me as

he patted his hand over his thinning blond, slicked-back hair, doing his best to tame a few unruly strands that refused to stay in place despite the Brylcreem weighing them down.

'Maybe, someday. But not tonight, O'Connor.'

With a snap of Reggie's fingers, the bouncers hauled me up. Taking full advantage of my weakened state, they half-carried, half-dragged me through the casino, past the flashing lights of the fruit machines and the watchful eyes of the men and women who were now huddled together on the far side of the room. The last thing I saw before they tossed me and my men out onto the pavement was Reggie standing in his booth, relighting his cigar, watching over the proceedings with a smirk of pure satisfaction pasted on his lined face.

The doors slammed shut, and I heard the unmistakable sound of the bolts locking into place. The cold night air bit into my skin as I pushed myself onto all fours. The exertion made me cough and spit blood onto the concrete slabs. I cast my eyes around. Niall and my men had fared better than I had.

My heart pounded as fury coursed through my veins, making my entire body vibrate with rage. Blood dripped from my split lip. My ribs screamed in protest. But none of that mattered. Orla was still out there, scared and alone. She needed me, and I wouldn't let her down. When something precious was taken away from you, it cut deep.

I wiped the blood from my mouth. My jaw tightened against the pain. I would tear Reggie Bennett apart piece by fucking piece when all of this was over. But first, I had to find out where he was holding Orla. When I got my daughter back, I would burn everything Reggie owned to the ground and see how he liked it. He'd poured petrol through my letterbox and threatened to torch Mary's flat, so that seemed like a suitable payback if you asked me.

20

REGGIE

Now that the scum invading my premises had been ejected, I leaned back with my legs spread wide and a smug grin pulling at my lips. I puffed on what was left of my cigar while I swirled a hefty celebratory measure of brandy around in my glass. The clink of ice cubes knocking together was the only sound at the table before I let out a low chuckle. Freddie and Pete looked a sorry sight, sitting opposite me, licking their wounds. A feeling of elation had chased my pain away.

'Cheer up, boys. You've got faces like slapped arses. Your ugly mugs are killing the mood. Either buck yourselves up or fuck off home,' I said, exhaling smoke through my nose.

Freddie and Pete instantly followed orders and shed their glum expressions. Freddie was fully on board, grinning like a fool, but Pete's laughter was more hesitant. His eyes kept darting towards the frosted glass window beyond the casino floor, no doubt worried Sean would reappear. There was no chance of that happening. Not on my watch. The big Dubliner had picked a fight with the wrong man.

'O'Connor and his band of merry men looked like proper mugs getting dragged out of here. Since Sean gave Crusher a hiding, it's gone to his head. He thinks he's untouchable,' Freddie said, shaking his head.

I took a slow sip of my drink, savouring the burn.

'Well, he's about to learn the hard way that no-body's untouchable, not when you hit them where it hurts. I'm the one in the power seat. Taking his little girl will break him proper.'

I leaned forward and placed my glass down with a thud. Pete jumped out of his skin and then tried to brush off his alarm by shifting in his seat. But his eyes were wild, and he was wearing an expression I wouldn't usually associate with him. Fear.

'You're acting like a proper tart. What's wrong with you?'

Pete cleared his throat before he answered me.

'Are you sure about this, Reg? I hope you know

what you're doing. O'Connor's an animal when he's pushed.'

'The big man didn't get very far throwing his bulk around tonight, did he?'

My grin widened. Then I knocked back the rest of my drink and slammed the glass down in front of Pete. He didn't flinch this time.

'The next time O'Connor comes through those doors... he'll be leaving in a box.'

Freddie let out a cackle, while Pete just swallowed hard as he stared at the amber liquid in his own glass. But even his doom and gloom, depressing demeanour couldn't dampen my spirits. I was on a high and the only way was up!

21

SEAN

Outside The Velvet Ace, the street lights cast long, twisted shadows against the pavement. London never truly slept, but there were quiet pockets in Soho, dark places where bad things happened and nobody asked questions.

'You might as well head off, lads,' I said to my men, gesturing to Niall with a flick of the head to join me in the alley at the side of Reggie's casino.

My ribs ached where Bennett's men had laid into me before they'd tossed me out like rubbish. I looked down at my hands, stinging in the cold night air. My knuckles were raw, but none of it mattered because Orla was still missing. Josie would be worried sick, but I couldn't go home until I found her.

Niall went ahead of me. By the time I rounded the corner, he was waiting, his face shadowed beneath the street lamp's dim glow. The rain was light but relentless, creating large puddles in the potholed asphalt.

'They worked you over good,' Niall muttered, stepping forward to take a closer look at my battle scars.

The taste of blood in my mouth turned my stomach, so I spat it onto the floor. Then I rolled my shoulders and cracked my neck.

'It's nothing I can't handle.'

Niall's eyebrows raised, and he clenched his jaw.

'Did Reggie tell you where he's taken Orla?'

I shook my head, eyes burning with fury. 'No.' I exhaled sharply. 'But we're going to jump Freddie and force it out of him.'

Niall nodded once, and then silence stretched between us.

Freddie wasn't the sharpest tool in the box, but his loyalty to Reggie was unwavering, which made him dangerous. Getting him alone would be challenging. He never strayed far from his boss's side, except to run errands or clean up a mess. But I'd have to try. It wasn't as though I had any other options.

'I think you'll want to see this, Sean,' Niall said, a sense of urgency in his voice.

He was standing in front of me, so he had a better

view of The Velvet Ace. I craned my neck and peered around the corner. Freddie had stepped out of the casino's entrance, whistling to himself. The collar of his brown wool coat was pulled up against the damp air on either side of his cream roll-neck jumper. I couldn't believe our luck. The gormless fucker was alone.

I flexed my fingers as I prepared to fight. 'Let's go and get the bastard.'

Without another word, Niall and I fell in step behind Freddie, our footsteps swallowed by the sound of city life. He walked with the cocky stride of a man who thought he was off-limits.

I moved first, emerging like a ghostly figure. My massive hand clamped over Freddie's mouth before he could so much as gasp. The look of horror on his face told me he hadn't seen us coming when I yanked him backwards into an alley, dragging him into the darkness. I shoved him hard against a brick wall. The impact knocked the air from his lungs. Freddie's eyes darted wildly. While Niall kept lookout, I drove a fist into his gut. Freddie doubled over with a choked grunt, coughing as he tried to catch his breath.

'Where is she?'

My voice was low and calm, but it was the kind of calm that promised violence. Freddie stayed silent. So

I didn't hesitate; I grabbed a clump of his brown col-lar-length hair and twisted it, forcing him to look up from his doubled-over position.

'Where. Is. She?'

'I-I don't—'

I interrupted his denial with another punch, this time to his ribs. Something broke.

Freddie yelped, and his body sagged against the wall.

'Where the fuck is my daughter?'

'I swear to you, I don't know.'

I leaned in close to Freddie and squeezed the man's throat. His eyes started to bulge as he clawed at my hand.

'I won't stop until I beat the truth out of you,' I snarled, getting up in his face. Then I took a step back and drove my fist into Freddie's gut again, harder this time. Freddie hit the floor, wheezing, his hands clutching his ribs.

I crouched beside him and grabbed his hand, my fingers tightening around his wrist.

'Believe me, you'll wish you'd spoken up sooner by the time I've finished with you.'

And then, with a swift, brutal twist, I snapped two of Freddie's fingers. The crack of bone echoed through the space. The scream that followed was guttural, raw agony. His face twisted in pain as his breath came in frantic bursts. I grabbed him by the collar and slammed him against the bricks.

'Now, I'll ask you one last time, or I'll really go to town on you. Where the fuck is my daughter?'

Freddie coughed, and blood speckled his lips. He looked at Niall as though maybe he'd be the reasonable one, but my brother stepped closer to him, his face set like stone to add weight to the threat.

'Sean can do this all night and not even break a sweat,' Niall said, his voice casual. 'Or we can skip to the part where you tell us what we want to know, and he'll leave you with enough bones intact to limp home.'

Freddie swallowed hard. Then he licked his lips. His eyes darted from side to side like he was searching for a way out. But there was no one around to help him. He knew only too well what I was capable of.

I was fed up with waiting for a reply, so I pressed my forearm against Freddie's throat, applying just enough pressure to make breathing difficult and give him some encouragement to cooperate.

'I'm tired of this, Freddie. You're really starting to fuck me off. Either you tell me where she is, or I'll finish you. Nothing would give me greater pleasure than killing you with my bare hands,' I threatened.

The words had barely left my mouth when Freddie wheezed, his fingers clawing at my arm. Something told me the bastard was about to blab, so I relaxed my arm a fraction.

'S-she's in a warehouse. A-an old t-textile factory down by the d-docks...' Freddie spluttered.

I exchanged a look with Niall. That made sense. Many of London's docks were abandoned. The isolated spaces had plenty of hiding places.

'Now that wasn't so hard, was it?' I said, petting him on the top of the head like an obedient dog as I freed his windpipe. 'Where's this warehouse located?'

The Thames was lined with derelict buildings, which were now being used as clandestine storage for illegal goods. Without insider knowledge, finding Orla would be an enormous task. I wouldn't know where to start.

'Greenwich Pier,' Freddie gasped. 'Honestly, that's all I know. Please let me go.'

'You'd better not be lying...'

'I swear to you, I'm not,' Freddie panted.

'If you are, I'll finish this properly.'

I smashed his head back against the wall for good measure before I let him go. Freddie's body slid down the brickwork. He sat on the wet ground in a daze.

He'd taken a pounding, but he was lucky he was still breathing.

I stepped back, rolled my shoulders and glared at Freddie. Then I stepped away, leaving him broken on the floor. Niall's fist came from nowhere and cracked against Freddie's jaw, making him slump against the bricks. He was out cold.

'The fucker deserved that for not speaking up sooner.' Niall smirked.

I didn't smile back. My jaw was tight. My head was pounding with one singular thought. I had a daughter to save. Once I got her back, Reggie Bennett would find out what happened when you took something precious from Sean O'Connor.

22

SEAN

The old docklands were eerily quiet. The smell of decay was thick in the damp air. Waves lapped at the pilings, a slow, rhythmic sound that did nothing to ease the storm raging inside me. The place was mostly abandoned at this hour, apart from the occasional drunk stumbling home or a late-night deal exchanging hands in the shadows.

The row of warehouses loomed out of the ground like ghosts against the misty glow of the London night. A single street lamp flickered outside the old textile factory. Niall and I stepped out of his car and looked at the building. Its corrugated walls were streaked with rust. By the looks of it, it hadn't been in use for years.

We moved like spirits through the mist, our bodies coiled with lethal intent. As Niall and I approached the entrance, our boots crunched over broken glass and gravel. The weight of my revolver felt heavy in my grip. My heart hammered against my ribs, but my hands were steady. My daughter and the men who'd taken her were inside that building. I was ready to tear the place apart.

As we drew closer, we hugged the shadows. Stayed in the darkness. Now that the warehouse was just ahead of us, I could see the door slightly ajar. Sloppy, I thought. An invitation for trouble, or a trap. I didn't care which. Niall glanced at me before he peered through a grimy window.

'By the looks of it, there are two keeping watch. One's sitting, the other's pacing.'

'And Orla?'

'I can't see her.'

Niall eased the door open just enough for us to slip inside. I gripped my revolver tightly. My pulse was a slow, measured drumbeat in my ears as I stepped through the doorway. The inside of the warehouse was cavernous, a rotting skeleton of a building. It smelled old and musty. Rusted conveyor belts, abandoned machines and shattered pallets littered the floor. Stacks of crates lined the walls, creating a maze of makeshift cover. A single hanging bulb swung from the rafters, throwing shadows across the concrete and revealing the men near the centre of the room.

One man sat on a wooden crate a few feet away, flipping a knife from hand to hand. The bigger, meaner-looking one was pacing back and forth near a stack of barrels, with a cigarette dangling from his lips. He was holding a crowbar in one hand.

I didn't delay. I stepped out from the shadows, raised my gun and put a bullet through the seated man's knee. His scream shattered the silence. Niall rushed forward and wrapped an arm around his throat, jerking him back. He'd been cradling his knee while holding the knife, but the pressure on his neck sent it clattering to the floor.

The big bastard with the crowbar charged. I barely had time to dodge as the iron bar swung past me. It smashed into the stacked-up crates beside me, inches from my head, sending splinters flying. I ducked low and drove my shoulder into the man's gut. The force pushed him backwards and slammed him against the barrels. The man grunted but didn't fold. Instead, he brought his elbow down hard against my back, making me drop to one knee. But I recovered fast and fired a shot at close range into his stomach. His eyes grew wide as his hands covered the wound, which sent the crowbar clattering to the ground.

For a couple of seconds, I watched blood seep across the fabric of his white shirt before I let my fury rain down on him. My fists hammered into his face until the man stopped moving. As his last breath left his body, I glanced down at my knuckles. They were weeping, but the satisfaction of beating him to death was worth every ounce of pain.

A groan from behind snapped me back to reality. I walked over to where Niall was guarding the injured man, grabbed him by the collar and hauled him onto his feet.

'Please don't kill me. I've got a wife and kids...'

'Haven't we all,' I growled, getting up in his terrified face. He could beg all he liked. It wasn't going to make me go any easier on him.

'Are there any more of Reggie's men lurking nearby?' I asked, holding the gun under the man's chin.

'No. He thought two of us would be enough.'

'Well, he thought wrong! Where's my daughter?' I demanded.

The man gestured with a flick of his head to the rear of the warehouse.

I drove the man's head into the nearest crate, letting him slump to the floor, unconscious as a parting gesture. Then I turned my attention to Orla and rushed to the back of the room. My heart was hammering in my chest.

The sight that greeted me made me gasp. My breath caught in my throat when I spotted my daughter's small frame hunched on a wooden chair. Her hands were bound in front of her, and a strip of tape covered her mouth. Her chest was rising and falling rapidly. Her cheeks were wet from the tears that had streaked her face. I crossed the distance in two strides and stood in front of her. She'd been looking into the middle distance but stared up at me when she saw me. Her big blue eyes were wide with terror, which made my blood run cold.

'It's all right, sweetheart. I'm here now,' I murmured, dropping to my knees.

I untied the ropes with shaking hands. Her tiny wrists were striped red from where the rope had bitten into them. Fresh rage roared inside me. Only a monster could do this to a defenceless child.

'Don't be scared. I've got you, darling.'

I pulled the tape from her mouth with a gentleness that didn't match the carnage around us. Then I cupped her angelic face. Her red curls were a tangled mess, but she was alive. A huge surge of relief swept through me.

'My mouth hurts, Daddy,' Orla whimpered, lifting her fingers to point out her injury.

Blood had dripped onto the front of her nightdress from her cut lip. I felt something inside me snap. Reggie had hurt my daughter, so he was going to pay dearly. This was far from over. Reggie Bennett had declared war.

'I think we'd better get out of here,' Niall said from where he'd been keeping watch.

'I want to go home.' Orla let out a sob as her small hands reached for my shirt.

'It's OK, angel. You're safe now,' I whispered, stroking her hair.

When I scooped Orla up, she threw her arms around my neck and held on to me like she'd never let go. She buried her face in my shoulder. I could feel her body trembling, so I kissed the top of her head. My heart thundered as I held her tight. I was scared I might crush her. She was as light as a feather, but I wanted to squeeze the fear out of her.

A slow clap caught my attention when it broke through the silence. Seconds later, Reggie Bennett stepped from the shadows, flanked by four of his men.

'Aww, ain't this touching? Real touching.' Reggie

grinned in the dim light, showing off his yellow teeth. My jaw flexed as we glared at each other. No love lost between us.

'You should never have touched my family...'

'And you should never have meddled in my business!' Reggie motioned to his men. 'Kill them. All of them. Start with the girl.'

Reggie had barely finished his sentence when the warehouse erupted into chaos. The man to his right wielded a baseball bat as he charged towards me. I reacted in an instant, shoving Orla behind a crate.

'Close your eyes, sweetheart, and stay here until I come back,' I said.

My daughter nodded and then buried her face in her hands, obeying without question.

I ducked the brute's first swing, but the second clipped my ribs, sending pain exploding through my side. I gritted my teeth and let the rage absorb the hurt, then I lunged and grabbed the crowbar mid-swing. With a yank, I pulled the man off balance and drove my forehead straight into his nose. A crack sounded as blood poured down the bastard's face. I didn't give him a chance to recover. I bashed his skull over and over with the crowbar. Once. Twice. Three times. By the fourth, the man's body had gone slack. His skull had cracked open like a watermelon. I let go of him, and his corpse dropped to the floor. For a second, I was mesmerised by the way his blood pooled around him. But the sound of gunfire tearing through the warehouse snapped me out of the trance. Bullets sparked off metal beams as the air filled with smoke and the stink of burning gunpowder. Reggie ducked behind a stack of crates, cursing as Niall went to battle. My brother fought like a savage, dodging blades and cut-throat razors. He was outnumbered. I had to help him before it was too late.

My finger tightened on the trigger of my gun as I moved through the chaos like a man possessed, desperate to get in on the action. One of Reggie's thugs grabbed Niall from behind. Niall drove his elbow into the man's ribs, then spun around and shot him point-blank in the throat. The man's head snapped back as blood started spurting out. He let out a wet gurgle before dropping to the ground.

Another man went to rush Niall, swinging a bat, but I caught it mid-air and wrenched it out of his hand. I slammed it into the bastard's face, sending his teeth scattering across the floor. He stumbled, recovered and drove forward. His fist connected with the side of my head, so I brought the bat down hard. The first blow shattered the man's knee. He screamed and began writhing around on the floor. The second cracked his skull. And the third made sure he'd never breathe again. Silence followed. Just the sound of my panting.

Niall was locked in a shootout with Reggie's last man. Spent ammo littered the floor as they desperately tried to finish each other off. Niall got lucky and fired two shots into the man's gut, which made him crumple. He clutched the gaping wound in his stomach as he slid to the floor with blood seeping out of him.

Only Reggie was left. I turned with my gun raised, ready to finish off the bastard, but I realised the coward had slipped away. I heard the side door swing open, followed by the faint echo of retreating footsteps disappearing into the night. I wanted to chase after him, but he'd have to wait. Orla was more important.

I rushed over to where I'd left my daughter and gathered her into my arms. At first, she whimpered when I cradled her, but then her tiny fingers curled into the damp wool of my jacket.

'Everything's going to be all right,' I said, pressing a kiss to her auburn hair.

Niall exhaled, wiping blood from his face. 'For now,' he said.

My expression darkened, and I threw my brother a

black look. Orla was scared enough without him making things ten times worse.

A low groan behind me caught my attention, so I tore my eyes away from Niall and turned around. The man Niall had shot in the gut was still alive, dragging himself across the floor, leaving a smear of blood in his wake in a desperate, pathetic crawl.

I handed Orla to Niall and walked over to the man. His breath rattled in his chest as I loomed over him like a reaper summoned from the pits of hell. He looked up at me and tried to speak. His lips were moving soundlessly. Then he coughed up blood, staining the front of his shirt. He was weak but stubborn. He needed to be put out of his misery, so I fired a bullet into his head before he could call for help.

The gunshot shattered the quiet and echoed through the warehouse. The only sound filling the cavernous space was Orla's crying. I walked back to where Niall was waiting and took her from his arms.

'Shush. Shush. Don't cry, darling,' I soothed.

Then I carried her out of the warehouse, stepping over the bodies of Reggie's men like they were nothing. Because to me, that's exactly what they were. They were the scum of the earth. They were evil bastards who were willing to hurt a kid to earn a crust.

As I walked to Niall's car, I felt something bitter,

something dark, begin to fester inside me. This was beyond business. Reggie Bennett had made it personal. He'd crossed a line. And there was no going back. I'd make damn sure he paid for what he'd done. This wasn't over. Not by a long shot. Not until Reggie Bennett was dead. And after I took his life, I was going to paint London red with his blood!

23

DECLAN

Dublin, November 1975

After the last fiasco, when Hargrove almost intercepted my shipment, I wasn't taking any chances. I'd travelled to Dublin with Fergal to escort the next batch of liquid gold back. I'd left Aidan holding the fort in London. He'd keep a close eye on what O'-Connor and his crew were up to in my absence. I'd have liked to have stayed longer, but I couldn't spare the time, so I was only home for a fleeting visit. Sean would try to muscle in on my territory if he got wind of the fact that I wasn't around.

Smuggling whiskey required a mix of corruption,

cunning and a network of reliable men willing to risk everything. O'Connor and I had once been allies. We'd worked together in the smuggling game for the same firm before we'd branched off to build our own empire, but as tensions rose between us, trust eroded. Sean's unpredictable violence was more than I could handle, so I tried to cut him out of the operation. Never one to take a slight, O'Connor retaliated by hijacking the first shipment. That act set the stage for full-scale war. We were now bitter rivals. Sean would stab me in the back if he got half a chance. The feeling was mutual.

The memory of that night was engraved in my brain in case my hatred for Sean O'Connor ever waned. Fergal and I sat in silence as I drove the borrowed van to the rendezvous. On the journey, I drifted back to when Sean O'Connor betrayed me.

The ship carrying my latest consignment of fine Irish whiskey, destined for London's underground bars, had just arrived from Belfast. The crates were being unloaded by dockers who'd moved with the efficiency of men who knew not to ask questions. But unbeknownst to us, Sean O'Connor and his younger brother, Niall, were watching from the shadows. They were crouched beside a stack of rusted shipping containers, waiting for the perfect moment to strike. We were relatively new to the game, so we'd been too comfortable. Overconfident. We were armed, but we hadn't been expecting trouble. That laziness cost us dearly.

There had been six of us. Three of them. The threat they'd posed should have caused us no bother. But they had the element of surprise on their side. My guys were laughing and joking, cigarettes glowing in the darkness, when O'Connor's crew made their move, carrying themselves with the precision of men who'd done stuff like this before.

One of my team had spotted three figures headed our way and had called out to raise the alarm, but Sean didn't let him finish his sentence. O'Connor was fast for a man of his size. His fist crashed into my guy's jaw with a crunch before the docker had a chance to dodge the blow. The punch floored him, and he crumpled onto the damp concrete, spitting blood from his injured mouth.

Then, chaos had erupted. Niall had swung a crowbar into another of my lad's ribs. The solid crack of bone echoed through the docks. While he was reeling from the strike, Niall had grabbed the back of his head and slammed it against a crate. Blood had

STEPHANIE HARTE

smeared the wooden surface as he collapsed in a heap.

'We'll handle this. You finish putting the last of the crates on the truck,' Sean had said to his other guy.

I'd been holding back. Calculating my next move. I'd never been one to act on impulse, unlike my hot-headed younger brother. I preferred to play the long game. To me, power was like a game of chess, and I was always three moves ahead. Putting myself in the firing line wouldn't stop Sean from stealing my shipment. I was more dangerous than these thugs because I didn't act out of rage. I acted with purpose.

A shot had rung out. One of the dockers on my payroll had panicked and fired into the night. The bullet had ricocheted off the steel hull of the boat but not hit O'Connor or his crew. Before he could fire again, Sean had grabbed him from behind and wrenched his arm backwards until the bones snapped like dry twigs. The man had screamed, his body convulsing in agony as Sean ripped the gun from his hand. Then O'Connor lunged at him with a knife and drove it deep into the man's stomach, twisting it hard before ripping it sideways. The docker had howled like a dying animal. Then he'd dropped to his knees and bled out on the floor.

I'd still been absorbing the gruesome events when I realised I was next in Sean's sights. As his bloodied footsteps had closed in on me, I'd pulled my revolver from the waistband of my flared cords and aimed the barrel at his chest. I'd squeezed the trigger, but the mechanism had jammed. Sean had run at me, slashing wildly. I'd sidestepped him and caught his wrist mid-swing. I'd struggled to take possession of the blade, and Sean had rained punches down on me with his free arm. My head had been spinning. I'd felt my legs start to buckle when I'd heard Niall call out into the darkness.

'Come on, Sean. We've got the whiskey. Let's get out of here.'

Sean had given me an almighty shove, which had made me lose my balance. I'd hit the deck as the loser. The dock had gone silent, apart from the groans of the wounded and the lapping of the tide.

Before Sean had driven away with my shipment, he'd wiped his knuckles on his coat and smirked over at me. Then he'd lit a cigarette with bloodied fingers, taken a drag and exhaled a long plume of smoke.

'Sorry you tried to double-cross me now, Kelly, are you?'

Sean hadn't waited for me to reply. I'd watched

from the floor, my pride bruised, as my precious cargo of whiskey disappeared into the night. While O'-Connor had been tearing into me, instead of coming to my aid, the two remaining members of my team had taken off with their tails between their legs. Fucking cowards. They'd been sorry they'd deserted me when I'd caught up with them. But no amount of begging was going to appease me. Neither of them were able to run anywhere again, now that they'd been kneecapped. I wasn't sadistic, but I was more than capable of cruelty. Violence, to me, was just another tool of business.

Sean may have won that round, but the war between us had begun. When I'd struck a deal with the Belfast Syndicate, a group of ex-paramilitaries who'd changed professions and were now smuggling whiskey across the Irish Sea concealed in legitimate shipments, I hadn't realised Sean had inside men at Bushmills. I'd paid them well for their discretion and their muscle. They'd moved my product in fake dairy tankers, hidden the crates among shipments of butter and cheese headed for England. But the greedy bastards had sold me out and tipped O'Connor off.

I had a new source now – McCarthy's Malt. A long-established but struggling whiskey distillery in County Cork with links to the Jameson empire. They operated legally by day but supplied illicit shipments at night, doctoring their books to cover missing barrels. After the Belfast Syndicate let me down, I strong-armed them into a deal, ensuring I got first pick of their best batches before they hit the legitimate market. The agreement was working well. For now.

24

JOSIE

London, November 1975

I'd been sitting by the window with my rosary clutched between tense fingers when Niall's car pulled up outside. I ran from my lookout point, but didn't make it to the front door before it burst open. My breath caught in my throat as I took in the sight that greeted me.

Sean was filling the doorway, wild-eyed, his face bloodied and bruised. Beneath his coat, I could see his shirt was torn and dirty, damp with sweat and something darker. Blood. Even though I was concerned about my battle-scarred husband, I tore my eyes away from him and fixed them on Orla.

My daughter clung to her daddy. Her protector. Her tiny arms were wrapped around his thick neck and her face was buried into his broad shoulder. She was shaking. Trembling from head to toe with fear. My knees nearly buckled as I imagined what she'd been through.

'My poor baby.'

A sob escaped from my throat as I rushed forward, hands outstretched. Orla lifted her head at the sound of my voice. Her tear-streaked face twisted with relief, and she managed a little smile.

'Mummy!'

My heart jumped with joy. I'd been terrified that I might never get to hold my child again. Sean barely had time to loosen his grip before I yanked Orla from his arms and crushed her against my chest. My fingers stroked her tangled red hair as my lips pressed down on her repeatedly, smothering her in kisses.

'Did they hurt you?' I asked as my eyes scanned over her.

I could see her lip was cut and swollen, but I was worried that she had other injuries that weren't visible.

Orla nodded. 'One of the men slapped me around the face because I tried to wriggle free when he was tying me to a chair.'

I glanced sideways at Sean and saw rage darken his features. Then I ran my fingertips gently down the side of Orla's face.

'What a horrible man to do that to you! I'll put something cold on it and that will take the swelling down,' I said to try to make her feel better.

'I was so scared when the men took me away, Mummy.'

Orla clung to me. Her tiny hands fisted into the fabric of my dress as she sobbed, so I clutched her tighter.

'Oh, my sweet girl, don't cry. You're safe now,' I whispered. I'd been so worried about her, so I held her like I'd never let her go again.

My tears fell as I rocked Orla. Her fingers gripped my dress for dear life, so I murmured soothing words into her ear. My heart was breaking in my chest, but I felt conflicted. On the one hand, I was so grateful to have my daughter home. But on the other, I was furious that Orla had become a pawn in the dangerous game Sean and Reggie were playing. Tension hung in the air around us. The only sound was Orla's sniffles.

When I slowly lifted my head, my eyes met Sean's. In that moment, I saw red. His injuries, his exhaustion and the fact that he'd fought and bled to bring our daughter home meant nothing to me. All I could see was the man who'd let this happen in the first place. I'd have to hold my anger inside for now and let it simmer because I didn't want to distress Orla any further. She'd been through enough already. But once my daughter was asleep in bed, Sean would feel the lash of my tongue good and proper.

25

DECLAN

Wicklow, November 1975

The Leyland van's headlights highlighted the outline of the Wicklow Mountains as we drove to the pickup point. They were vast and dark, wrapping around us as they stretched as far as the eye could see. Away from the bright lights of the city, the night sky hung low over the National Park. It was heavy with the weight of an impending storm. We'd chosen the location in the middle of the wilderness for privacy, but it suddenly seemed like a bad move. If the weather was about to turn, we were isolated, cut off from civilisation.

I stopped the van and killed the engine. When I

stepped outside, my breath misted in the cold, clean air, so I pulled my coat tighter around myself as I leaned against the warm bonnet. I trained my eyes on the winding road, which was barely visible as it snaked through the forest. There was no sign of anyone approaching. The only sound was the wind whistling as it whipped through the trees, carrying the scent of damp earth and pine.

I climbed back into the truck to shelter from the bitter gale when the wind stepped up a gear. Fergal and I sat in silence, chain-smoking the Major we'd bought in the duty-free to pass the time. Where the fuck were the McCarthys? I checked my watch. They were almost an hour late. The brothers were never this sloppy. I was usually patient, but even I had my limits. I glanced at Fergal as he sat beside me. He was resting one hand inside his coat where his revolver lay.

'They should've been here by now,' Fergal muttered as he turned to face me. 'Something's off. Do you think we should abandon the meeting?'

I could see he was rattled. I felt edgy myself, so I didn't respond. I lit another cigarette and inhaled deeply as my eyes scanned the treeline. It would be easy to panic. Our location was remote. The Wicklow

Mountains had swallowed people whole before, and tonight I sensed they felt hungry.

'If they're not here in ten minutes, we'll hit the road,' I said.

I took another look at my watch. Darkness was closing in on us. The only light was from the dim glow of the moon as it tried to push through the dense clouds. The air had grown damp, and now fog had started to roll in fast, spilling down the mountainside like a living thing. One moment, the trees stood stark and black against the night sky; the next, they were nowhere to be seen, their jagged outlines vanished into the creeping mist. It thickened with every breath, curling low around the ground, muffling sound, distorting shapes, heightening our nerves. An eerie, unnatural stillness had settled around us like a cloak, which sent a chill down my spine.

Time inched by as we watched and waited. Just as we were about to make tracks, the sound of an approaching engine broke the suffocating silence. A moment later, headlights appeared in the forest. They attempted to cut twin beams through the fog but couldn't illuminate the road for more than a few feet ahead. They bounced along the uneven dirt track before the battered Bedford lorry emerged from the trees. I let out a slow breath but didn't relax.

The truck rolled to a stop a few feet away. The driver's door creaked open, and Gerry, the older of the McCarthy brothers, climbed out, his frame stiff with tension. Owen surfaced from the passenger's side a heartbeat later. He moved slower, his hands raised slightly, not enough to be obvious, but enough for me to notice.

I opened my van's door, flicked my cigarette onto the ground and stepped forward.

'You took your fucking time. We were about to give up on you,' I said.

Gerry swallowed hard. His eyes darted backwards and forwards.

'I'm sorry we kept you waiting, but we ran into a delay.'

My gaze switched to the lorry. I noticed the back doors were shut, but we were behind schedule, so we needed to load the whiskey into my van straight away.

'What kind of delay?' I asked, suddenly suspicious that this was a set-up.

Gerry turned to look at his younger brother, which made Owen shift uncomfortably. He was twitchy, and his hands were trembling.

'We had to make a bit of a detour. There was a Transit...'

Before Gerry could finish his sentence, a branch

snapped, and a rustling sound came from some undergrowth in the distance.

Tension coiled tightly around me as I reached for my gun. Fergal mirrored my action, drawing his own weapon.

'Who did you bring with you?' I demanded.

My voice carried the weight of Dublin's inner-city streets. Gerry looked alarmed. He took a step back and shook his head from side to side.

'Nobody. It must have been an animal...'

I knew he didn't believe that any more than I did. The frantic bobbing of his Adam's apple had given away his fear.

Another crack came from the woods in front of us. Then the unmistakable click of a rifle being cocked pierced the silence. I didn't need anyone to tell me we were about to be ambushed.

'Get down,' I hissed with fury bubbling inside me.

Fergal and I dived behind the truck as the McCarthys scattered. Seconds later, the first gunshot tore through the night. The woods exploded as four figures emerged from the shadows, their rifles spitting fire, faces half-hidden under scarves.

Gerry got caught in the open as he moved position and took a bullet in the leg. A strangled scream escaped from his lips as he fell to the ground before he dragged himself behind the truck. Fergal returned fire to cover him. The revolver bucked in his grip as he dropped one of the shooters.

'Fuck! I'm sorry, Declan, we thought we'd lost them, but they must have tailed us,' Owen blurted out in a panicked voice.

His eyes were wild as they darted around the forest.

'Tailed you? You set us up more like!' My words were measured. Deliberate. My jaw clenched as the reality hit home. I didn't take kindly to being sold out.

'I swear to you, we didn't set you up,' Owen replied without missing a beat.

But I wasn't sure I could believe a word he said. 'Who are they? The Belfast Syndicate?' I wouldn't put it past them to try to move in on my supply.

'Honest to God, I've no idea,' Owen insisted.

He threw his left hand up while his right clutched tightly to his weapon. I didn't know what to think. Until now, the McCarthys had proved to be reliable and trustworthy. Although I was well aware that everyone had a price. But if the brothers were in on it, surely Gerry wouldn't be lying injured behind the van. Maybe Owen wasn't lying.

I peeked over the truck and spotted a man re-loading behind a boulder. Without hesitating, I fired one shot, then another two. The man's body slumped lifelessly against the stone. Gunfire crackled through the trees in response, muffled by the thickening fog that twisted through the Wicklow Mountains like a ghostly figure.

As the gunfire raged, I crouched behind the battered Bedford lorry, my heartbeat steady, my mind sharp. These bastards were chancers, thinking they could rob me blind so close to my own backyard. Well, they thought wrong. I was never going to let them walk away with my shipment. Not while I still had breath in my body.

Fergal reloaded beside me, muttering a curse as a bullet ricocheted off the truck's metal frame. Gerry clutched his leg, his face pale with shock as blood oozed through his fingers. If he was behind this, I was glad he was paying the price for his disloyalty.

A shadow moved through the fog, silent, creeping. Fergal raised his gun and fired several rounds. A pained cry travelled through the air, and then came the thud of a body hitting the dirt.

During the break in gunfire, my mind started working through our options. I had one goal, which was to get the whiskey away from here without sustaining any more casualties. Both vehicles were still intact, but transferring the crates from the Bedford to my Leyland van would be an impossible task. We'd weakened the other side, but they still had two men who were armed and dangerous. The thought had just entered my head when more shots and shouting began to echo around us.

Fergal reloaded beside me. He was gritting his teeth. His face was set in a grim line.

'I think they're lining themselves up to take the lorry,' he said.

I narrowed my eyes, squinting into the darkness. 'As if I'm going to stand for that! We need to move now and finish this,' I replied.

He nodded, understanding that I had no intention of trading bullets all night. When I gave the signal, Fergal and I broke cover and surged forward, shooting as we went. Bullets whizzed past us as the men fired off rounds. They weren't expecting the counterattack, and their aim was all over the place. I caught one of the bastards reloading and put a bullet clean between his eyes. I barely felt the recoil of my gun because my mind was on winning the fight.

The other man tried to run, but Fergal dropped him with two shots into his back. Job done. Fergal and I glanced at each other with victorious grins pasted on our faces. We thought we'd defeated the enemy, but we suddenly heard footsteps crashing through the undergrowth.

'We need to get to the van. If they take it, we're fucked,' I said.

My eyes darted between the parked vehicles. I wasn't going to hang around. I started running back towards the Bedford with Fergal at my heels. When I got closer, I grabbed Owen by the collar and shoved him towards the driver's door. Then I stooped down and dragged Gerry to his feet. He groaned in pain but helped to haul himself into the passenger's side.

'Don't wait for us, just drive,' I instructed.

I ran over to the Leyland and opened the door. Fergal jumped onto the back bumper, rifle at the ready, keeping watch as I climbed into the driver's seat. Once the engine roared to life, he joined me in the cab. The van lurched forward, its tyres skidding on the damp earth.

A shot rang out as we moved in convoy. There was a sniper in the trees. He'd hit the side mirror of the Bedford, which exploded. The sound of glass shattering filled the cab. Then another shot came. This time, it missed. I clenched my jaw. My hands were steady on the wheel. We couldn't afford to take a hit. It would draw attention to the van.

As the trucks tore down the winding mountain

road, the fog swallowed the scene behind us. Blood-soaked bodies cooling in the dirt vanished into the darkness. Once we'd put some distance between ourselves and the shooters and were sure they weren't following, I flashed my lights at Owen, signalling him to stop.

'Let's get the cargo swapped over and go our separate ways,' I said, pulling alongside the Bedford as the road had widened.

Whether I ever dealt with the McCarthys again would depend on what came to light. If I found out they had anything to do with the ambush, they'd be dead men walking.

26

JOSIE

London, November 1975

It seemed to take forever for Orla to drop off to sleep.
Every time her big blue eyes threatened to close, they
sprang open again and darted around the room as she
took a moment to familiarise herself with her surroundings. It was clear my daughter was traumatised
by the ordeal. Sean was going to pay for subjecting
her to the terrifying event.

'Why did you let this happen to us?'

My voice was hoarse, raw with sadness and fury.
Sean flinched as though I'd struck him. He swallowed
hard as he fixed his eyes on me.

'Now, just a minute, Josie...'

'Don't Josie me!' I stepped closer to my husband, my body trembling with rage. 'Orla could have been killed, Sean! She could have been...'

I choked on the word. I couldn't bring myself to say it out loud, but I could tell by the pained expression on his face that he'd filled in the blank.

'Don't even go there... I got her back, didn't I?'

My chest rose and fell rapidly. My emotions were warring with each other. I wasn't disputing that he'd brought Orla home. But everything I'd been through suddenly crashed down on me like a tidal wave. The fear. The helplessness. The sound of the front door being kicked in. The force of Reggie's punch when it connected with my face. The taste of the blood from my split lip. The pain in my stomach from his kicks. The panic I felt as he tore my dress from my shoulder. The overpowering smell of the Old Spice he'd doused himself in. And the sheer terror that coursed through my veins when Reggie finally left the house and took our child with him.

Sean had warned me off. He didn't want me to confront him over this, but he had no idea what I'd been through. What Orla had been through. Every time I caught sight of my reflection, everything came flooding back. One of my eyes was almost swollen shut, and there was a bruise blooming across my cheekbone. My injuries were visible. Orla's not so much apart from her cut lip. But that didn't mean she wasn't deeply scarred.

'You should never have let this happen. You should have taken notice of Reggie's warning,' I said, not willing to let the matter go.

Sean's jaw tensed, and then his shoulders slumped under the weight of guilt. He had no argument. No defence. This was his fault, and he knew it. He was the one who'd brought trouble to our door.

Silence stretched out between us. It was thick and suffocating. You could cut the tension filling the room with a knife. Finally, Sean let out a slow, shuddering breath.

'I promise I'll fix this, Josie,' he said.

But I didn't answer him. I turned my back on him. I couldn't bear to look at him. How could he fix this? The damage had already been done.

The house seemed colder than usual, or was it just the frostiness cooling the air? Sean stood near the door, arms braced against the frame, his broad shoulders hunched as he watched me move around the small kitchen. I hadn't looked at him once since we'd had words. He knew I was furious.

'You're not safe here, Josie.' Sean's voice was low and controlled, but it had an edge to it. A whisper of desperation had crept into his tone. 'You need to go back to Ireland with Orla until all this blows over.'

I slammed a plate into the drying rack. The clatter was sharp against the silence. My fingers were shaking as I gripped the sink. I spun around and glared at Sean while I dried my hands on a towel.

'I can't just take off with our daughter and pretend none of this is happening. Do you seriously think running away will fix this?'

'I'm trying to keep you both safe,' Sean countered, skilfully avoiding answering my question.

He took a step closer to me. I could see his fingers twitching. He wanted to reach for me, to hold me in his arms, but he was hesitant. I threw him a black look. My eyes flashed with anger, giving him a visual clue to stop him from making a move.

'It makes perfect sense to me. Treat it as a holiday.' Sean smiled.

'A holiday?'

It was the middle of November. Ireland wasn't famed for its climate even in the height of summer, let alone at this time of year.

Sean nodded as he continued to beam. I couldn't believe he thought he'd talked me around so easily, as if I was going to buy into that notion.

'Why don't you come with us then?' I suggested to wipe the smile off his face.

'I can't, Josie. Who knows how long you'll be gone for? My business and my livelihood are here. I can't just walk away from everything I've worked so hard to build up,' Sean replied, putting my idea to bed.

'But you expect me to leave my life behind? Leave you behind? And what about Orla? Her friends? Her school?'

Sean exhaled sharply and raked a hand through his dark brown hair.

'I hear what you're saying, but the thought of you and Orla getting caught in the crossfire makes my stomach twist. I won't put you at risk while I finish things with Reggie.'

I folded my arms across my chest and lifted my chin defiantly.

'What if you can't finish things? What if this feud costs you your life?'

My voice wavered as I spoke, and I knew Sean had seen the fear I'd been trying to hide.

He reached for me and pulled me towards him. Then he cupped my face in his large hands.

'I know you're scared, Josie, but I have to stand my ground. I promise you nothing's going to happen to me. But there'll be no peace until I end Reggie. I can't protect you or Orla from him...' Sean's words caught in his throat. He paused, then shook his head to drive the thought away. 'I'm going to destroy everything that bastard owns before I send him off to meet his maker.'

'I know the risks, but we're not leaving, and that's final!' My voice was strong and insistent as I blinked back tears.

Sean's jaw clenched. He knew my mind was made up. 'There's no point in me trying to reason with you. You're not going to budge, are you?' His blue eyes searched my face.

'No,' I replied, holding eye contact with him.

He shook his head from side to side. 'Jesus, woman, you're as stubborn as a mule.'

Sean knew he'd lost this fight, but he ran a hand over his face while choosing his next words. 'So you're determined to stay...' he began.

'I am.'

'Then we need to stay one step ahead of Reggie, so he can't hurt you or Orla again,' Sean said.

A heavy silence fell between us. The war was coming. There was no turning back. Whatever we were about to face, we'd do it together. Stand strong and put on a united front.

27

DECLAN

Dublin, November 1975

The load in the back of the Leyland was well-secured, but I could still feel its weight pulling ever so slightly as I took a sharp turn. Barrels of whiskey clinked together, a reminder of the risk we were taking.

I knew the Garda and customs officers were looking for any reason to pull vehicles over. If we were caught, we'd be looking at a long stretch behind bars. I glanced in the rearview mirror and saw a blanket of fog. But I couldn't shake the feeling that we were being followed. My heart was thudding in my chest. Was I being paranoid? Maybe, but the threat felt real.

The first raindrops began to spatter against the

windshield as the truck climbed the hill on the outskirts of Howth, a fishing village about ten miles northeast of Dublin city centre. I leaned forward and flipped the wipers on. Then I reached for the small tin on the dashboard and pulled out a cigarette. Fergal and I had smoked the last of the Major. Lighting it with a single practiced motion, I inhaled deeply, letting the smoke fill my lungs before exhaling in a slow stream. The tang of tobacco steadied my nerves, grounding me for the moment.

The amber glow of the twinkling lights dotted around the peninsula broke through the gloom. Relief began to creep in, but I wasn't about to celebrate just yet. Hargrove, Sean and other faceless bastards were sniffing around, keeping me on my toes. They wouldn't let me rest easy. But if any of them came for me, I was ready. This was a well-planned operation.

Howth Harbour had long been a hub for smuggling, thanks to its strategic position along the Irish Sea. Its mix of commercial vessels and smaller trawlers provided the perfect cover for illicit cargo.

Our journey would mimic a legitimate trip, taking advantage of established fishing routes and the busy maritime trade. We'd head towards UK waters and meet a smaller boat for a mid-sea transfer. To avoid mooring in a large port, we'd land at an isolated inlet along the English coast and offload the whiskey onto a waiting vehicle for the final leg. The plan sounded good on paper, but I knew only too well how things could go catastrophically wrong.

The Leyland's tyres were noisy as I slowly drove along the stone quay. I rolled down the window to flick my cigarette outside and saw something move up ahead. My grip on the wheel instinctively tightened and I glanced sideways at Fergal. He'd spotted the potential threat, too, and had his revolver at the ready. For a split second, I thought there might be a guard lurking, but as the figure stepped into the dim street light, I recognised the familiar face of a trusted contact. It was Duffy, the skipper of the boat taking my cargo to England. He was a burly man with a thick Donegal accent and a scar down his left cheek.

As I stepped onto the dockside, the salty air was heavy with the scent of diesel and rotting fish. The wind from the water was bitter, slicing through my coat as I walked towards the worn wooden pier. The fishing trawler *Storm Chaser* bobbed slightly in the midnight swell. Its hull was weathered, and its nets were hanging loose.

The few dim lamps along the water's edge barely cut through the fog rolling off the wild Irish Sea. The hazy glow turned the stacked lobster pots into hulking shadows. I stood with my back against a rusted metal crate, surveying the scene as my breath misted in the cold night air.

As we looked on, a dozen men worked in near silence. Their boots scuffed against the damp wood as they shifted the barrels under the cover of darkness. Fergal stood beside me with his hands in his pockets. But I didn't make conversation. My eyes were sharp, locked on the cargo as I oversaw the offload from the Leyland, scanning for any sign of trouble. The labels on the barrels read 'salted herring', but every man here knew they held something far more valuable than fish. Pure, triple-distilled whiskey was inside them, Cork's finest.

A lot was riding on this, so Fergal knew better than to bother me with trivialities. Instead, he stared out at the inky water, enjoying the respite. This shipment was huge. The payoff from this run alone would see my crew through the winter and put me back on top after Sean's betrayal. The bastard had cost me a fortune, but I'd get even with him in my own time.

'This is the last of it, Mr Kelly,' one of the men said as he rolled a barrel towards the ship.

I nodded in acknowledgement.

The dock workers had moved quickly, strength in numbers. They'd done a good job, so they'd been paid well, and so had the harbourmaster. He'd been happy to turn a blind eye for the right amount of punts. But that didn't mean the operation was without risk.

'Where's Duffy?' I asked.

'He's up top, making sure there's no unwelcome guests hanging around,' Fergal replied with a jerk of his chin.

I walked over to the Leyland and slipped the keys under the wheel arch as agreed. Then I climbed onto *Storm Chaser*. Fergal was already on board. Duffy was at the wheel. We were in good hands. He'd smuggled more contraband across these waters than he'd ever admit to.

'Why were you so late? What kept you?' Duffy grumbled, not looking away from the dark sea as he steered the trawler ahead.

'We ran into a problem in the mountains. The weather was atrocious,' I replied.

I didn't want every man and his dog to get wind of the ambush. But Duffy didn't ask any further questions. He just nodded, flicked a switch, and the dull thrum of the trawler's engine rumbled to life beneath our feet.

I went below deck and watched as the men secured the barrels, hiding them beneath layers of genuine fish crates. Once I was happy they'd been properly concealed, I went back outside and gave the skipper the nod.

'Right, let's go. We've got time to make up,' Duffy said.

Storm Chaser pulled away from the dock and sliced through the blackness of the Irish Sea. The lights of Howth Harbour faded behind us, swallowed by the fog. I stood on the deck, trying to ignore the contents of my stomach swirling around as the salt spray stabbed my face like needles. We'd barely left the harbour's protection, but the trawler was already lurching violently as it cut through the churning waters.

As we headed away from land, the wind howled through the rigging. *Storm Chaser*'s hull groaned with each brutal slap of the waves. The swell sent the trawler pitching skyward before slamming back down, the force rattling the whiskey barrels hidden below.

I gripped the railing, my stomach twisting as another wave crashed over the bow, drenching me to the bone. Duffy fought the wheel, his scarred knuckles white, eyes locked ahead on the black horizon. I clenched my jaw, but it was no use. My insides were rolling worse than the sea beneath us.

'Christ, you look like shite.' Duffy laughed.

He spared a quick glance at me as he tried to keep

the trawler from being swallowed whole by the relent-less waves.

I willed the sickness to pass, but it was clawing up my throat like a vengeful spirit. I considered myself a good sailor, but this trip seemed cursed. I'd thought we were on the home straight when we'd set sail, but we had a long way to go before we reached land and solid ground. I would have focused on the horizon to help my nausea, but it was too dark to make it out. Sky and sea blended into one. I squeezed my eyes shut as the trawler rose and slammed while rocking from side to side like a drunk on his way home from a lock-in.

'Don't tell me the big man's got a weak stomach,' one of the deckhands said with a grin, lighting up a cigarette with ease despite the howling wind.

I wanted to tell him to go and fuck himself, but I was scared to open my mouth, worried I'd puke all over the deck, so I shot him a glare, but cold sweat beading on my forehead undermined the threat. I turned away from him, braced myself against the railing and prayed that my last meal would stay where it belonged.

'I didn't realise you were so delicate. You should stay in the middle of the boat where the movement's less extreme,' Duffy said with a smile on his face, which immediately got my back up.

'If you know what's good for you, you'll shut up and steer,' I growled through gritted teeth.

Before I had time to take his advice, another swell hit, and this time there was no stopping the contents of my stomach. I leant over the side, emptying my guts into the frothing sea below as the crew roared with laughter.

I wiped my mouth on the back of my hand and forced myself upright. My legs were unsteady, my stomach was still twisting, but there was fire in my eyes when I flashed the still chuckling men a look, which was enough to silence any more comments. I glanced over at Duffy. He was grinning too as he steadied the wheel.

'Don't die before we get paid!' Duffy yelled.

I ignored his comment and dragged myself away from the railing, but my stomach started rebelling again. I'd never experienced a sea this rough. The waves crashed against the hull with bone-rattling force. Duffy held *Storm Chaser* steady, navigating the dangerous waters with the skill of a man who'd made this run more times than he could count.

'This trawler better not go down,' I said, muttering a silent prayer.

'She won't,' Duffy shouted.

I wasn't convinced. Anyone could see the skipper

was battling to steer the boat through the relentless surge. I fixed my gaze forward and stared out into the blackness. I had whiskey to deliver, so I hoped this bastard weather wouldn't sink us. We still had a long way to go before we reached dry land.

* * *

We'd been at sea for hours when another vessel emerged from the fog. The small fishing boat's lights flickered through the mist, and I could just about make out the shapes of men moving on the deck. My spirits lifted along with the contents of my stomach, but I swallowed down the nausea.

Duffy positioned *Storm Chaser* alongside the boat, keeping the distance tight for the transfer. One wrong move and the whiskey would end up in the water. I wiped the rain from my brow and locked eyes with the man standing at the bow of *Sea Ghost*, the other vessel. He looked like a hard bastard with a face like an old leather boot.

'You're late,' he called to Duffy over the roar of the sea.

'Stop fucking whinging. Let's get this done,' Duffy shouted back.

The words had barely left his mouth when his crew threw ropes across to *Sea Ghost*. I watched with my heart in my mouth as the first barrel of whiskey was hoisted from the hold. It swung precariously between the two boats as the men worked together to transfer it from one craft to the other. The swell fought them at every turn; each shift in the waves threatened to send my cargo, and possibly a member of the crew, tumbling into the black depths. The men grunted as they heaved the barrel onto the deck of the smaller trawler. They scrambled to secure it before it rolled overboard.

'One down, only eleven more to go,' I said.

Then I trained my eyes on Duffy, watching him like a hawk for any sign of betrayal. Trust in this business was hard to come by. Deals could turn sour at sea, where no one could hear a gunshot or a man's last scream. But his crew kept moving. They were focused on getting the job done. Another barrel swung across the gap between the boats and crashed onto *Sea Ghost*'s deck with a heavy thud.

'There's a light on the water!' one of the crew shouted.

I narrowed my eyes and looked out to sea. From the fog, there was a sudden, unfamiliar flicker. As I watched, I saw another flash, a signal maybe. My bowels rumbled as the faint glow crept closer through the mist.

'It could be another fishing boat, but it might be the coastguard,' Duffy replied.

My hand was already on my gun as I cursed under my breath. My blood turned to ice. If the authorities were onboard, we'd surely be arrested. If it was a rival gang, there was every chance we'd end up losing our lives as well as the whiskey.

'Get the last barrels over, now!' Duffy barked at his men.

Both crews doubled their efforts, working frantically as the light grew brighter while my heart pounded against my ribs. We came dangerously close to losing one barrel when it swung out of control in mid-air. The men gripped the ropes with white-knuckled hands, guiding it to safety as the sea lurched beneath it. As it landed on the deck of *Sea Ghost*, I breathed a sigh of relief.

'Declan, have you got the rest of my money?' Duffy asked.

I pulled an envelope from inside my coat.

'Every penny's in here,' I assured, knowing he couldn't count it. The deck was too exposed. I had no intention of double-crossing him. Duffy had kept his side of the bargain. He'd well and truly earned his fee.

'You and Fergal need to change boats now,' Duffy said as the last barrel landed on the deck. 'Hold them steady,' he said, instructing the crew on both vessels.

My heart was in my mouth as I transferred onto *Sea Ghost*. I couldn't afford to put a step wrong.

'Good luck, fellas!' Duffy called out when the crew dragged Fergal and me on board. 'Pull the ropes in, lads, we're heading back to land.'

Duffy's voice was carried away by the wind as he turned the vessel. His men gave *Sea Ghost* a shove, and both trawlers peeled away from each other, groaning as they battled the open sea.

The low, menacing hum of a larger engine was closing in on us.

'That's no trawler. It's the coastguard,' Fergal said, appearing at my side with his shotgun in hand.

As the words left his mouth, a searchlight burst through the fog behind us. Its beam was harsh as it cut like a blade through the mist.

'Get those barrels concealed below deck now!' I ordered, throwing my cigarette into the sea.

Sea Ghost's engine roared and water churned as her twin motors screamed to life and sliced through the ink-black waves. The silhouette of the coastguard's vessel loomed behind us. Its lights were fixed on our trawler as we tried to outrun them.

'This is Her Majesty's Coastguard. Cut your engines and prepare for us to board,' a man with an English accent said over a loudspeaker.

Sea Ghost surged forward, ignoring the command. Waves battered the hull as the fog closed in again, swallowing all visibility. I gripped the rail, bracing myself as the boat lurched hard to starboard. Another spotlight cut through the mist, followed by a warning shot. Fergal fired a flare across the water. It screamed through the air and exploded in a burst of red in front of the coastguards, to momentarily dazzle them. Our skipper seized the opportunity to change course, but the chase continued. Spray crashed over the bow, and metal groaned under pressure.

'I'll cut through the rocks. They'll never risk following us in this fog,' the skipper shouted over the wind.

He steered the trawler towards the ragged coastline. *Sea Ghost* snaked between the dark outcrops like a serpent as the skipper barked orders at his crew. I could see the stars glinting faintly in the sky above when we burst through the fog. Behind us, there was only frothing sea and darkness. The call of the coastguard's horn faded into the distance. The boat had disappeared from sight. They'd vanished.

I exhaled a long breath. My chest was heaving.

That was too close for comfort. I was trembling from head to toe, not from the cold, but from the weight of it all. I looked out into the darkness, and for a moment I thought I saw the shadow of the ship re-emerge, but it was just my imagination playing tricks on me. I staggered over to the wheelhouse while the boat rose and lurched and huddled down inside it to shelter from the elements until we reached dry land.

By dawn, the first hazy outline of the small cove we were heading to had appeared. My men would be waiting with their trucks at the isolated drop-off point, ready to move the barrels north to London.

When I stepped off the trawler, I was relieved to finally have solid ground beneath my feet. I lit a cigarette and watched the men offloading the barrels. As I exhaled a slow stream of smoke, I knew danger could still be lurking. Everything had been against us on this run. We'd have to keep our wits about us. I wouldn't relax until my precious cargo was secured inside the basement of The Black Harp.

28

JOSIE

London, November 1975

Our small kitchen hummed with the low murmur of Fleetwood Mac playing on the radio. The smell of fried eggs still lingered in the air, although our plates were clear, just the faint smear of bright yellow yolk and dollops of ketchup remained.

I was sitting at one end of the table, stirring sugar into my tea. I knew my hair was a mess without checking in the mirror. I could see a few stray pins were hanging on to yesterday's bun like grim death out of the corner of my eye. I hadn't washed or dressed yet. I was still wearing my pastel-blue floral nightdress and quilted dressing gown. Sean was at the opposite end of the table. His chair was pushed back from the edge to allow his legs to splay. His dressing gown hung open, exposing a dark hairy chest, a white singlet and checked pyjama bottoms. Orla sat between us, in her pink Bagpuss nightdress, rubbing her eyes while swinging her legs under her chair.

'Would you like some toast and jam, love?' I asked, already knowing what my daughter's answer would be.

Orla bobbed her head.

'What do you say?'

I was big on manners, so a nod wouldn't suffice.

'Yes, please, Mummy,' Orla replied.

'Good girl.' I smiled and smoothed down her deep auburn curls tangled from sleep. Then I pushed my chair back and got to my feet. 'Do you want some, Sean?'

'No, thanks.'

He rubbed at the hint of dark stubble on his face before resting his elbows on the table in front of him. He seemed distracted by something. Distant.

While I prepared Orla's food, the only sound in the kitchen was the music playing softly in the background and the shuffling of my slippers as I moved around the room.

'Here you go,' I said as I put the slice of thickly buttered jammy toast on the table.

'Thank you, Mummy,' Orla replied unprompted. Her eyes were wide with glee as she stretched to reach her food. She nibbled away while clutching Madame Cholet, her favourite Womble, under her arm.

I lifted the teapot from the centre of the table and refilled my mug. After putting it down, I added milk and sugar.

'It's all been decided, Josie,' Sean suddenly said.

I stopped stirring my tea and let the spoon clink against the side of the cup.

'What's been decided?' I lifted my head and fixed my eyes on Sean. He had my undivided attention.

'You need to pack a bag. You and Orla are going to Biddy's for a while.'

Sean's voice was firm as though this wasn't up for discussion. He could think again. I let out a laugh. I couldn't believe what I was hearing.

'It might surprise you to know, but you can't just send us away when the mood takes you.'

'For the love of God, it's not like that.'

Sean shook his head. He had a defeated look pasted on his face as though he was done with butting heads with me over this, but I wouldn't be pushed around. Not by him. Not by anyone.

I scraped my chair back and stood glaring at my husband with my hands on my hips. But Sean wouldn't meet my eye.

'Listen, Josie, there's no point in us falling out over this. It's for the best.'

'Really?'

Sean's jaw tightened. 'Yes.'

I shook my head, aware that Orla was watching us going back and forth. Her blue eyes were shifting between us like a spectator at a tennis match. She was the kind of child who noticed everything. She could be sweet and innocent one moment, then sharp and knowing the next.

'No way, Sean. You don't get to decide this!'

I was boiling mad, and my voice came out louder than intended. I didn't like arguing in front of Orla, but at least she had the sense to pretend to be focused on her breakfast when I glanced in her direction.

'It's too late, Josie. I've already made the arrangements.'

Sean's voice was calm, but his words hit me like a punch to the stomach; there was so much power behind them. I stared at him as I tried to take in what he'd just said, opening and closing my mouth as I searched for something to counter with that would make him back down.

'Why now?' I asked. They were the only two words that came to mind.

Sean threw me a look.

'You know why.'

I turned away so he wouldn't see the tears welling up in my eyes. Every second dragged by as I counted to ten to try and compose myself. I heard Sean push his chair back, but I didn't turn around. A moment later, he placed his hands on my shoulders. I felt myself tense.

'What's the problem, Josie?'

'How will sending me and Orla to stay with Biddy change anything?'

'She's like a sister to you. You trust her, don't you?' Sean's voice softened slightly.

'Of course I do, but that's not the point!'

'It'll be like old times. Like when the two of you used to lodge together...'

If Sean thought sending me on a trip down memory lane would nudge me in the right direction, he was wrong. Biddy and I went way back. We'd both been placed in the same hostel for single women by the Irish Chaplaincy when we arrived in the UK. We'd secured jobs as cleaners at The Ritz, and once we'd saved up enough money, we'd moved into the same lodging house. She'd been with me the night I met Sean all those years ago. She was my best friend, but that didn't mean I'd roll over and do as I was told.

'Niall's already spoken to Biddy and she said she'd be delighted to have you and Orla staying with her. She said—'

I spun around, my eyes blazing, which cut Sean off mid-flow. I was furious with him.

'How dare you go behind my back and arrange this without my consent!' I ranted.

Orla peeked over her half-eaten toast at us. She could feel the tension crackling in the room, but she knew better than to say anything.

'I'm not going. And that's final!'

I crossed my arms over my chest and glared up at Sean defiantly. He stooped and whispered in my ear so Orla wouldn't be able to eavesdrop.

'This isn't up for discussion, Josie. Either you go back to Ireland or you need to stay with Biddy until I settle things with Reggie.'

Although quiet, Sean's tone was firm. No-nonsense.

Silence stretched out between us, thick as syrup. I clenched my teeth together. My whole body was taut as I dug my heels in. I wasn't sure why I was being so stubborn. He was only trying to keep me and Orla safe. It was the way he'd handled the situation. If he'd gone about things differently and consulted me, instead of going behind my back, I'd have been more compliant. Nobody liked to be pushed around, did they?

'I'm going to talk to Reggie and call a truce.'

Sean's words hit me like a slap around the face.

'Do you really think Reggie Bennett's the kind of man who'll shake hands and let bygones be bygones?'

Sean ran a hand through his dark brown hair.

'We'll soon find out. Something needs to change. This war can't go on forever.'

I craned my neck to look up at my husband, searching his face to see if he was telling the truth.

'You'd better not be lying to me, Sean O'Connor.'

A muscle started to twitch at the side of his jaw, which sent a fresh surge of fury coursing through my veins.

'You're not calling a truce, are you?'

My voice trembled, but it wasn't with fear. It was with anger and pent-up frustration.

'For God's sake, Josie! What did I just say to you? Something needs to change or we'll never be able to move forward.'

'I don't doubt you'll end this, one way or another. But I'm pretty sure you're not looking for a peaceful outcome.'

My heart started hammering in my chest. Tears threatened to spill, so I sank my teeth into my bottom lip while attempting to steel myself. But I knew I was fighting a losing battle.

Sean reached towards me and cupped my face in his huge hands. His calloused thumbs felt scratchy as they brushed against my cheeks.

'Listen, love, I know you don't want to go, but I need you to trust me. I won't let you down. I promise it won't be long before you're back where you belong.'

Sean's voice was soft as he stared deeply into my eyes, reducing me to tears. But I had a bad feeling that this was all going to end in disaster.

29

JOSIE

Biddy's front room was crammed with mismatched furniture, but it was homely, warm and cosy. I sat perched on the edge of the two-seater sofa with my hands clenched around a mug of strong, sweet tea. Orla was cuddled in beside me with Madame Cholet tucked under her arm. Sean stood on the opposite side of the room, his huge frame tense, his blue eyes locked on mine.

Biddy had made herself scarce, to give us some privacy so we could say our goodbyes. Part of me wanted to rush into Sean's arms and stay there, but the other part wouldn't allow it. My stubbornness was winning the battle of wills, and I wasn't about to budge. My husband had forced me into this situation, so I wasn't going to make this easy for him.

Sean walked towards Orla and me. He dropped down on his knees in front of our daughter and opened his arms. Orla uncurled herself from me and fell into them, burrowing her freckled face into his broad chest. He stooped and closed his eyes, inhaling the scent of her hair for the longest moment.

'I'll see you soon, darling,' he murmured.

Sean gave Orla a tight squeeze before he released her. She looked up at him. Her big blue eyes were wide and innocent. He smiled at her and then pressed a kiss onto her forehead.

'Bye, Daddy,' Orla said before she snuggled in next to me on the brown corduroy sofa again.

Sean stood up and towered over us, which made my stomach twist.

'I better get going,' he said.

A lump formed in my chest. He waited a couple of beats for me to respond, and when I didn't reply, he gave me one last lingering look before walking across the room. My heart started hammering in my chest. No matter how angry I was, I couldn't let him walk out the door without saying something.

'Sean, wait,' I called, leaping to my feet.

He stopped in his tracks and turned around to

face me. I grabbed hold of his arms and looked up into his handsome face.

'Please be careful. I don't want to lose you,' I mouthed.

I didn't want Orla to hear what I'd just said. She adored her father, so she didn't need the weight of my worry on her tiny shoulders.

'You won't. This will be over before you know it. I promise.'

Sean smiled and then planted a tender kiss on my lips. I wanted to believe him. I wanted to stay like this forever. I wanted time to stand still. But it didn't matter what I wanted. My gut was telling me something terrible was about to happen.

I stood in the middle of the room with a pain radiating in my chest and dread swirling inside me as my husband walked out the door.

'Are you OK, Josie?' Biddy asked, rubbing my arm with her fingertips.

I hadn't realised she was standing next to me. My mind was a blur.

'I'm fine,' I lied, keeping up the pretence for Orla's sake.

Biddy gave me a sympathetic smile. She knew that wasn't the case.

'I don't know about you and Madame Cholet, but

I'm starving. How about we go for a Wimpy and chips, an ice cream float and a knickerbocker glory?' Biddy suggested to take Orla's mind off everything.

'Oh, yes, please.' Orla's blue eyes were shining. 'Can Mummy come too?'

'Of course she can,' Biddy replied, flashing me a bright smile.

My stomach had tied itself in knots. I wouldn't be able to eat a bite, but I kept that to myself. Orla was ready to burst with excitement, so there was no way I was going to disappoint her.

30

SEAN

When Niall and I arrived at my speakeasy, the basement bar was thick with cigarette smoke and the ghosts of late-night deals. Dim lights flickered above the polished mahogany bar, casting long shadows across the stone walls. The hum of low conversations from the few trusted men huddled together at the back table buzzed like static. Heads were bent. Drinks were barely touched.

'Evenin', lads. Thanks for coming,' I said, grabbing a bottle of Irish single malt and two glasses from behind the bar before walking over to them.

'We heard about the dreadful business with Josie and Orla,' Paddy said, shaking his head.

I slumped down in the nearest chair, unscrewed

the lid and poured myself a large measure, which I downed in two gulps. The whiskey burnt a blazing trail down my throat. I glanced at my knuckles as I gripped the glass. They were still raw and bruised, but I felt no pain. All I felt was rage. I reached into my pocket, grabbed my fags and lighter and lit one. Inhaling deeply, I allowed the smoke to soothe my nerves as it snaked its way around my lungs.

Niall flopped down next to me, poured himself a drink and leaned towards the centre of the table.

'Reggie overstepped the mark. He thinks he's untouchable. But everyone's got a weak spot,' he said.

I flicked my cigarette into the ashtray and narrowed my eyes.

'His weakness is money. He's amassed a fortune ripping people off who can't afford it. Reggie doesn't give a shite about loyalty or his men. But threaten his business? That's a different story. Having pots of cash is all that matters to him.'

Niall nodded, and then he fixed his dark brown eyes on mine. 'So what are you suggesting? We clean him out?' A slow grin spread across Niall's face.

The weight of the last few days was bearing down on me. I leaned back in my chair and stretched my shoulders as I took a long drag on my cigarette.

'We won't clean him out. We'll burn him to the ground.'

It seemed symbolic when smoke from the tip curled upwards as I spoke.

Niall let out a short, humourless chuckle. 'Now you're talking. I like the sound of that!'

My fists were clenched on the table as barely contained fury boiled under my skin. The walls felt like they were closing in on me. But the claustrophobia hadn't come from my surroundings. It was the rage pressing against my ribs, begging to be unleashed.

Reggie had given me the idea when he'd poured petrol through my letterbox while Orla was asleep in bed. Dragging an innocent child into the war was an unforgivable act in my eyes. It was a low blow. Josie and I had scrubbed the hallway until our hands were raw, trying to get rid of the smell, but it had penetrated deep into the wood and had clung to the grain for days on end, filling our lungs every time we breathed.

I'd witnessed what fire could do. The power it held. The destruction and devastation. I'd helped pull bodies from the burnt-out building after the gas explosion that killed Mary O'Hara's husband. They were charred beyond recognition. The smoke was thick with the stench of melted flesh. My stomach twisted at the memory, so I forced the thought down before it consumed me. Reggie had to be stopped before he unleashed any further damage. He'd visited my home twice now. I wouldn't let him come back a third time.

'So what did you have in mind?' Paddy asked.

'His backstreet gambling den would be an easy target.' Niall jumped in before I had a chance to reply.

His eyes shone with excitement as his face broke into a huge grin.

I understood where Niall was coming from. I'd briefly considered torching the place where Reggie's punters pissed away their wages and stacked up debts like bodies in a war but quickly dismissed the idea. The basement beneath an old East London pub he used for his illegal fights was a shithole, half falling apart as it was. Burning it down would do the bastard a favour. And besides that, he didn't own the gaff. He just gave the brewery a cut of the winnings to turn a blind eye to his fixtures.

'Easy isn't always the best option, though. I've got my eyes fixed on The Velvet Ace.'

My men's heads turned from side to side as they muttered to each other. Most of them were wearing looks of concern.

'Don't you think that's a bit risky, Sean?' Niall asked.

His grin had faded, and his expression had turned serious.

'Nah.'

'The lad's right. Reggie's got in-house security watching the place,' Paddy piped up.

'That's as may be, but the casino's Reggie's crown jewel. The beating heart of his empire. And best of all, he lives above it on the top floor. I wouldn't want to be in his shoes if a fire broke out. He couldn't jump from that height and survive. He'd have a hell of a lot of stairs to climb down to get to safety.'

A lazy smile spread across my face before I took a final drag of the cigarette that had burned low between my fingers and then stubbed it out in the ashtray. I flexed my fingers as I exhaled the smoke through my nose.

'No offence, Sean, but I don't think we'll be able to pull it off. I think we should pick an easier target,' Niall said with worry etched into his features.

'No offence, Niall, but I didn't ask for your opinion.'

I flashed my brother a black look. The last thing I needed was for him to start making waves. I could see by the expressions on my men's faces as I glanced around the table that none of them were overjoyed with my suggestion. But I paid their wages. So I made the decisions.

I was born and raised on the streets of Dublin and learned to fight before I could walk. Growing up in a tough working-class neighbourhood did that to a person. Survival meant being able to use your fists and your wits. I'd mastered both at a young age. Niall, not so much. Things were easier by the time he came along. I'd moved to London when he was a child and sent money home every week to help out. I'd arrived with little more than the clothes on my back, but I'd brought the sharp instincts of a street fighter along for the ride, and my ability to scrap had put me on the path to success.

I reached for the bottle and refilled my glass, but I didn't drink the whiskey. My fingers tightened around the tumbler as I swirled the amber liquid around. I needed my fellas on side. Otherwise, the plan would never get off the ground.

'I really think you should reconsider this. The Velvet Ace is like a fortress. Reggie's got men watching every door,' Niall continued.

He wasn't going to give up trying to talk me around. I admired his determination, but he was making the men jumpy, so I'd have to slap him back into place.

'And I think you should mind your own fucking business,' I seethed through gritted teeth before knocking back the whiskey in my glass.

Niall blinked furiously. I met my brother's gaze. Saw the fear in his eyes. I knew all about fear. I fought bare-knuckle for money before moving into the boot-legging trade, and I faced some formidable opponents. My time in the ring taught me discipline and persistence, and how to break a man with a single punch. But it also taught me to be more than just a brawler. It taught me to be a strategist.

Beneath the hardened exterior, I was still the street kid from Dublin who wanted more than just violence and bloodshed. I wanted a life where my wife and daughter were free of the war I was fighting. The war they'd been dragged into through no fault of their own.

'I wasn't planning to walk through the front door,' I said, breaking the fingers of tension that had stretched out between us.

Niall raised an eyebrow.

My jaw clenched as my mind worked through the plan. The logistics. The risks. The goal. This wasn't just about revenge. I had to make sure neither Josie nor Orla ever had to live in fear of Reggie Bennett again.

It was poetic, really. The bastard had threatened to burn my family alive. Burn Mary's family alive, and no doubt countless others who'd crossed his path. I'd be delighted to repay the favour. The thought of Reggie feeling the heat licking at his heels and the smoke choking his lungs as his property melted around him while he scrambled to escape, before realising he was trapped, filled me with joy. Bennett considered himself untouchable while he was in The Velvet Ace, lording over his kingdom. It was about time somebody cut him down to size. I couldn't wait for justice to be served.

'We'll only get one opportunity to get this right. When we hit Reggie, we're not just going to hurt him. We're going to finish him.'

I poured myself another whiskey, lifted the glass to my lips and took a slow sip, letting the burn settle deep in my chest. I cast my eyes around the table, expecting to see nods of agreement, but my men were avoiding my gaze. They shifted uncomfortably in their seats, nursing their drinks as though they could ignore the tension that had begun pressing in from all sides. I let my sights settle on Paddy, one of my oldest allies. He cleared his throat and knocked back his drink to give himself the courage to speak.

'I'm sorry, Sean, but I think your proposal is madness.'

My jaw ticked as his words registered.

'I'm not sure I heard you right. Did you say my proposal was madness?'

I glared in his direction, but Paddy wouldn't meet my eye.

'We've done some bad things over the years, but torching The Velvet Ace? That's taking things too far. Reggie's got powerful friends in high places. If you go through with this, we'll all be marked men,' Paddy said while tipping loose tobacco onto a sheet of Rizla and rolling himself a cigarette.

A murmur of unease rippled through the room.

'We've got wives and families. Are you going to tell me Reggie won't come for them? You know he will, Sean,' Paddy continued.

My fists curled. This wasn't the response I'd been expecting. Where business was concerned, I was loyal to the core. I prided myself on that. I thought my men shared the same quality. They'd never given me a reason to question their allegiance before. I liked to think I was a reasonable man, but I wasn't somebody to be crossed. Paddy should know that.

'So what do you suggest we do? Nothing? Let Reggie call the shots and do whatever he wants?' My gaze swept around the table. My expression was dark with contempt as fury bubbled under the surface. 'I never pegged any of you for cowards!'

My words were bitter, and I could see by the look on the men's faces that I'd hit a nerve. But nobody spoke up. None of them were brave enough to challenge me. I'd thought so highly of these men who'd stood shoulder to shoulder with me countless times, but my respect for them was going down the pan.

'Reggie threatened to burn my house down while my daughter was asleep in her bed. He kidnapped her and threatened to kill her. And you're saying my plan for retaliation is madness?'

'No one's saying we don't want blood, Sean. But we have to be smart about it,' Niall said, which got my back up even further.

'So you're saying my idea isn't smart?' I spat, turning on my brother. My blue eyes were blazing. 'Reggie made it personal when he brought Josie and Orla into this.' My voice cracked slightly from the weight of emotion swirling inside me, but then I steadied myself. 'If we don't finish him off, he'll keep coming. He'll keep targeting my family. He knows they're my weak spot.'

What I'd said was powerful. I'd intended it to be. I was hoping to provoke a reaction, but my men kept their heads bowed and their lips clamped shut. The air in the speakeasy remained thick with tension, cigarette smoke and the scent of whiskey.

Faced with a wall of silence, I pushed my chair away from the table and walked to the back of the room. My towering frame cast long shadows under the dim light as I mulled over my next move. I wasn't prepared to deviate from my plan, but the chance of a successful outcome was unlikely without backup.

I looked up as Niall came to stand beside me. He patted me on the shoulder in a show of support. Then he crossed his arms over his chest and turned away from me to watch the others. I'd called this meeting expecting loyalty. Instead, I'd got mutiny.

Paddy shifted in his seat, which caught my attention. My gaze settled on him as he stared into my face.

'Jesus, Sean, you know I'd go to hell and back for you, but this...' Paddy paused and shook his head. 'It's too far, Sean. It's way too far.'

Paddy pushed back his chair and stood looking around the table before he headed for the door. One by one, my men followed his example. None of them would meet my eye. None of them uttered a word. All of them walked out. As I watched them go, a word sprang to mind. Traitors.

'Christ, I never expected the lads to react like that,' Niall said, shaking his head from side to side.

Neither had I, but I didn't respond right away. My eyes were glued to the empty seats. The room had taken on a ghostly feel. Years of unwavering loyalty had turned to dust before my eyes.

'Fuck the lot of them! We'll do it ourselves if they want no part of it.'

My reputation was at stake. Reggie was about to find out he couldn't target my family without serious repercussions. But I was seriously worried about our safety now that Niall and I were doing the job alone.

31

SEAN

The cold night air hit us as we stepped out of the speakeasy. The streets of Kilburn were deserted apart from the distant sound of traffic and the occasional drunk staggering home.

I lit another cigarette with steady hands, although my insides were churning with something darker than anger. Rage was bubbling, close to erupting. As we headed to the car, Niall walked beside me, his collar turned up against the chill.

'Sean,' Niall said, stopping in his tracks. 'Let's not rush things. We need to think about this.'

Niall's shoulders slumped like the weight of the world was resting on them.

'What's there to think about? I've thought about

nothing else since I found Josie on the floor, beaten to a pulp. You saw what Reggie did to Orla. She's just a child, for fuck's sake, but that didn't stop him from tying her to a chair and splitting her lip. He's overstepped the mark, so I want his blood.'

My grip on my cigarette tightened as I glared at Niall, daring him to desert me, too.

He shook his head. 'Listen to yourself, Sean. You're not thinking straight. You're seeing red. You're being impulsive, and that's how men like us end up six feet under. Remember what happened to Rory?'

My eyes were blazing as I faced my brother. Silence hung heavy between us, thick and suffocating.

'What sort of a question is that? Of course I remember.'

It might have been years ago, but I'd never forget my brother's blood seeping through my fingers as I'd cradled his body splayed out on the pavement. I'd whispered useless reassurances to him as his young life drained away. Declan Kelly's men had made sure he'd never grow old.

'I still sometimes wake in the night and hear Rory's voice calling me, begging me to help him. The way they left him to die in the middle of the street like a fucking dog...'

I let my sentence trail off. I could feel my nostrils

flaring as I tried to shake the memory from my head. My hand twitched, so I glanced down at the scars on my knuckles, the ones I'd got the night Rory died from punching the pavement in helpless rage after he passed away. I also carried emotional wounds from losing my younger brother in the prime of his life. It was a tragedy, and the experience hardened me.

'I'm sorry to bring it up. I know how badly it affected you, but I'm trying to get through your thick skull. What Reggie did to Josie and Orla was outrageous. I'm not disputing that. I just want you to think about the consequences before you steamroll ahead with your plan. Declan Kelly went one step further than Bennett when he took Rory's life over a turf war, and we never tried to get justice for him, did we?'

My lip curled as his words registered. I didn't like his tone, so I threw him a black look. I didn't appreciate him implying I hadn't avenged our brother's death.

Niall's eyes bore into mine. I saw them drop to my hands when he noticed me clenching and unclenching my fists. He was trying to stay composed and steel himself for what was to come, but he began blinking rapidly as his nerves got the better of him. He knew my temper was looking for an escape route.

'I'm not a coward, Niall. You don't have to worry,

one day I'll get even with the Kellys for taking Rory's life. But for now, I've got Reggie Bennett in my sights and he's going to pay.'

'Jesus, I wasn't suggesting you're a coward. Far from it! I didn't mean to offend you.' Niall held the palms of his hands up in front of him. 'God knows, you're feared across the whole of London and beyond, but your weakness is your loyalty to Josie and Orla. It's so fierce it's stopping you from seeing sense. I just want you to think about this for a bit longer. You can sometimes be careless in your rush to get your own back. I'm worried you're going to start something you'll end up regretting,' Niall warned.

'So what are you suggesting? That we do nothing? We roll over and let Reggie win?'

Niall blew out a loud breath.

'I thought you were built of stronger stuff than this. Paddy and the boys have spooked you good and proper. I don't care what you lot think, I won't ignore what Reggie did to my family.'

'I'm not asking you to. Everyone knows your love for Josie and Orla is unwavering. But you don't need to burn The Velvet Ace to the ground to prove that. You're intelligent. You're calculated. You're disciplined—'

'Enough of the compliments. They're making my

head swell,' I cut in, silencing Niall mid-flow. 'You know as well as I do, I'm merciless, if the need arises.'

I wasn't a man who wasted time with words. I preferred to let my fists do the talking.

'I know you are, but don't be reckless, Sean.'

Niall's jaw tensed. Worry had etched its way into his features.

'We'll find another way to get even with Reggie. You can't burn down his casino, his home—'

'Let's not get too dewy-eyed about this,' I interrupted before Niall had a chance to finish the sob story. 'There's no other way to get the message across. I'm going to turn that bastard and his property to ash.'

Niall exhaled sharply, then he rubbed his hands over his face.

'Jesus Christ! Can't you see this would be a suicidal move? Bennett knows a lot of people. He's got half the city on his side. If we torch The Velvet Ace, the shit's going to hit the fan and there'll be no coming back from it.'

'Bring it on,' I replied, holding on to each word.

Niall threw his eyes to heaven. 'What if something goes wrong? What if the fire doesn't take hold? Or Reggie walks away unscathed?'

I took a step closer to Niall as barely contained fury battled to get out of me.

'That's not going to happen. You said my Achilles' heel was my loyalty to Josie and Orla, but family isn't my only weakness. Reggie's about to find out that I sure as fuck never forgive or forget either.'

32

REGGIE

The Velvet Ace pulsed with merriment and the chatter of conversation, but I tuned out the noise as I sat at the head of the table, drumming my fingers against the wood. A half-empty glass of brandy sat in front of me. I felt my face contort with barely contained fury. My jaw was tight as I ground my teeth and glared at the men gathered before me. All of them wore wide lapels, bold patterns and an air of menace. I was always the best-dressed in the room. My air force blue three-piece suit and brown tasselled shoes were polished to a shine.

Pete and Freddie sat opposite each other on either side of me. Their heads were bowed. They knew better than to make eye contact with me when I was in a mood like this. The air was thick with smoke, curling from the cigar nestled between my fingers. I leaned back in my chair with my legs spread wide apart. As I exhaled a slow stream of smoke, Freddie looked up. My eyes never left his face as I took in the dark bruising blooming across his ugly mug. He squirmed in his seat from the intensity of my gaze, which made a lazy smile play on my lips.

'I didn't get a wink of sleep last night, Freddie.' My voice was intentionally calm.

'Didn't you, Reg?' Freddie replied, acting all innocent as beads of sweat broke out on his upper lip.

'Any idea what might have been keeping me awake?'

Freddie swallowed hard. As he looked me in the eye, guilt was written all over his face.

'Umm, I, I...' Freddie stammered as he tried to buy himself some time.

I could see by the look on his face that he was struggling to think about what to say next, so I saved him the trouble and cut him off with a wave of my hand.

'I couldn't drop off because I was racking my brain, trying to work out how Sean O'Connor had managed to track down his little girl. I mean, how the fuck did he find the warehouse without being tipped off?' Anyone would think somebody had given the man a map!'

I tapped the cigar against the ashtray without taking my eyes off Freddie. His cheeks were getting redder by the minute.

'Every time I go over it, I land in the same place.'

Freddie's nostrils flared, and his eyes grew wide. 'Reggie, I swear to you I didn't say nothing,' he said, pushing his chair back from the table.

'Where do you think you're going?' I barked.

'I'm desperate for a slash,' Freddie replied.

'Well, you'll have to hold it until I finish with you. We're in the middle of a fucking conversation, shit for brains. Now ain't the time to go and take a leak!'

Freddie stood before me, shifting his weight from foot to foot, wringing his massive hands in front of himself. I couldn't help noticing that the ring finger and pinkie on his left hand were taped together.

I glanced sideways at Pete, but he didn't catch my eye. He was staring straight ahead with an unreadable expression on his face. I wasn't going to make this easy for Freddie, even though the tension in the room was suffocating.

'Don't fucking lie to me!' I roared, slamming my fist down on the table. My voice boomed off the walls, which made Freddie flinch. 'I know you told O'-Connor where I was holding his daughter.'

My eyes narrowed as I glared at him.

'I'm s-sorry, Reg, I d-didn't have a ch-choice.' Freddie bowed his head in shame, and I let out a cold, mirthless laugh. He was pathetic. I'd lost all respect for the heavy who'd worked for me for donkey's years. I'd always considered him my right-hand man. Not any more!

'You didn't have a choice? Let me tell you something, Freddie, you've always got a choice. And you chose O'Connor over me!'

My expression darkened.

'It wasn't like that, Reg. I did my best to resist, but Sean and Niall beat me black and blue and broke two of my fingers before knocking me out cold,' Freddie replied, showing me his injured hand to back up his story.

'You're pathetic. I expected more from you than this. You sold me out to save your own sorry arse,' I raged.

Freddie squared his jaw, and his body tensed. 'I'm sorry you feel like that, Reg.'

Freddie was built like a brick wall, but his bulk hadn't been enough to stop him from being scarred from his run-in with the O'Connors. The bruising on his face was the same colour as the dark blue double-breasted velvet blazer sitting snugly over his broad frame.

I wasn't impressed that he'd lied to me or sung like a canary, even though I knew he hadn't given up the information willingly. He'd taken a pounding from the Irish brutes before he'd blabbed.

'There's no denying those two bastards are a pair of savages, but if you hadn't opened your big cakehole, Orla would still be in my clutches.'

My jaw tightened as I threw him a black look.

'I'm sorry, Reg, but I think it's out of order that you snatched a little girl. That ain't business. That's crossing a line,' Freddie announced, suddenly finding his balls.

'Since when did you have a conscience?' I asked Freddie, then I turned to face Pete, shaking my head. 'I can't believe what I'm hearing. This fucker's been breaking legs for me for a decade. Now he's discovered his morals and he's gone all righteous on us!'

Pete shrugged, but said nothing, preferring to stay out of it. That wasn't an option. I expected him to back me up.

'I can't help the way I feel. I didn't sign up to hurt kids.'

I didn't appreciate Freddie implying I was some

kind of sadistic maniac. I saw myself as a gentleman, and a charismatic one at that. I was a cut above the rest, not some common thug, but I tilted my head to one side to let him think I was considering his words. A heartbeat later, I pushed back my chair. The sudden movement sent it toppling backwards. Pete scrambled to put it back on its feet while I glowered at Freddie. His face was a picture when my fist connected with his gut, knocking the air from his lungs in a loud grunt.

Freddie doubled over, gasping for breath. I would have loved to have taken all the credit for his suffering, but I wasn't stupid. I knew he was already in a weakened state from the beating Sean had given him.

'If you think you can pick and choose which side you're on, you're wrong, Freddie. Loyalty ain't optional. It's an essential part of the job, and if you can't give that to me after everything I've done for you, you're out on your ear. Understand?'

Menace coated my words. The threat filled the room.

Freddie coughed and then straightened his posture, towering over me.

'I know that. And I know I fucked up, but you can count on me, Reg. It won't happen again.'

'Because of you, that fucking bastard walked into

my warehouse and took his little brat right out from under my nose, humiliating me in the process.'

'I tried not to blab, but they were going to kill me. I swear to you, I'll make the O'Connors pay,' Freddie said, with an edge of desperation creeping into his voice.

I let out a laugh and glanced in Pete's direction.

'How do you propose to do that? You didn't come off too well the last time you came face to face with Sean and Niall, did you?' I roared, my voice thick with rage.

I was goading him to provoke a reaction. Freddie shifted from foot to foot as he desperately tried to formulate a plan, but nothing materialised, so he stayed silent and stared at me with a gormless look on his face.

'Niall is a waste of space. Sean's the brains of the operation. That fucker's been a thorn in my side for as long as I can remember. I'm going to make an example of him and send shock waves through the Paddy community, so none of them try stepping out of line again. They think they can waltz into our country and start taking over. If it was up to me, I'd send the lot of them back to where they came from. You know my mantra is no Irish, no blacks, no dogs!' I stepped closer to Freddie and jabbed my finger in his face. 'If you want to get back in my good books, you need to put a bullet between Sean O'Connor's eyes. His outfit will fall to pieces once he's out of the equation.'

I could see by the look on Freddie's face that he was regretting suggesting he'd take revenge on Sean.

'Kilburn's crawling with his kind. If you go after O'Connor too hard, the rest might—' Pete piped up.

'Might what?' I interrupted.

'Join forces with the O'Connors and rise up against us,' Pete said in a voice so low I could barely make out what he was saying.

'All the more reason to come down hard on the big man. Sean's the top dog. Everyone, the Kellys included, knows that. Doing away with him will be my warning to the rest of them. It should keep them in their fucking place, in the gutter where they belong. They're the dregs of society. They come here, breed like rats and act like they own the streets. This is my city. Not theirs!' I sneered and slammed my fist onto the table.

Freddie cleared his throat. 'How do you want me to handle it?'

I pulled my chair out from the table, plonked myself down and leaned back to consider Freddie's question. As I thought about it, a slow grin spread across my face.

'I want you to gun him down in public, preferably in broad daylight with a large crowd watching. Sean thinks he's untouchable. He thinks people worship the ground he walks on. So we'll take him apart, piece by piece, until there's nothing left but a cautionary tale of what happens to the likes of scum who overstep the mark.'

The men around the table shifted in their seats as they exchanged wary glances.

Pete exhaled loudly enough to catch my attention. I eyeballed him as he got up from the table and walked over to the other side of the room. He was a wiry man with enough nervous energy to power the National Grid. As he turned to face me, he shoved his hands into the pockets of his light brown leather bomber jacket to stop them from twitching. The oversized collar of his patterned polyester shirt peeked over the top of the zip. His flared trousers were mustard coloured and slightly too short for him, so they revealed the white socks he wore with a pair of scuffed tan loafers. His thick sideburns and greasy hair completed the look of a man who tried too hard to be stylish but fell short.

'O'Connor has a formidable reputation. What if he fights back?' Pete asked.

'Sean won't live long enough to fight back,' I countered.

I took a fresh cigar out of my pocket, bit the end off it then lit it with the butt of the one I was smoking. The orange glow danced before my eyes as I took a slow drag. I savoured the taste for a moment and then put the other one out on the table. Pete and Freddie should have counted themselves lucky neither of them were any closer, or I'd have used them as a human ashtray.

'This city needs a reminder of who's in charge. And Sean O'Connor is going to be my message.'

I exhaled a thick cloud of smoke, then watched it curl towards the ceiling with a large grin on my face.

33

SEAN

'Are you absolutely certain you know what you're doing? If you go through with this, there'll be no walking away,' Niall said.

He was making one final attempt to talk me out of torching The Velvet Ace, but he was wasting his time. I had murder on my mind. There was nothing left to say. I flicked my cigarette into the gutter, then fixed my eyes on my kid brother.

'When have you ever known me to walk away from anything?'

This wasn't just about revenge. I was sending a message. If somebody threatened my family, they'd pay in blood.

'Are you coming or not? I'm doing this with or without you.'

I didn't wait for Niall's reply. I opened the car door and placed one jerrycan of petrol in the passenger footwell and the other behind the passenger's seat before getting behind the wheel. Niall lingered on the pavement for just a moment, then he climbed in beside me. I could see he was hesitant, but his loyalty was unwavering.

'You sure about this? You don't have to come.' I felt obliged to offer him a get-out clause.

'Like hell I don't!' Niall replied.

The streets around Kilburn were nearly deserted at this unearthly hour, but the back alleys still pulsed with the usual undercurrent of trouble. I gripped the wheel of the battered Ford Cortina and tried to block out the smell of the petrol, but it was overpowering in the confined space, so I wound down the window.

Niall sat in tense silence, staring straight ahead, his features set like carved stone. I reached forward and turned on the radio. It crackled to life, but the music was too slow, too depressing, so I turned it off again and fixed my eyes on the road ahead.

The neon lights of Soho still flickered despite the late hour. As I turned into Old Compton Street, the sight of The Velvet Ace at the far end made my pulse speed up. I glanced at its entrance as I drove past. One of the back windows was glowing faintly. There must still be a few stragglers inside, drinking, gambling, wasting their lives away, lining Reggie's pockets.

I pulled the Cortina into an alleyway a few streets down and cut the engine.

'I'm going to ask you one last time, are you sure about this?' Niall sounded like a broken record.

'Shut the fuck up!' I shouted. Then I exhaled, long and slow, as I tried to calm my building nerves. I flung the door open and stepped out of the car. I wanted to get this over and done with before doubt started to creep in. The cold night air hit me like a sobering slap as I stood on the pavement, jerking me into action. I opened the rear door and grabbed the jerrycan wedged behind Niall's seat.

'You ready?' I asked when Niall climbed out of the Ford.

He nodded, gripping onto the canister that had been sitting between his feet with white knuckled hands.

As we paced towards the casino, the street was quiet. The late-night revellers who'd spent the evening in Soho were long gone. Niall and I slipped into the alley leading to the back of The Velvet Ace and disappeared into the shadows, moving like ghosts, staying low, staying silent.

The cold metal of the jerrycan's handle was biting into my palm, so I was glad when I was able to put it down. I crouched by the rear entrance, uncapped the can and tilted it, sloshing the petrol onto the wooden door. Then I made a trail along the wall, splashing the liquid up the bricks and across the window ledges, drenching every inch of the place. Niall mirrored my movements on the other side. We moved quickly. Eager to get the job done and be on our way. The fumes were so strong they made my eyes water and burned the inside of my nose.

'Are you ready?' I whispered. My heart was hammering inside my chest.

Niall nodded, then he stepped back and stared up at the building.

I reached into my pocket and pulled out a box of matches. There was no time for hesitation or second-guessing. I struck the match before my nerves got the better of me. Nothing happened, so I dragged the stick down the box again. A tiny spark ignited, producing a small flame that danced in the breeze. I flicked it onto the trail of fuel snaking towards The Velvet Ace before it went out.

The fire took hold instantly, roaring to life. It raced

up the petrol-soaked walls, greedily devouring every-thing in its path, swallowing wood, metal and glass. Within seconds, the flames started licking higher, and a blistering wave of heat surged towards us, which forced us back. Then the windowpanes began to shat-ter. Common sense told me it was time to go, but I couldn't resist the urge to watch Reggie's pride and joy turn to ash.

'Come on, Sean. We need to go,' Niall said.

He'd already turned his back on me.

'We will, but let's just wait a while longer. I want to be sure it doesn't go out,' I said with a smile on my face.

34

REGGIE

By the time we noticed thick smoke snaking its way through the casino, blackening the walls and destroying everything in its path, we were already trapped. The chandeliers overhead shattered one by one, plunging us into darkness. Their glass rained down on us like jagged hail as we tried to look for a way out.

The heat was unbearable. My face was slick with sweat. The scent of burning wood clawed at my throat, and I started to cough. I dragged the sleeve of my expensive suit across my mouth to stop my lungs from filling with smoke, then I turned to Freddie and Pete.

'Where's the bloody door?'

My voice was hoarse. Panicked.

'I think it's this way,' Pete replied, leading the way.

Being plunged into darkness while smoke filled the room was pure torture. Terrifying. We were disorientated, so we couldn't think straight. The walls groaned as if the whole building was taking its last breath. We had to get out before the place collapsed.

We'd only taken a few steps when we stopped in our tracks.

'Go back. It's blocked,' Pete gasped, clamping his hand over his mouth.

The flames had already eaten away part of the ceiling, which sent a stream of fiery embers cascading down as debris started to fall. The rolling smoke blanketed our surroundings as it billowed through the rafters to the floors above. I reached out, but my hands found nothing. It had swallowed everything and turned the air into a choking fog. Every breath was acrid, making my throat raw and my chest tighten.

In the commotion, Freddie tripped, landing hard on his knees. He started coughing his guts up on all fours with his hands out in front of him.

'I c-can't br-breathe!' he stuttered.

Neither could I. The smoke was suffocating, wrapping around me like a shroud, making my breath ragged. But I wasn't ready to die. Not yet. Not like this.

Pete and I grabbed him on either side and hauled him up.

'Move, you useless bastard, or we'll be burned alive!' I bellowed above the roar of the fire.

Freddie stumbled and knocked into Pete.

'Watch where you're going, you clumsy fucker,' Pete shouted.

Things were snapping, crackling and popping around us. Sound was distorted. The darkness felt endless as we searched for an exit. I wasn't sure there was a way out. The fire was spreading fast. My heart was pounding against my ribs. My pulse was racing. We were running out of time.

'We're done for!' Freddie cried out as his head twisted from side to side, looking for an escape route.

'Shut the fuck up. The last thing we need is you running around like a headless chicken,' I barked.

My lungs were screaming, desperate to suck in clean air that didn't exist.

Suddenly, a door loomed out of the blackness. Pete reached for it, then let out a blood-curdling scream as his palm sizzled when it made contact with the metal handle.

'Jesus Christ!'

He jerked back in agony, shaking his burned hand. His eyes were wild with pain.

'We're trapped!' Freddie boomed in a voice like a foghorn.

He was a useless person to have around in a crisis.

My eyes darted around the room and landed on the window over the sink in the galley kitchen at the rear of the building. It had already cracked from the heat, so I grabbed a cast-iron trivet from the counter and flung it through the glass. It shattered, allowing a gust of cold air to rush in, but it also brought a fresh surge of flames. They roared towards us like a wild animal hungry for our blood.

The smoke was stinging my eyes, making my vision blurred. But I somehow managed to haul myself onto the counter and squeeze through the broken window, shards of glass slicing into my flesh. I'd never felt relief like it when I landed outside with a thud on the cold, damp ground. Then I scrambled to my feet and stuck my head through the opening. Freddie was doubled over, barely able to breathe. Pete wasn't much better. His knees were buckling beneath him.

'Get a move on you fuckers or you're going to be toast!'

Pete suddenly found his strength and fired through the window a moment later, like a ball from a cannon. He landed at my feet with a bang. Freddie made a half-arsed attempt to join us, so we had to drag him through the gap. He was in a bad way by the time we got him out and lay sprawled on his back, gasping for air.

I wasn't about to hang around. The building was unstable, so I paced to the far corner, which led to the side alleyway, as Pete crouched beside Freddie while he caught his breath. That was when I noticed the overpowering smell of petrol and the empty jerrycans. The fire that had gutted my casino hadn't started accidentally. It was arson. The cowardly act had Sean O'-Connor written all over it. If that bastard had deliberately doused my place in petrol, he wasn't going to get away with it.

As I turned the corner into the alley, which was cloaked in smoke and shadow, I spotted the unmistakable shapes of the Irish brute and his twiggy sidekick metres away, gazing up at the inferno they'd created. I ran back to Pete and Freddie, being careful not to make a sound. I didn't care if my men were injured; I needed reinforcements. And there was no better man for the job. They didn't call him Pistol Pete for no reason. He was a mad, trigger-happy fucker with a quick-draw response and he was a good shot to boot.

'Sean and Niall torched the place. They're in the alleyway. Don't let them get away.'

The moment the words left my mouth, Freddie and Pete scrambled to their feet.

35

SEAN

'Come on, Sean, we have to get out of here,' Niall said, yanking me by the arm.

I could see he was keen to put some distance between us and The Velvet Ace. He fidgeted nervously, but I wanted to stay and gloat. I was mesmerised by the flames licking the blackened brickwork, even though the smell of smoke and petrol was suffocating.

Moments ago, panicked shouts and frantic movements were coming from inside the inferno near where we were standing. I'd heard the screams of trapped people echoing in my ears, but now everything had gone quiet.

'Sean, for God's sake, come on,' Niall called with desperation creeping into his tone.

I reluctantly began to walk down the alleyway, glancing over my shoulder every couple of steps. The fire had really taken hold. As we retreated, the heat roared at our backs, and thick smoke curled into the night air.

While we were moving away from the scene towards the safety of the car, I realised we weren't alone. Reggie and his crew had somehow escaped from the building and were coming after us, seeking retribution. A sudden burst of gunfire erupted from the shadows, forcing us to dive for cover behind the rubbish bins choking the narrow passage.

'For fuck's sake! I told you to get a move on. I knew it was a mistake hanging around here,' Niall ranted as he pulled his weapon from the waistband of his flared jeans.

'Shut your mouth and concentrate on the job in hand,' I barked back.

This was neither the time nor the place to start pointing the finger of blame. We had a battle to fight. A bullet ricocheted off the brick wall beside my head, sending dust and mortar into the air. Niall fired back. The muzzle of his revolver flashed like lightning in the dark.

'Fucking Irish scum! Thought you could torch my

place and walk away, did you?' Reggie's cockney voice rang through the alley.

His words were laced with venom. Seconds later, he stepped out of the shadows with his gun raised and a grin pasted on his face. Pistol Pete was beside him, wielding a weapon as they closed in on us.

When they fanned out, I spotted an opening to take Pete down. He was the bigger threat. He was a maniac. His draw was fast. He wouldn't hesitate. He'd pump me full of bullets without breaking into a sweat.

'We need to get out of here. Stay down and get as far away as possible. I'll cover you,' I said to Niall.

'No, Sean, don't!' he yelled.

But I didn't listen to my brother's objection. I stepped out into the open, firing at Pete as I retreated backwards, hoping to take him out of the equation. My bullets cut through the alley, deafening in the enclosed space, forcing Pete back behind an old dumpster. I hadn't realised Freddie was hidden in the shadows when I'd started shooting.

Freddie's first bullet cracked me like a whip. I barely had time to register it before the second one hit. White-hot searing pain exploded through my ribs. My stride faltered as my breath caught in my throat. I stumbled, landing like a sack of spuds on the ground.

'Sean!' Niall shouted, emptying his cylinder as he tried to cover me.

His voice was frantic. His eyes were wide with fear.

I was down, but I wasn't done. It would take more than a bit of lead to stop me. I dragged myself back onto my feet and lifted my pistol, determined to finish this. But before I had a chance to fire, another shot hit me. The bullet tore through my stomach, the force of it doubling me over. The world spun as my knees hit the floor.

Niall rushed over, grabbed my arm and tried to drag me along. But it was no use. I was too heavy. Too weak. As I lay in the alleyway shielded by a large industrial bin, cold seeped into my bones. Niall fussed over me, pressing his shaking hands to my stomach, trying to stem the flow of blood pouring out of me.

Another round of shots rang out. Niall fired back, but he was outnumbered.

'Get out of here before they shoot you too,' I rasped.

'No way. Not without you,' Niall replied, his revolver still smoking. His voice was tight with panic.

My thoughts flickered to Josie and Orla. To the future we should have had ahead of us as the fire raged behind me, swallowing The Velvet Ace and devouring everything in its path. I'd set out to destroy

Reggie. And I had. His empire was burning to the ground. But he'd destroyed me too. I'd fought my whole life. But this fight was over. I'd been desperate to seek revenge. In the end, none of this mattered.

Niall said something else, but I couldn't make out the words. They were jumbled together. I felt light-headed. Weak. My head was spinning. I was so cold. My teeth were chattering. My vision was tunnelling. Was I dreaming, or was I floating on air? I couldn't be sure. I felt disorientated. Confused. I couldn't fight the drowsiness pulling me towards sleep.

36

JOSIE

I didn't remember deciding to leave the flat. I didn't remember asking Biddy to watch Orla. All I remembered was that I was pacing the front room one moment, and the next I was outside, hurrying towards the Hillman Imp Sean had bought me for my thirtieth birthday. Something was wrong. I could sense it with every fibre of my being.

I heard the sirens before I saw the flames. They were distant, but getting closer. I stopped the car near Reggie's casino and jumped out. My heart was pounding inside my chest. I froze for a minute as I took in the scene. The Velvet Ace was burning like a beacon in the night. The air was thick with the smell of smoke. I pulled my coat tightly around my body and started running towards it.

The street outside the casino was chaotic. Men were shouting as they tried to help people out of the burning building as smoke poured out of it. It was suffocating. I started to cough, so I pulled the lapel of my wool coat over my mouth and nose to protect myself from the worst of it.

My heart skipped a beat when I heard gunshots crackling in the side alley. I knew it was going to be bad even before I saw him. I took off like a rocket, shoving past fleeing figures. When I rushed into the mouth of the passageway, I saw shadows moving towards me. Sean was on the floor. Niall was dragging him in my direction, firing rounds in front of them. Reggie's men were at the other end of the alley, shooting back.

I screamed Sean's name, but the sound was lost in the fray. As shots rang out around me, my breath caught in my throat. I swallowed down my fear and forced my hesitant feet to move. Sean needed me. Now wasn't the time to be a coward, so I raced to help him.

I dropped to my knees beside him. His breath was coming in short, shallow gasps. His hands were covered in blood as he pressed them to his stomach. I barely registered the heat. I was concentrating on Sean.

'No, no, no,' I cried, laying my hands on top of his to apply more pressure to the wound, desperate to stop the bleeding. 'You're going to be OK, Sean. Help is on the way.'

The wail of approaching sirens sliced through the night. They were getting louder by the second, which made the gunmen retreat.

'You should've stayed out of my way, O'Connor. London belongs to me!' Reggie shouted before he disappeared from view.

Sean's blue eyes found mine. He looked dazed, and at first he had trouble focusing, but then his lips curled into the smallest of smiles.

'What are you doing here?'

Sean's breath hitched as his blood seeped between my fingers. Time seemed to slow as I watched him battling to fill his lungs with air. I blocked out the chaos going on around us. All I could focus on was my husband's life slipping away.

'Shush, shush,' I soothed. 'You're going to be fine.'

I had a horrible feeling I was wrong. Something told me there wouldn't be any coming back from this.

'I'm sorry, Josie.' Sean's voice was barely above a whisper.

I pressed against his wound with trembling hands.

'Don't try to talk. Save your strength.' A sob threatened to rip from my throat.

Niall dropped down beside us. His face was pale. Haunted.

'We can't stay here. We need to move him.'

Hearing what his brother had just said, Sean grunted as he tried to shift, but his body wouldn't cooperate. His hand found mine. His grip was weak as he clutched my fingertips.

'You've got this, Josie. Don't, don't let Reggie win.'

Sean sounded breathless, which made panic build inside me, but my gaze never wavered as I looked into his eyes. His pain was clear for all to see.

'Stay with me,' I pleaded, my voice hoarse from the smoke in the air.

'Take care of Orla...'

'Stop talking like this. Do you hear me? You're not going anywhere. You're not leaving us, Sean. You promised!' The tears welling up in my eyes were blinding me.

'Goodbye, Josie...'

I shook my head, frantically muttering prayers under my breath. 'Don't you dare say goodbye. Help is coming. Hold on, Sean. Please hold on. It won't be much longer. Look at me.'

Through laboured breaths, Sean did as I'd asked, but the light in his eyes was fading fast. 'Always remember that I love you,' Sean whispered.

'I love you, too.'

Tears were pouring down my cheeks now.

Sean tried to speak again, but all that came was a weak gasp. He squeezed my fingers briefly. Then his grip loosened. His breath hitched, and he lay motionless on the ground as the life drained from him.

'No!' I cried before a raw, guttural wail of agony poured out of me.

Niall's hands were shaking as he pressed them against Sean's neck.

'Don't you dare leave us like this.' His voice sounded desperate before he began to sob.

I dropped forward and clutched Sean's lifeless body as blue flashing lights bathed the soot-streaked walls of The Velvet Ace. Seconds later, ambulance crews were on the scene.

'Help, over here, my brother's been shot.'

Niall jumped to his feet and waved his arm in the air to attract their attention.

'Mind out, love,' one of them said.

I reluctantly peeled myself away from my husband and stood beside my brother-in-law as the ambulance man rushed towards us carrying a battered green canvas medical kit. He knelt beside Sean and ripped open his shirt, which exposed several bullet holes just below his ribs. I'd never seen so much blood. The man pressed two fingers against Sean's neck, then, a short while later, he dropped them to his wrist. The medic looked at his partner.

'There's no pulse. He's gone,' he said. His voice was flat and professional.

I stood frozen to the spot with my hands clamped over my mouth. My legs threatened to buckle, but they somehow managed to hold me up. My breath was coming in sharp, ragged gasps.

'There must be something you can do to help him,' Niall shouted.

The ambulance men exchanged knowing glances. My hands trembled at my sides. I'd curled my fingers into fists, and my nails were biting into my palms.

'I'm sorry, mate. It's too late,' the man replied, his face grim.

And with that, the men rushed back down the alleyway to help with the casualties being evacuated from the front of the building, leaving Sean lying motionless on the ground.

The ambulance man's parting words sucked the air from my lungs as a sob clawed its way up my throat, but no sound came out. Gone. How could Sean be gone? My husband, the man who'd survived every-thing life had thrown at him, who'd fought tooth and nail to keep his family safe, couldn't be gone. He couldn't be dead. I was struggling to take it in. I wanted to shake him and tell him to get up, but Sean would never do that again. His massive frame was still. His blue eyes were open but empty.

I heard Niall let out a strangled noise and slam his fist into the wall. I flinched but stayed rooted to the spot, swaying where I stood. I couldn't tear my gaze away from Sean. My legs were barely able to support my weight, so when Niall's body started heaving with grief as he began to cry his heart out, I collapsed into him.

My sobs were muffled against the scratchy fabric of his donkey jacket. We stayed locked together for the longest moment, trying to comfort each other while coming to terms with the enormity of the situation. A bitter taste coated my tongue. I'd spent all night with a weight in my chest, fearing something was wrong. And now here was the proof. My worst fear lay in front of me.

The heat from the fire was more intense than be-fore. My ears were ringing with the roar of the burning casino. The world had blurred around me, so it took me a moment to realise that someone was speaking to me. I dragged myself out of Niall's embrace. A fireman was touching my arm. He was telling us to move out of the alleyway, but I didn't want to leave Sean. I let out a strangled cry and dropped to my knees beside him. My trembling fingers brushed against his cooling skin as my tears fell onto his bloodied shirt.

'What about my husband?' I asked, looking up at the fireman.

'Don't worry, we'll look after him,' he said.

His words bounced around in my head, drowning out the crackling of flames, the wailing sirens and the garbled voices of the emergency services tackling the blaze.

I was still registering what he'd just said when two of the ambulance crew draped a sheet over Sean's lifeless body. I gasped as the fabric covered his face, making it final. Niall and I clung to each other as they lifted Sean onto a stretcher and carried him away from the scene. We followed two steps behind them.

Niall stood beside me, fists clenched at his sides, his face pale beneath the layers of soot and sweat as they loaded Sean into a waiting ambulance. The Velvet Ace's orange glow cast long shadows that flickered like ghosts across the faces of those who stood watching. Everything was spinning. The murmur of onlookers faded into a dull hum.

The fire raged on behind us. Flames continued to lick the old brickwork. Sean had achieved what he'd set out to do, but it no longer mattered. Nothing mattered any more. The feud had cost him his life. He'd taken his last breath and spoken his last words. Reggie Bennett was the cause of the tragedy. And I would never forgive him for taking my husband away from me.

37

REGGIE

I sat in the back of my motor as Freddie drove away from what was left of The Velvet Ace like a man possessed. His eyes were wild, and his knuckles had turned white from gripping the steering wheel. Pete was in the front passenger seat, his pistol still in his right hand, primed and ready for more action.

Smoke clung to our clothes, a bitter reminder of what we'd just been through. Sean O'Connor was dead. I'd finally managed to cut out the thorn in my side. I should have been elated. But it had cost me dearly. The casino I'd poured blood, sweat and tears into was gone. She was more than just a business to me. She was my life. My flagship. My pride and joy, and O'Connor had burned her to the ground. He'd paid with his life, but his sacrifice wasn't enough to make up for what he'd done to me. My jaw was locked so tightly it ached.

The car sped through Soho, past the flickering neon signs of late-night clubs and the shuttered shopfronts lining the narrow streets. We tore down Charing Cross Road, weaving through what little traffic remained at this hour. The city stretched out before us. Its towering buildings were cold and indifferent. The British Museum was on the left. St Paul's Cathedral was on the right.

London never slept, and neither would I, not after this. I could feel the weight of the disaster pressing down on me. I was seething. My kingdom had been reduced to smouldering ruins.

On the journey to Greenwich Pier, I plotted my revenge. An act like this couldn't go unpunished. Sean was no longer in the running, but the O'Connor family would be wishing the big man had stayed out of my way by the time I'd finished with them. None of them were off limits. I had Josie and Orla firmly in my sights.

The briny stench of the Thames filled the air inside the car as we neared the warehouse. The huge row of industrial buildings loomed out of the night sky. Their frames looked like skeletons under the orange glow of the street lamps. It was quieter here. The roads were wider and emptier than in Soho.

Freddie stopped the car outside the old textile factory and went to unlock the metal padlock, which had rusted from exposure to the elements. Pete and I joined him as the doors groaned open. We bundled inside, and I flicked the light switch, which made little difference. The dim bulbs swung from the ceiling of the draughty lock-up, casting jittery shadows as I paced the concrete floor, trying to clear my head. But it wouldn't be easy. My mind was whirring. My thoughts were jumbled.

'What a fucking shit show!' I said, bitterness coating my words.

I shook my head and dragged my hands down my face.

Pete let out a burst of laughter. An inappropriate response to say the least, but the mad fucker was still riding the high on the adrenaline rush of the shootout. He liked nothing more than pumping lead into moving targets. It was his favourite thing to do.

'I thought you'd be over the moon that we got the bastard,' Pete said, grinning from ear to ear.

'I got the bastard!' Freddie corrected. 'I told you I'd make it up to you, Reg. And I did!'

I stared at the two morons with disbelief written

all over my face as they both tried to take the credit for finishing O'Connor off.

'Cheer up, Reggie, you've got a face like a slapped arse. You should be celebrating the event of the century,' Pete said.

I turned to glare at him. My eyes burned with fury.

'Celebrating? What have I got to celebrate, you dimwit? That casino was my life's work. My empire. My legacy. Do you think I enjoyed watching her go up in flames while I was trapped inside?' I felt choked up just thinking about it.

Pete shrugged, pulled a packet of fags from his pocket and lit one up. He took a long drag and then blew smoke rings into the air.

'Your empire was just bricks and mortar, mate. You'll be able to rebuild it in time,' he said.

I didn't like his tone. He was trivialising my loss. I knew for a fact he wouldn't be so blasé if somebody had torched his precious gun collection.

'The revenue from those bricks and mortar, as you so callously put it, pays your wages. Do you want to find yourself out of a job?' I fumed.

'Pete's got a point, though. We've got a lot to be grateful for. I thought we'd had it. We were lucky we didn't die in the fire,' Freddie piped up.

'You don't need to tell me that!' I boomed, still reeling from the shock.

'You need to get things into perspective. Possessions are replaceable. People aren't,' Pete replied, then he ran his soot-stained hand through his greasy hair.

His bolshie attitude was getting right on my tits. He'd do well to keep his trap shut before he was on the receiving end of my temper. I didn't know if the fire had claimed any lives, but I was pretty sure not everyone had escaped unharmed. We'd all managed to walk away unscathed, albeit traumatised.

Freddie stepped forward, his eyes darting between us.

'Something's just occurred to me. O'Connor's lot won't take his death lying down. Niall's still out there. And Josie, too. We should keep a low profile,' he said.

I sucked in a deep breath, which made my nostrils flare.

'Niall's a dead man walking. And as for Josie, the scrawny little excuse for a woman is too pathetic for words. She's no fucking threat to me.'

Silence settled, heavy and thick, between us. The distant sound of water lapping at the docks was the only noise cutting through the tension. I rubbed my temples. The war wasn't over, not yet. I still had to lock Kilburn down and claim everything the Irish fucker owned as compensation for what he'd taken from me. But I had other enemies lurking in the shadows who would try to beat me to it. It was a stressful situation. The only good thing to come out of it was that Sean O'Connor was gone. That was worth something, even if it had cost me everything.

38

JOSIE

Biddy's flat in Kilburn was eerily quiet with the kind of deafening silence that pressed down on you and made your chest hurt. The curtains were drawn, but open just enough for me to see daylight trying to break through the thick clouds. The start of a new day. My first without Sean by my side. I couldn't bear the thought of it, so I turned my tear-stained face away from the window.

'Shall I make some tea?' Biddy asked.

Neither Niall nor I replied. We were both lost in our grief. Numb. Rocked to the core.

A moment later, I heard the tap open and water flow, followed by the soft hum of the kettle on the hob. The clock on the wall ticking filled the void as I sat at

STEPHANIE HARTE

the table, staring down at the rosary beads twisted in my fingers. Niall was opposite me. His face was set in a grim expression. His red-rimmed eyes were glassy with pain. I didn't need to ask him how he was feeling. I knew he was broken. I was broken. Life would never be the same again.

Biddy moved around her kitchen like a ghostly form. Warming the pot, adding loose leaves and boiling water. She gave the liquid a quick stir and then placed the lid and a cosy on top before setting the brewing tea on the table between us. I watched my best friend moving around on autopilot, assembling mugs, spoons, milk and sugar, placing everything we'd need within easy reach.

Biddy was doing her best to look after us even though she was exhausted. None of us had slept a wink. We'd sat in her kitchen waiting for morning to break. Knowing there was worse to come. I was only hours away from breaking my daughter's heart. She would be devastated when she found out her father was dead. I didn't want to be the one to shatter her world, but nobody else could do it. The news had to come from me.

'I'm dreading telling Orla.' My voice cracked as I spoke.

Biddy rushed over, pulled a chair up next to mine and then put her arm around my shoulder.

'I know, Josie. It won't be easy, but we'll do what we can to help. Won't we, Niall?'

Biddy looked over at my brother-in-law, but instead of backing her up, he buried his face in his hands and started sobbing his heart out. Niall's distress reduced both of us to tears. I wanted to go to him, to comfort him, but my body had other ideas. My muscles had turned to jelly. All I could do was shake. None of us spoke for the longest time. Our grief was palpable.

'Please don't think badly of me, Josie. I tried to talk him out of it,' Niall said, breaking the silence.

His voice was raw. Emotional. I looked over at him. I could see he was finding it impossible to hold it together. Pain was etched into his face like letters on a gravestone. Before I had a chance to reply, he started speaking again.

'I did everything I could to stop him, but he wouldn't listen.' Niall shook his head.

'I know you did. When Sean got an idea in his head, there was no talking him out of it. You're not to blame for what happened...'

I tried to reassure Niall, but my words sounded flat. Guilt was eating away at him even though he wasn't responsible for his brother's death. My husband had been a grown man and a stubborn one at that. He'd known his own mind. Nobody had forced him into this situation.

After the brief exchange, we fell back into our thoughts, and silence stretched out between us again until the soft creak of a floorboard in the hallway broke the quiet. It was Orla. She was awake. Life as she knew it was about to be shattered. The moment I'd been dreading had arrived. My heart started galloping in my chest. I knew I should go to her, but my reluctance pinned me to the chair.

Orla stood in the doorway in her nightdress with her precious Womble tucked under her arm. Her toes curled in on themselves against the cold floor. Her dark auburn hair was messy from sleep. She looked so young and innocent. Her big blue eyes, the same shade as her father's, blinked as they tried to adjust to the light.

'Have you been crying?' Orla asked, rubbing sleep from her eyes as she walked towards me. 'What's the matter, Mummy? Aren't you feeling well?'

My daughter stopped in front of me and brushed my hand with her fingertips as she stared into my face. My heart was breaking, but I couldn't afford to let her see my pain. I had to stay strong for her even though everything was crumbling around me.

Orla glanced around the kitchen, and when the words left her mouth, my breath caught in my throat.

'Where's Daddy?'

Tears sprang to my eyes and rolled down my cheeks before I could stop them. I pulled Orla towards me, wrapped my arms around her and then buried my face in her mass of curls, steeling myself for the difficult conversation I was about to have.

A few seconds later, I straightened my posture and looked her in the eye as she searched my face for the answer to her question. Hard as it was going to be, I needed to get this over and done with. I wasn't being fair to her. She didn't understand what was going on. She looked confused; dare I say, frightened.

I brushed Orla's hair back from her face before stooping towards her.

'I'm so sorry, sweetheart, but Daddy's not coming back,' I said.

My voice shook when I spoke. This was the hardest thing I'd ever had to do.

Orla's brow furrowed, and she pursed her lips as she tilted her head to one side, considering what I'd just told her. She'd always been curious and observant beyond her years.

'But where's he gone?'

Orla's words cut me like a knife. I should have re-alised she wouldn't understand that I meant he was dead. Why would she? She was five years old. Far too young to lose her father. Far too young to contemplate the enormity of what had just happened. I needed to be clearer. Leave her in no doubt.

'Daddy's gone to heaven. He's with the angels now.'

My bottom lip quivered as I battled to hold on to my tears. This was confusing enough for her without me going to pieces.

Orla stared at me with a look of bewilderment on her face. I knew she'd heard what I'd just said, but my words made no sense. She couldn't take it in. None of us could. Her eyes grew wide, and her cheeks flushed. Two rosy apples sat in the middle of her pale, freckled face as she tried to absorb the news. Niall turned away from us, unable to watch the heartbreaking scene. Orla didn't say a word. She didn't cry. She just stood rooted to the spot, looking stunned, lost, so I pulled her back into my arms and held her tightly while I rocked her backwards and forwards.

'He died trying to protect us. He was so brave...' I mumbled into my daughter's hair while tears slipped down my cheeks.

Orla's body stiffened, and Madame Cholet tumbled from her hand and fell to the floor with a soft thud. She wriggled out of my hold and took a step backwards so she could look me in the eye.

'Daddy can't be dead,' she said, panic making her voice rise.

'I know it's a lot for you to take in, but he is.'

A lump formed in my chest as I stared into my daughter's haunted eyes.

'No! He can't be!'

Orla's expression darkened, and she shook her head from side to side, refusing to believe what she'd just been told. Watching her process the awful news was heartbreaking. I was barely able to hold things together. I went to pull her back into my arms, but she pushed me away. While I was still reeling from her rejection, she rushed over to where Niall was sitting and looked up into his face.

'Where's my daddy?'

Orla's voice was urgent. Demanding. Niall seemed out of his depth. Unwilling or unable to answer her question. His eyes teared up, but she didn't look away. She stared into his soul with her piercing blue eyes as she waited for him to reply. The silence stretched on until Niall finally buckled.

'He's gone to heaven, darling.'

'No! He can't be in heaven. I never said goodbye to him...'

Orla's face scrunched in confusion, so Niall went to stroke the side of her face, but she began to scream. As the high-pitched sound pierced the air, I rushed over to her and scooped her into an embrace. She thrashed about in my arms as I cradled her, pushing me away and clinging on to me at the same time. Her small fists banged against my body as she let out her emotions.

'I'm sorry, love. I'm so sorry,' I whispered over and over.

Orla eventually stopped trying to fight me and collapsed into my arms. Her sobs turned from agonised wails to hiccups as she cried herself dry. Then she buried her tear-stained face into my chest. She stayed like that for a while. Still. Quiet. And then all of it started again. Sniffles to begin with, which grew with intensity until the heart-wrenching sound of a child's world falling apart surrounded us. I held her close, rocked her gently while whispering words that wouldn't make her feel better. Nothing I said would ease her suffering. Nothing would ease my suffering. All of us were feeling it, but nothing would take our pain away.

39

JOSIE

The small front room of our house was barely recognisable. The curtains were drawn tight against the outside world, and candles flickered on every available surface, their soft glow casting long shadows against the floral wallpaper. The air was thick with the scent of lilies and melted wax. In the centre of the room, resting on two wooden trestles, was Sean's coffin.

Neighbours and friends had trickled in to pay their respects during the course of the evening. Some whispered prayers, others drank quietly in the kitchen. Now they'd gone, the house had fallen into a heavy, church-like silence. I sat in the armchair beside the coffin with my hands clasped in my lap and my rosary tangled between my fingers. I hadn't spoken to anyone for hours. I was exhausted; my bed was calling, but I refused to leave Sean's side.

When I glanced up, I saw Niall standing in the doorway, cradling a mug of tea. He was watching me with a hollow look on his face. I'd never seen him like this before. He was lost without Sean and consumed by grief.

Orla wanted to stay close to her daddy, too. She'd fought off her tiredness, but when it finally got the better of her, she'd curled up on the settee under a blanket and drifted off instead of going to her room. Her small body was twitching in her sleep. The toll of the last week was written across her face. She looked troubled, not peaceful. Even her new favourite toy, a teddy that Sean had won her at the fair last year, wasn't comforting her as she clutched it tightly in her arms.

I tore my red-rimmed eyes away from my daughter, eased my stiff limbs out of the chair and stood in front of Sean's coffin, staring at the brass name plate. I slowly ran my fingertips over it before resting my palm on the smooth mahogany.

'You should be over there by the fire with Orla on your knee, telling her the stories she loved about life in Dublin, not lying in this,' I whispered to Sean's coffin, and my lips began to tremble.

I hadn't heard Niall crossing the room, but when he gently touched my shoulder, I jumped.

'I'm sorry, Josie. I didn't mean to startle you,' he said. 'Would you like me to carry Orla up to bed?'

'No. Leave her be. I'm going to sleep down here as well. I don't want Sean to be alone. We'll have one last night together as a family...'

I tried to hold it in, but I couldn't stop a sob escaping from my lips. Niall swallowed hard, and then he pulled me into his arms. We clung together, united in grief, for what felt like the longest time.

'I suppose I'd better turn in. We've got a long day ahead of us tomorrow. I'll be in the spare room if you need anything,' he said before placing a kiss on the top of my head.

When Niall left the room, silence settled again. There was just the ticking of the clock, the gentle crackle of the fire and the candle flames to keep me company. It was going to be a long night. I was shattered, but I knew I wouldn't sleep a wink.

'I don't know how to do this without you,' I whispered once I heard the bedroom door close. 'Why did you have to be so stubborn? So reckless?' I let out a bitter laugh. 'You promised me everything would be OK, that you would finish things. But Reggie was too powerful. You couldn't destroy him. He destroyed you...' My voice cracked as my tears started to flow again. 'Why wouldn't you listen? To me? To Niall? You always thought you knew best. Always had to have the last word. And now look what's happened.'

I glanced down at the rosary digging into the palm of my hand, and my fingers traced the crucifix. It was the same one I'd prayed with every night while Sean had been out until all hours trying to hold on to his patch of Kilburn.

'I urged you to go straight. Encouraged you to sign a lease on a pub. Why couldn't you do what I'd asked? Why did you have to make a living from smuggling whiskey with all the risks that involved? Your precious business had already cost Rory his life, but instead of learning from the tragedy, you followed in his footsteps. Followed him into an early grave. How could you do this to me? How could you do this to Orla? You're one selfish man, do you know that, Sean O'Connor?'

What was wrong with me? Was I losing my mind? I was talking to my dead husband inside the coffin as though we were having a conversation. But it wouldn't matter how many questions I asked him, he wasn't going to answer me. He was no longer of this world. I knew that. I just couldn't accept it.

My emotions were swinging like a pendulum. One minute I was distraught, the next I was fuming. Surges of grief and anger kept coming in waves as I mourned the loss of the only person who truly understood me.

'Please watch over us, Sean. Watch over Orla. Keep her safe. She needs you the most,' I murmured as the fight seeped out of me.

I leaned forward and pressed my lips onto the polished wood before I sat back in the armchair and began to pray as I kept vigil over him. I hoped my faith would bring me the strength to face the future without the man I loved. Only time would tell.

* * *

Nobody was stirring as dawn broke. The house was still. I hadn't slept. I'd sat slumped in the same chair beside Sean's coffin all night. My hands were clasped in my lap, with the rosary tangled between my fingers. The crystal beads were nearly worn smooth from use.

I glanced around the room. The candles had almost burned down to pools of wax, but they were still just about flickering.

Fear gnawed at my insides as I sat alone with only

my thoughts for company. It tightened itself around my chest like a vice, crushing my spirit and zest for life. However I looked at it, the future seemed bleak without Sean. Nothing would ever be the same again.

Movement in the hallway suddenly brought me back to reality.

'Did you manage to get some sleep?' Niall asked from the doorway.

'No. Did you?'

Niall shook his head. His eyes looked hollow. Dark shadows had nestled beneath them.

The sound of our voices woke Orla. She looked around the room, unsure of where she was until her eyes settled on Sean's coffin. She threw back the blanket and padded across the room barefoot, with her bear tucked under her arm. My heart felt like it was going to split in two when she ran her tiny fingertips along the side of the polished wood.

'Today's the day we have to say goodbye, sweetheart,' I said as I reached forward and wrapped my arm around my daughter's waist. 'Even though Daddy's gone, he'll always be with us, watching over us.'

Orla turned towards me and buried her face in my chest.

'Why don't you go and get dressed? I'll make us some breakfast,' Niall said.

He didn't wait for me to reply before he headed off in the direction of the kitchen.

* * *

I was just finishing the washing up from our boiled eggs and toast when there was a loud knock on the door which sounded like a thunderclap.

'I'll get it,' Niall said.

Two men from the funeral home wearing black overcoats, bowler hats and solemn expressions were on the doorstep. I stood in the kitchen doorway with a pinny tied around my waist, drying my hands on a towel. Niall's girlfriend Philomena, Biddy, Mary O'Hara and Sean's men arrived a moment later.

I took Orla's hand and led her to the row of hooks at the bottom of the stairs. I lifted down her wool coat and fed her arms into the sleeves, buttoning it up slowly with shaking fingers. Then I slipped mine over my black lace dress, pulling the folded back piece of my mantilla down to cover my face.

Orla and I clung to each other as we watched Niall and the other pallbearers, two of Sean's cousins who'd made the journey from Dublin, Paddy and a couple of his closest friends, carry his coffin out of the front room. Some of the men were red-eyed, some were stony-faced. We followed behind, heads bowed, as they made their way down the hall. Silence fell around us like a shroud.

'Are you OK, pet?' I asked, stooping down to Orla's level.

She nodded, but I could see her chin trembling and her eyes welling up, so I squeezed her hand tightly.

'Stay strong for Daddy,' I whispered as I towed her along behind her father's casket.

The hearse was parked outside the house, polished to a shine. The street on either side of it was lined with neighbours, shopkeepers and drinking mates from the pubs. There was a good turnout, as expected. Sean was well-liked within the Irish community and further afield. The people who'd gathered to pay their respects stood in the drizzle with their heads bowed as Sean's coffin, draped in the green and gold flag of his local GAA club in Dublin, was carried out of the front door for the last time.

I'd been trying to put on a brave face although I was close to breaking down, but I didn't want Orla to feed off my distress, so I kept my eyes trained on the pavement to avoid the well-wishers' sympathetic gazes. If anyone had offered me words of comfort or compassionate looks, I wouldn't have been able to hold it together.

I stood on the cracked pavement outside our house, my breath fogging in the cold air as I stared at the coffin inside the hearse. It was hard to believe Sean was inside it. I felt like I was in the middle of a bad dream I couldn't wake up from.

Orla and I climbed into the black limousine along with Niall, Philomena, Biddy and Mary. As the hearse pulled away from the kerb, I caught sight of my reflection in the glass. My face was deathly pale as I sat beside my daughter, both of us cloaked in black. Both of us in mourning.

The hearse rolled to a stop at the front steps of St Jude's a few minutes later. Our limo pulled up behind it. I stepped out first. As I got out of the car, the bell began tolling. Slowly. Mournfully. The sound echoed off the brickwork of the tower. Each chime hit me like a blow to the chest. Orla stood beside me, clinging onto me. Her beautiful red hair was tied back from her face with a simple black ribbon. Her blue eyes, Sean's eyes, were rimmed with red. I wished I could take her pain away, but all I could do was hold her hand, so I gripped it tightly. Niall and the others joined us. He put his arm around my back and squeezed the top of my shoulder before he walked over to the hearse.

The heavy wooden doors of St Jude's creaked open, and Father Riley appeared. The church stood solemn in the morning mist, its stone facade watching over the mourners as they filed inside. I nodded to the priest who was waiting at the top of the steps, Bible in hand, his lips pressed into a line of sympathy.

Niall and the pallbearers stood for a moment in silence before lifting the coffin out. The shiny mahogany was adorned with a small crucifix and a brass name plate. I'd placed a prayer book inside, and Orla had added a drawing of her and her daddy holding hands in front of the sea at Skerries. She'd never been herself, but Sean had told her all about the place, and she knew how much he'd loved it.

The priest led us inside in a slow procession as the choir sang 'Here I Am Lord'. Soft light filtered through the stained-glass windows of saints and martyrs as we made our way to the front, bathing the walls in red, blue and gold puddles.

The old church looked beautiful, lit by flickering votive candles. It was packed. Every pew was filled. The local community had turned out in force as we prepared to lay my husband to rest. Footsteps echoed on the stone floor as the coffin was brought down the centre aisle and left in front of the altar. The under-taker placed a photo of Sean, broad-shouldered and laughing with that famous twinkle in his eye, on the lid.

Orla and I sat in the front pew. I had my black veil pulled over my face, my shoulders were stiff, and my hands were knotted in my lap, clutching my rosary and a sodden handkerchief. My daughter was pressed against my side, staring at the floor. She was wearing her Sunday best under a new black coat, which she'd yet to grow into. Her slight frame was lost inside it. A brooch Sean had given her, shaped like a shamrock, was pinned to the lapel. Her fingers kept reaching up to touch it as though it might bring her closer to her father.

When she leaned in close to me, I held her tightly as silent tears slid down my cheeks. Niall was on the other side of Orla. His fists were clenched on his knees. His jaw was locked as he stared straight ahead, fighting to hold in his emotions. The priest stepped forward, and the choir faded into silence. He paused and cast his eyes over the silent congregation to gauge the weight of the man being laid to rest before he began the service.

'We are gathered here today to commend the soul of Sean O'Connor to God. He was a son, a husband, a father, a brother, a friend, a man who walked the path he chose with courage, even in the darkest of hours.'

As Father Riley spoke, goosebumps broke out all over my skin. Hearing him talk about Sean in the past tense made the world spin. It was more than I could bear, but what choice did I have? Whether I liked it or not, my husband was gone.

I closed my eyes and remembered the happy times we'd shared. He'd been too handsome for his own good. He wasn't saintly or unblemished; none of us were. But he was my rock. The only man I'd ever loved, and I was lost without him. His passing had left a huge void.

When Orla started tapping me on the arm, it brought me back to my senses, and I turned to face her.

'Is Daddy in that box or is he with the angels?'

Her innocent face crumpled in confusion.

A pain stabbed me in the chest as my heart splintered again.

'He's with the angels, love. And he's watching over us now.'

As I cast my eyes up to the vaulted ceiling and the painted scenes of the saints in Heaven, I felt Sean's presence in the quiet of the church.

Father Riley invited Niall to speak, so he rose

slowly to his feet. His hands trembled as he approached the lectern. Once he was in position, his dark eyes swept the pews as he plucked up the courage to begin.

'My brother wasn't perfect. Far from it. He was stubborn, and he had a temper. But he was brave. He never backed down from anything. He was a powerhouse. A force to be reckoned with.' Niall's voice cracked, and he looked at the coffin for strength. 'Sean loved his family, and he protected us until the end. As sure as God is my witness, I promise each and every one of you, his sacrifice won't be for nothing.'

My breath caught in my chest. I knew Sean's death had hit him hard and that he was struggling to cope with his grief, but this was neither the time nor the place to be talking about getting revenge. He should have had more respect than to air his views at his brother's funeral. I didn't care how much Niall was hurting; there'd already been too much bloodshed, without him vowing to retaliate. As far as I was concerned, the war with Reggie was over. I didn't want any more lives lost.

I glared at Niall as he stepped down from the altar, but he didn't meet my eye. He looked straight ahead as he walked back to his seat with his jaw set and a scowl resting on his face.

'Sean O'Connor was many things. He was a man forged in fire, who loved his family with a passion. He worked hard, and protected his own. Today, as we lay him to rest, we pray for peace and strength for those left behind,' Father Riley concluded.

His eyes swept over the congregation as he spoke, but as he uttered his final words, his gaze settled on Niall as if pleading with him to reconsider the promise he'd made.

My faith had been my anchor for as long as I could remember, but now it felt distant.

When 'Abide With Me', the final hymn, began, I joined in with the chorus. My lips were trembling, which made my voice shake. Orla nuzzled her head against my arm, so I placed it around her shoulder. I knew by the small tremors coming off her in waves that she was finally letting her tears fall. They were silent. Endless. My darling girl had been so brave. Sean would have been proud of her.

The bells tolled outside as the pallbearers raised the coffin and carried it down the aisle. I kissed my fingertips, reached out and placed them on the polished mahogany as the casket passed my pew.

'Goodbye, Sean,' I whispered, then sniffed back my tears.

40

DECLAN

I'd decided to keep The Black Harp closed to the public today. Even though my rivalry with Sean ran deep, I understood the importance of appearances in the underworld. Shutting up shop sent a clear message to the community. I might have been his enemy, but I wasn't without honour.

The bare bulb swinging overhead cast shadows across the worn table. I sat nursing a whiskey, staring at the grain of the wood as though it might offer me an answer to my dilemma. Aidan and Fergal were opposite me, watching me with a wary expression.

'You seem out of sorts,' Fergal said, breaking the silence.

'I can't imagine why!' I snapped back.

'Anyone would think you're upset about Sean O'-Connor. He was your enemy, Dec. Reggie did us a favour when he finished him off,' Aidan said without an ounce of sympathy.

My brother was right, but that didn't stop me feeling rattled by what had happened. Tomorrow wasn't guaranteed for any of us. We weren't on good terms with Bennett either. None of the Irish crews were. He wanted all of us out. Sean's death had sent shock waves through everyone. It could have easily been one of us in his shoes. Reggie was more powerful than all of us put together.

Aidan leaned forward and narrowed his eyes.

'Please tell me you're not thinking of attending the funeral?'

I threw him a black look as I swirled my drink. 'And what if I am?'

Aidan shook his head as though he was scolding me.

'I'm just planning to pay my respects—'

Aidan leapt out of his chair and slammed his fist down on the table, cutting me off mid-flow.

'Jesus, Dec, what's got into you?'

I was never one to act on impulse, unlike my hot-headed younger brother. I prided myself on having self-control, so I didn't appreciate his outburst.

'It's common knowledge that Sean and I were arch-enemies, but he was a family man at the end of the day, and now his wife and kiddie have been left without their provider. I'm not going out of respect for him. I'm doing it for what he stood for. For the war we're still fighting. You don't have to like a man to recognise he was a leader. And if Reggie can bring down the likes of O'Connor, we should be shitting ourselves,' I replied in a calm manner.

I didn't need to raise my voice. When I spoke, men listened.

'I'm not sure showing your face is a good idea. What are you hoping to achieve? You're not suggesting we have a truce, are you?' Fergal asked with a horrified look on his face.

'Of course not.'

'O'Connor's crew might see it as weakness if we go and pay homage to their fallen leader,' Fergal warned.

'Weakness?' I laughed. Nothing could be further from the truth. He was underestimating my mindset. It was a case of respect versus opportunity.

'I don't see it like that at all. It could be good for business. Sean's operation will turn to shit unless somebody experienced steps in and runs it.'

'As if Niall's going to sit back and let you muscle in on O'Connor territory,' Aidan scoffed.

'Why don't you do us all a favour and shut the fuck up!' I said as I resumed nursing my whiskey.

The air in the room was thick with tobacco smoke, tension and quiet calculation. Fergal stood up and walked over to the map of London pinned on the wall. He turned his back on us and silently traced the boroughs with his finger, mulling over what I'd just said while Aidan slouched in his chair. His arms were folded across his chest and a bitter scowl was resting on his face.

Fergal stopped what he was doing and glanced over at me. 'So what are you thinking?'

'I'm proposing we go to the cemetery. We'll keep a respectful distance, but we want them to feel our presence. We'll be humble. No gloating,' I replied.

'It's a good idea to be on neutral ground to gauge the reaction. Emotions will be running high, so we don't want to cause any unnecessary drama,' Fergal said.

'Seems like a waste of time to me. Sean's dead and his crew have no backbone. We could take their operation tomorrow if we wanted to,' Aidan countered, doing a U-turn on what he'd just said.

He changed his mind like the wind. I couldn't keep up with him. My brother's approach was so different to mine. I didn't need his senseless chatter clouding my thoughts, so I fixed him with a cold look.

'We will take over Sean's turf in time, but we're civilised human beings. We're not vultures. The local community will turn on us if we swoop in too soon. Without them, we'd have no customers. And Niall's so full of anger and grief, there's no telling what he'll do. He's a wildcard. We mustn't underestimate him. Let things settle before we make our move. Then, when they least expect it, we'll steal their patch from under them.'

The worried expression Fergal had been wearing lifted, and his lips stretched into a smile. He walked back over to the table and poured himself a drink. 'I get where you're coming from,' he said, nodding slowly.

'I don't. Fergal's right. It feels like weakness to me,' Aidan muttered under his breath.

I leaned forward so that he'd feel my breath on his face. 'Well, nobody asked for your opinion. Turning up at Sean's burial won't show weakness. Cowards don't court danger. It'll prove to the O'Connors that we possess a strength beyond measure. That they could only dream of.' My voice was calm but steely.

Aidan glared at me before he knocked back the

rest of his whiskey, then set his glass down with a sharp clink.

'You don't have to come if you don't want to, but I'm going to stand at the edge of the mourners and keep myself to myself. I'm not looking to stir up trouble,' I said. My lips curled in the faintest of smiles. I was looking forward to lulling Niall into a false sense of security before I took everything the O'Connors owned.

'What if you turning up at the cemetery causes heat? You'll be outnumbered ten to one,' Aidan pointed out.

'He won't be going alone. I'm going with him,' Fergal said.

I turned to face my closest friend. Aidan was flaky, but I could always rely on my right-hand man to have my back.

'We'll keep our eyes open and if it looks like things are going to kick off, we'll bow out,' I said to Fergal.

'If you're hell bent on doing this, you can count me in as well,' Aidan said, reluctance heavy in his tone.

As we filed out of The Black Harp, our mood was as cold as steel. The sky was gunmetal grey. Ominous dark clouds were gathering overhead as though they knew trouble was brewing. I'd never admit it, but I hoped we weren't walking into more than we could handle.

41

JOSIE

The sky hung heavy over Kensal Green Cemetery. Dark grey clouds had gathered overhead, threatening rain, but as yet they hadn't delivered. The funeral procession moved slowly through the wrought-iron gates. The hearse crawled ahead, leading the way. When I stepped out of the limo, the chilly breeze lifted the hem of my coat and made my black veil flutter against my cheeks that were damp with tears.

Orla looked smaller than ever as she stood beside me, clinging to my coat. Her Mary Janes scuffled the gravel as we began to walk. Her eyes were wide. Vacant. Disbelief was etched into her young face.

Behind us, mourners spilt from their cars. There

had been a good turnout for Sean. Neighbours from Kilburn mingled with tough-faced men from the speakeasy. They moved like shadows among the crooked gravestones, their clothes solemn. The men wore dark wool overcoats and stiff collars, while the women clutched handkerchiefs and rosary beads. As we made our way to Sean's final resting place, the only sound was the distant hum of traffic and the squelch of shoes on the damp grass.

I stood like a statue at the edge of the open grave, clutching Orla's hand. She stared into the gaping hole, her eyes blank. Her face was paler than usual, which made the dusting of freckles across her nose and cheeks more apparent. She wasn't crying, but her lips were trembling from the effort to stay composed. I swept a strand of my fox-coloured hair that had escaped from my bun back from my face and then exhaled a long breath.

Father Riley came to stand beside me as Sean's coffin was carried to where we were waiting. Niall's eyes were red-rimmed. His steps were forced, almost robotic, as he drew closer. As the pallbearers nudged the casket into position on the platform, my eyes were drawn to a red Ford Capri pulling up at the edge of the cemetery, its tyres crunching on the loose gravel.

When Declan Kelly emerged from the car and straightened the lapels of his overcoat, my heart skipped a beat. He was wearing a wide black tie over a crisp white shirt, the collar sharp against his clean-shaven jaw, and his brown, wavy hair was slicked back with precision.

Declan moved with the deliberate gait of a man used to commanding attention. He was flanked by Aidan and Fergal as he made his way towards us. I stiffened. My free hand curled into a fist at my side. The unexpected sound of footsteps made heads turn, and that was when Niall saw them, too. His jaw clenched at the sight of the intruders.

'What are those bastards doing here?' Niall muttered, more to himself than anyone.

I didn't reply. My eyes were fixed on the three men as they approached the edge of the crowd. They stayed far enough away to avoid confrontation, but close enough to be seen. I sensed it was a tactical move. They hadn't come here out of respect or to offer words of sympathy. They'd come here to watch and make their presence felt.

Declan, Aidan and Fergal's appearance drew uncertain murmurs from the crowd. A few of the mourners cast uneasy glances towards the group, but it didn't look like they'd come here for trouble. They were keeping their hands in their pockets and their heads bowed.

'Who does he think he is? I should go over there and tell him to fuck off,' Niall said. His shoulders were rigid, and his fists were clenched down by his sides as he kept his eyes on Declan. I tried to break his focus by touching his arm.

'Don't even think about it. The last thing we want is for Sean's funeral to turn into a circus. We all know they're not here to mourn. They're here to see if we break. Don't give them the satisfaction,' I said.

Niall's nostrils flared, but he nodded in agreement.

Declan didn't try to catch anyone's eye or look directly at me or Niall. He stood at the perimeter, staring at the coffin, and then his gaze settled on the priest as Father Riley prayed over the yawning grave in a solemn voice.

Paddy leaned towards Niall and muttered under his breath, but I overheard what he said.

'At least there's no sign of Reggie. I figured he wouldn't show. We were worried about nothing.'

I'd had no idea they'd thought Reggie Bennett turning up was even a remote possibility. I was glad they hadn't shared that fear with me.

'He's a fucking coward,' Niall mumbled back.

His eyes didn't waver from the graveside. From Father Riley. From Sean's coffin. But he continued to speak in a hushed tone.

'This crowd would've torn Reggie apart if he dared to show his face.'

As the coffin was lowered into the ground, my knees buckled slightly. Niall placed a steadying hand on my back. I stepped forward with Orla beside me and stared down at the mahogany casket. I stood like that for a moment as if willing myself to draw strength from Sean before I dropped a single white lily into his grave. It landed softly on the polished wood as the cold wind swept across the opening.

'I'm sorry I didn't get to say goodbye to you, Daddy. I promise I'll be a good girl for Mummy,' Orla said.

Her soft voice quivered with emotion as tears slipped down her cheeks.

A lump formed in my throat as we watched the grave being filled in. Earth hitting wood was a sound I'd remember for the rest of my life. As the last handfuls of soil were scattered, Declan turned and walked back to his car. His men fell in step behind him. He hadn't said a word to us, but he'd intended to send a clear message. The balance of power had shifted since Sean's murder, and if we weren't careful, Declan Kelly would try to take over. I couldn't stand back and let that happen. I had a daughter to provide for and bills to pay. Raising Orla alone was a daunting prospect, but I didn't have another choice. Reluctant as I was to take hold of the reins, I owed it to Sean's memory to keep the business alive. His empire was thriving, so I'd be a fool to throw it all away.

I stood numbly at the edge of the grave, gripping Orla's hand like it was a lifeline. Her tears had stopped, but her eyes were glazed with confusion. She was too young to understand the enormity of what had happened. We were facing a desolate future. The idea of that made a sob escape from my lips. A heart-beat later I felt Biddy and Mary close in around me, forming a silent shield of sympathy.

The other mourners had pulled back to give us some space, but they were slow to disperse, as if walking away meant truly accepting that Sean O'-Connor was never coming back. Although he was gone, his presence still lingered.

Orla clung to my side. It was to be expected; her whole world had been turned upside down. It would take time for her to adjust to life without her daddy.

Niall stood a short distance away from us, chain-smoking. His eyes were fixed on the treeline beyond the cemetery wall as though he was sensing something bad was about to happen. But the Kellys were long gone. Declan hadn't hung around. He was no doubt plotting how to bring our business to its knees. But I had enough on my plate to be worrying about that. I still had to get through Sean's wake.

42

DECLAN

Smoke curled towards the ceiling from the half-burned cigarette resting in the overflowing ashtray. Fergal stood by the window, staring out at the slick London street as rain pelted against the glass. Aidan sat at the table opposite me, nursing a pint of Guinness. None of us spoke, but my eyes flicked between them. My mind was full of silent calculation.

A bottle of Powers was open in the centre of the table. Three glasses had been poured from it, and two of them were untouched. I picked up my tumbler and knocked back the contents. I let the whiskey burn on my tongue before I swallowed it.

'So, what are you planning?' Aidan smirked.

'Who says I'm planning anything?'

Fergal started pacing backwards and forwards in front of the window as his agitation got the better of him.

'Reggie's casino's in ashes, the O'Connors are in mourning, and their lads are leaderless. Are you trying to tell me you're not going to take advantage of the situation?' Aidan asked, fixing his eyes on mine.

'You know me too well,' I replied as my mouth lifted into a smile.

'So come on then, tell us what we're in for. Don't keep us in suspense,' Aidan said.

Patience had never been my brother's strong suit.

'We need to take things slowly, so you'll have to rein yourself in,' I said to Aidan, throwing him a knowing look. 'I'm going to set up covert meetings with Sean's men and offer them a future working for us Kellys. As a reward for switching sides, they'll have our protection and money in their pocket.'

Fergal stopped pacing and eyed me with suspicion from a distance. 'And what if they refuse? Do you really think they'll forget about Sean that easily?' he asked.

My mouth twisted in a half-grin. 'Sean had the kind of physical strength that made men think twice before crossing him, but he's gone now, and Niall's not cut from the same cloth. The men don't respect him the way they did Sean. And besides that, loyalty fades when the rent's due. Grief won't feed their families.'

Aidan started to laugh. 'I like where you're coming from.'

'I want the speakeasy in Kilburn and that place Sean kept in the arches he used as a stash house. We'll take everything he owned brick by brick. If we don't swoop in and claim it, somebody else will.'

Aidan nodded in agreement.

'What about Josie?' Fergal asked, cracking his knuckles.

My gaze narrowed. His sudden concern surprised me.

'What about her? She's not our problem. She's got a kid to look after and with no army behind her, I reckon she'll go back to Kerry and in a year or two she'll marry a lonely old farmer twice her age who'll raise the kid as his own.'

'And what about Reggie? He's down a casino. He'll be bleeding money. He's not going to walk away without compensation,' Fergal pointed out.

'That's a fair comment. We'd better put the plan into place soon. We'll let the men give Sean his send-off, and tomorrow when they're nursing bad heads, we'll bring them in. Show them what needs to happen. Kilburn's wide open. We'll need to step into Sean's shoes before Reggie beats us to it.'

I lifted the bottle of Powers and filled my glass before raising it to my lips and swallowing down the contents. If Sean had still been with us, he'd be wishing we'd never fallen out. I'd have had a different attitude to things if that had been the case. But the man had been my enemy, so I didn't have an ounce of guilt about what I was proposing to do.

43

JOSIE

I sat in the corner furthest away from the door with Orla beside me. Her small frame was curled against me as though she'd been glued to my side. She wasn't crying now, but sadness was carved into her face. She was pale. Exhausted. Confused. There was too much pain for a young child to deal with. I would have given anything to take her suffering away, but there was nothing I could do apart from stay close to her.

The air in the backroom of Sean's speakeasy was thick with smoke and sorrow. The sound of laughter usually filled the space, but a low hum of conversation had taken its place.

A lone fiddler was in the corner playing 'Danny Boy'. The slow, haunting music drifted through the room, wrapping itself around the mourners like a shroud, bringing even the hardest of men to tears.

As the night wore on, the whiskey flowed and the wake stepped up a gear. Nostalgia and shared memories gave me a sudden longing for home. Maybe Sean had been right. I hadn't been prepared to consider it before, but going back to Ireland might be good for Orla and me.

The fiddler lowered his bow to give his gnarled fingers a well-deserved break after he'd played 'When Irish Eyes Are Smiling'. It was so incredibly moving that it made goosepimples break out all over my body.

The musician nodded over to Dorothy, an elderly woman sitting in the far corner. She'd been a singer before she left Ireland's shores for a better life in the early thirties. I'd come to London when I was only eighteen, lured, like her and so many others, by the promise of prosperity. But contrary to popular belief, the London streets weren't paved with gold.

I'd settled in Kilburn, an area popular with Irish immigrants. Although the move had been testing, I hadn't expected to face discrimination from men like Reggie Bennett and was surprised by the blatant hostility shown to people who were honest and willing to work hard. But I had no regrets. If I hadn't come to England, I'd never have met Sean.

A hush fell as Dorothy slowly got to her feet. Her eyes misted as she looked over at Orla and me. Then she offered us a sympathetic smile before she began to sing.

'In Dublin's fair city, where the girls are so pretty, I first set my eyes on sweet Molly Malone...'

Dorothy's voice echoed around the room as she belted out the Dublin anthem, a staple at Irish wakes, which seemed particularly fitting as Sean and many of the mourners were born and bred in the county. The old lady's body was weak and feeble, but her vocal cords were as powerful as ever as she put her heart and soul into her performance.

'Alive, alive, oh. Alive, alive, oh. Crying, cockles and mussels, alive, alive, oh.'

Some mourners joined in with the chorus; their voices were husky from years of smoking, but they hit every note.

The song carried the weight of loss, love and home, which brought a tear to my eyes and made my lips tremble. By the final verse, the whole room was singing. Sean would have loved it. I glanced over to where Niall was sitting near the doorway. His eyes were tightly closed. Memories of his brother were too painful to bear.

As the last notes of 'Molly Malone' faded into the

whiskey-scented air, a heavy silence fell over the room. The kind of quiet that settled deep in a person's bones.

Niall seemed to be guarding the entrance, albeit with a glass of whiskey in his hand. I could tell by his stiff posture that he was on edge, rattled by Declan's appearance at the cemetery. His eyes were scanning the crowd, looking for signs of danger.

Niall picked up a bottle from a nearby table and started refilling people's glasses. I couldn't help noticing how pale his face was from stress and grief when he poured me a tumbler of Sean's finest, the stuff he reserved for friends and favours.

'Thank you for the beautiful song, Dorothy,' Niall said when he passed her.

'No bother,' she replied, before sitting back in her seat.

Niall lifted his glass high, and his voice rippled through the hush. 'I'd like to raise a toast to my brother...' He paused to swallow the lump that had lodged in his throat. 'Sean O'Connor was many things. A fighter. A rogue. A stubborn bastard. But above all, he was loyal. To his family. To his friends. To his crew.'

The mourners murmured in agreement, glasses raised in unison.

'To Sean. May the streets of Kilburn never forget

his name.' Niall's hand shook slightly as he held his drink aloft.

'To Sean.' The voices in the room echoed, as though a thousand ghosts had joined in with the toast. Sean's speakeasy was usually a lively venue, but it was cloaked in loss.

'May the road rise to meet you. May the wind be always at your back...' Niall began as he recited the traditional Irish blessing in Sean's honour.

There wasn't a dry eye in the place by the time he'd finished his moving tribute, so I asked the fiddler to play one of Sean's favourite songs, 'The Wild Rover', to lift the mourners' spirits. I was aware that the weight of the grief in the room was taking its toll on Orla. Niall came to stand beside us. Sensing she was struggling, he ran his fingertips down his niece's cheek as she stared up into his face with innocent blue eyes.

The tender moment came to an abrupt end when the back door creaked open and a gust of cold air blew in. The room held its breath. The fiddler's bow froze mid-stroke as he was building up for the ending of 'The Wild Rover'. I followed my brother-in-law's gaze, and my heart skipped a beat. Conversations dried up. Heads turned. The atmosphere thickened. Reggie Bennett was standing in the doorway with a smirk on his face. You could have heard a pin drop.

He didn't belong here. He was dressed more like a gangster than a mourner. No black suit or tie. Instead, he wore a wide-legged slate-grey three-piece. The jacket and waistcoat were cut sharply against his frame; rain droplets glinted on the shoulders. Every thread of his clothing screamed Soho, not Kilburn. His shirt was unbuttoned just enough to show a medallion hanging on a gold chain. His thinning blond hair was slicked back. His blue eyes were hidden behind tinted aviators despite the hour and the bad weather.

Reggie looked like he belonged to another world. One of smoke-filled parlours, whispered deals, and debts that were paid for in blood. I could just about make out Freddie and Pistol Pete behind him, looming out of the darkness, shadows with eyes.

I pulled Orla towards me when I felt her flinch. Her eyes were wide. Her body was trembling. The threat in the room was real, even though our numbers were greater. Orla and I had suffered at Reggie's hands – Sean had too – so we knew how dangerous he could be. He was more powerful than my countryfolk gave him credit for. Many of the Irish had a reputation for displaying courage and confidence and for being outspoken. But bravado got you nowhere in certain situations.

It seemed Sean wasn't destined to have a peaceful send-off. First Declan. Now Reggie. Who else was going to invade the private gathering? These people had no respect. They shouldn't have come within a hundred miles of Kilburn today. Anger started bubbling inside me. These men did nothing but create chaos and I'd had enough of it. I was sick of the way their whims and fancies were affecting mine and Orla's lives.

Niall glanced down at us, huddled together. Then he stepped in front of us without giving it a second thought. He was ready to defend us, already making plans to intercept the enemy, which was way out of his comfort zone. He wasn't used to being the first into the battle. He usually brought up the rear. Sean would have been so proud to see his younger brother stepping into his shoes willingly. I wished he could have been here to witness it himself.

'You've got some nerve coming here. You weren't invited. You're not welcome. Get out before I sling you into the gutter,' Niall growled.

His fists were clenched by his sides, ready to spring into action if needed. I gripped his wrist tightly.

'Don't, Niall. Not here. Not in front of Orla,' I whispered.

Reggie ignored his warning anyway. He slowly removed his sunglasses and strolled in with a lazy arrogance like he owned the place. He saw himself as a gentleman, but the grease under his fingernails and his ruddy face told another story. It was lined from years of smoking and drinking, and dodgy dealing. I detested the man. He made my skin crawl.

'Easy now, tiger,' Reggie said, his cockney voice smooth and mocking. 'I'm not here to cause trouble. I come in peace. I'm just paying my respects, that's all. Thought I'd raise a glass to the dearly departed.'

'That's never going to happen. Now piss off back to whatever sewer you crawled out of. You've said your bit.' Niall's voice was unwavering.

Reggie's smile faltered just a little before his smirk came back stronger than ever. The corners of his mouth curled as his eyes scanned the room. The crowd bristled. Men stood tall. Women pulled their children closer. Tension coiled around the group, building with intensity, waiting for somebody to snap. Reggie's gaze eventually landed on me as I knew it would.

'Oh, there you are, Josie.'

Reggie's eyes never left mine as he walked towards

me. People stepped aside like reeds parting in the wind to let him pass. As he drew closer, the unmistakable smell of Old Spice wafted up my nostrils. My stomach somersaulted in response.

'I wanted to offer my condolences.' Reggie smiled. 'It's a great turnout.'

His voice was loud and casual, like he was walking into a club instead of a wake. I would have loved to have slapped him around the face, but maintaining my composure sent a more powerful message than lashing out at him ever would.

'It's a shame it had to come to this, but Sean brought this on himself, sweetheart. Your man knew the rules. He chose to break them. He crossed a line and got too big for his boots, but maybe, just maybe, your lot will learn from this and know their place,' Reggie said, his eyes scanning the room again.

Orla let out a sudden sob. The sound was unexpected. Raw and sharp. I held my daughter tighter in my arms.

'Haven't you done enough? You didn't need to come here to gloat!' Niall hissed, his fists clenched as he glared at Reggie.

Bennett took a step closer, and Orla buried her face into my side as her fingers twisted the fabric of my dress.

'Don't get any ideas, Niall. The war's over. Sean lost. You'll only make things worse for yourself by getting out of line.'

I glanced over at Reggie's men. Pete had his right hand inside his coat while the fingers of his left one were twitching. That wasn't a good sign. This was a volatile situation. Emotions were running high. The last thing I wanted was for more bloodshed at Sean's send-off, so I peeled Orla away from me and stood up. My hands were shaking, but my voice was as clear as cut glass.

'That's enough! Get out!' I shouted. My frustration over the way these men kept fighting, today of all days, had got the better of me.

My response was brief and to the point. I wouldn't waste any more words on Reggie.

My knees were knocking together as I faced him. I was terrified of him, so I had to channel every inch of strength within me. I didn't want things to escalate. Enough lives had been lost.

'Shut up and sit down, you stupid bitch. We'll go when we're good and ready. You don't get to call the shots,' Pete roared back.

Reggie raised a hand to silence him.

'I was about to leave anyway,' he replied. Then he turned slowly and paused beside Niall, squaring up to him. Their bodies were inches apart. The tension between them was palpable.

'Unless you want to end up like your brother, I suggest you stay out of my way,' Reggie said.

Niall didn't reply. He just stared at his enemy as though Bennett was the devil himself. He kept his jaw tight as his chest rose and fell.

Reggie paused by the back entrance and cast his eyes around the room before he delivered his warning.

'Things around here are about to change. Kilburn doesn't belong to Sean any more. I'm the one in control now.' Reggie's voice rang out, low and clear for all to hear. The sound of glass shattering behind him cut through the room like a gunshot. Niall had thrown his glass in a fit of temper. It had landed inches from Bennett's head, but he didn't flinch.

'You'll be sorry you did that, O'Connor,' Reggie growled.

I muttered a silent prayer to the Almighty. Pistol Pete was armed, and he was a dangerous man with a weapon. He wouldn't need to be asked twice. He'd happily blow Niall's brains out. He was giving off that nervous, cornered-dog energy. He was fidgety. Twitchy. It was never a good idea to upset a man with an unpredictable trigger finger.

Reggie stood glaring at Niall for the longest moment, then he turned and walked away, leaving the door to slam shut. Pete and Freddie scuttled out behind him.

Silence followed their exit for a couple of beats, and then hushed murmurs swept around the room. I collapsed into my chair and scooped Orla into my arms. The tears I'd been holding back spilt down my cheeks. Reggie wasn't content with taking Sean's life; he wanted revenge. Despite what he'd said, instead of ending the war, the fire Sean had started had ignited the next chapter.

'As if I'm going to let Bennett take over,' Niall said with bitterness coating his words. A muscle moved in his jaw. He opened his mouth to release the spasm and raised his glass again. 'To Sean, and the legacy he built!'

'To Sean!' the crowd echoed.

The music resumed, but the fiddler had lost his spark. The atmosphere in the room had shifted. The air was still heavy with grief, but now rage was simmering just under the surface. The day couldn't be over soon enough for my liking. Sean's death had left behind a gaping hole I had no idea how to fill apart from with rage.

44

REGGIE

Freddie, Pete and I were wandering around looking for a place to while away time when I heard the sound of music playing. I stopped outside the club in Soho near the remains of The Velvet Ace. It seemed a fitting place for me and the lads to drown our sorrows. I'd never been inside the venue before. Why would I? It was within spitting distance of my own gaff, but thanks to Sean and Niall, I needed to find an alternative place to drink.

The club was called The Phoenix, which felt like a prophecy. A sign. I promised myself as I stood on the rain-slicked street that if it took me until my dying day, I would rebuild my beloved casino. In time, she'd rise from the ashes and be the beating heart of Soho again.

I pushed open the door and immediately liked what I saw. No chaos. No shouting. No riff-raff. Just a smooth rhythm coming from the corner stage. Warm lighting, clinking glasses and velvet booths. It was classy with the faintest undercurrent of danger wrapped in elegance. The kind of smoke-hazed place where the bartender didn't ask questions as long as you tipped him.

My shoes sank into the plush carpet as I walked to the bar. The floor covering softened footsteps, soaked up secrets and screamed money. I ordered a bottle of brandy with three glasses, and Freddie carried them up the stairs to a quiet area where we could talk without being overheard.

I poured myself a stiff measure, and while Freddie and Pete made themselves comfortable, I stood on the balcony above the main floor, one hand resting on the brass railing, the glass gripped in the other, drinking in the atmosphere.

The Phoenix reminded me of how The Velvet Ace had been in its heyday. Low light spilt from ornate art deco chandeliers as cigarette smoke curled lazily towards the ceiling fans. Conversations blended with the hum of the jazz band. The lounge singer wearing a black sequin bell-sleeved dress and wedge-heeled shoes like skyscrapers had a voice so smooth it could stop fights and start affairs.

A wave of bitterness washed over me. Being here was like a slap in the face. A harsh reminder of what I'd lost. The Velvet Ace hadn't just been a casino. She used to breathe like she had lungs of her own. She was a sanctuary. A safe haven. No weapons past the door. My bouncers saw to that. The card tables hummed, dice clattered and waitresses glided like dancers. She was an oasis in a city that never slept. An addiction for some.

People came from London and beyond, lured by the hope that fate could be fair. That the house didn't always clean up. But it did. A winning streak was just an optical illusion designed to lull a punter into a false sense of security so they'd place larger bets and make reckless decisions after kissing their partner for luck as though that would influence the outcome.

The Velvet Ace had been a gold mine. Losing her had hit me hard. But it wasn't just the money. She was my life. My one true love. Sean's stunt couldn't go un-punished. He'd thought he could topple me from my throne. He'd done damage, but he should've finished the job. Because now I'd make sure every person who meant anything to the bastard would suffer at my hands.

I'd ignored the stares and murmurs of disapproval when I'd stepped uninvited into Sean's wake. The O'-Connors knew I wasn't there to mourn. I was there to make a point. They'd done their best to make a stand. Their best wasn't good enough.

'Are you all right, Reg? You're very quiet.'

The sound of Freddie's booming voice brought me back to reality. I tore my eyes away from the singer and fixed them on him. The big oaf was standing next to me, staring at me with a concerned look pasted on his ugly mug. I'd been on the verge of giving him his marching orders after he'd told Sean where I was holding Orla, but he'd redeemed himself when he'd fired the fatal bullets that had ended O'Connor's life.

'I was just thinking about the casino. This place reminds me of it.'

'We can go somewhere else if it's upsetting you,' Freddie offered.

My jaw flexed. I didn't answer him because my thoughts had drifted back to my memories again. The Velvet Ace hadn't just been bricks and mortar. She'd been my world. My home. My family. The O'Connors had made it personal when they'd burned her to the ground.

I turned away from Freddie and went to join Pete in the booth half-shadowed by an enormous plant. The cheeky fucker had made a huge dent in the bottle of brandy I'd paid for, so I picked it up and swung it in front of his face to make the point. He had the good sense to look embarrassed.

'Sorry, Reg, I got a bit carried away, but I thought we were celebrating Sean's downfall,' he said.

Then he took his cigarettes out of his pocket and lit one. The flame of the match briefly illuminated the scar beneath his left eye, which he'd got in a pub brawl when he was a lad.

I ran my thumb around the rim of my glass. I didn't blame Pete for raising a glass to Sean being six feet under. I would have joined in if bitterness hadn't been eating me alive. Rage and hatred were still burning inside me even though the fire was out. I had a thirst for revenge.

'Do you know what's fucking me off?'

Pete shook his head. Freddie gave me a gormless look. Nobody was around to overhear what I was about to say, but I leaned towards them anyway.

'Sean's family are still living and breathing,' I said. My voice was low and full of menace.

Pete gave me a knowing look and then took a long drag from his cigarette. The end flared orange like a dying star. Freddie stayed silent, taking in what I'd just said.

'I built The Velvet Ace up brick by brick. Ran the tables myself the first year...'

'I know you did, Reg.' Freddie gave me a compassionate smile, but I didn't want his sympathy. I wanted my business back.

'Do you know what I'm missing the most?' I quizzed.

'No,' Freddie replied.

'The hum. Not from the machines, but the buzz of the place. The room used to come alive when punters were there. The sound of cards shuffling. Dice hitting the felt. Laughter over the clink of glasses. The tension in the air as the ball raced around the roulette wheel. I miss the lot...'

The words died on my tongue as my hand curled into a fist.

'The O'Connors didn't just burn down my building. They tried to finish me off as well. Finish all of us off. We're lucky we escaped with our lives!'

My voice was louder now, powered by pent-up rage.

'And because of that, I'm going to make Sean's lot pay ten times over. Anyone with even the faintest connection to the O'Connors is in my sights. Before you go all noble on me, I don't care what you think, Fred, women and children aren't out of bounds.'

I picked up my glass and tossed back the brandy in one go. Freddie swallowed hard as the gravity of what I'd said registered. He'd made it clear how he felt about kids being used as pawns. But he didn't make the rules. I did! If he had a problem with following orders, I'd show him the door.

45

JOSIE

I stood in the doorway for a moment longer than I meant to, staring down the hallway like I was facing a cornered dog threatening to bite me. The air inside the house was still, too still, like it had been holding its breath since Sean left that day.

'What's wrong, Mummy?' Orla asked, sensing my unease.

I turned and looked down at her with a painted smile on my face as she clung to the back of my coat.

'Nothing, pet,' I replied, trying to make my voice light and cheery.

We stepped inside. The click of our shoes on the floor echoed loudly around us. The sound was hollow, empty, like the house was reminding us that somebody was missing. Sean's presence was embedded in the walls, so his loss felt huge.

My stomach lurched as I prepared to walk past the photos in the hallway. I didn't look at them. I knew them by heart anyway. I loved the one of us at the beach. Sean's arm was snaked around my waist as I held Orla in my arms. Our smiles were carefree because we'd had no idea what lay ahead for our family. We'd thought we had all the time in the world.

I glanced at Orla. She was jaded. Dark circles nestled under her eyes, and she was as white as a sheet. It was well past her bedtime. The stress of the day had taken its toll on her.

'Would you like a nice mug of cocoa before you go to bed?' I asked, and then I made my way into the kitchen.

I didn't need to wait for Orla's reply. I knew what she was going to say. It was part of her bedtime ritual, although she'd have to skip her bath tonight or she wouldn't get to sleep until the early hours of the morning. Hopefully, the warm milky drink would help to relax her body and calm her mind. She looked like she had the weight of the world resting on her slender shoulders.

Once Orla had drifted off, I sat alone in the kitchen as the rain tapped the windowpanes like impatient fingers. It felt strange being back in the marital home without Sean. The silence wasn't peaceful. It was loud. Crushing. It taunted me as I imagined every word Sean had left unsaid. The quiet reminded me of every fight we hadn't finished. We'd argued about anything and everything over the years. Our relationship had been volatile.

We'd regularly fallen out because Sean would stay out late while I waited at home, worrying myself sick. Because he'd refused to give up bare-knuckle fighting. Because he'd insisted on making a living from smuggling whiskey. The list went on. But the row that had left the biggest mark on me was the one we'd had about the barmaid. I hadn't pressed him on what was really going on between them for obvious reasons. I was scared to hear the answer.

She hadn't been his only indiscretion, but she'd been the most hurtful because I'd witnessed the betrayal with my own eyes. The recollection stung, so I pushed it out of my head. I didn't want to taint the memory of my husband by thinking about his infidelity. For all his lies, for all his faults, Sean had filled this house with joy. His voice. His laughter. His chaos. And now? Only emptiness remained. A hollow shell. A feeling of loneliness suddenly wrapped itself around me. I was here with nothing but his ghost.

The wake had left me wrung out. Reggie and Declan's appearance at Sean's sending-off haunted my every thought. Having his enemies invade our privacy was unforgivable. It only added to the stress.

Dwelling on it was getting me nowhere. I needed to sleep, so I reluctantly climbed the stairs. I paused in the doorway for a moment before I went to sit on the edge of the bed Sean and I used to share. I ran my fingers over his side of the mattress, tracing it like a scar. Then I reached over and picked up his lighter from the nightstand. The silver was worn, but his initials engraved on one side were still clear. I flicked it open, sparked the flame, and watched it dance for a moment before I snapped it closed.

'How could you do this to me? How could you leave me like this?'

The emotional turmoil was overwhelming. Tears started rolling down my cheeks again. Mine and Orla's future was uncertain. I wasn't sure what to do for the best. Time wasn't on my side. Reggie and Declan were going to close in on me if I let them. I felt uneasy with the way Sean made a living. But if I lost everything he'd built up, I'd feel disloyal. I prayed for clarity and some divine intervention. Hopefully, my path would seem clearer after a good night's rest.

46

DECLAN

The rain hadn't eased in the slightest. It had been tapping rhythmically against the windows of The Black Harp for hours now as though London was in mourning. Word had reached me that Reggie had gatecrashed Sean's wake. A move that had taken me by surprise, as he was the reason the big man was lying in the box in the first place. It was the height of disrespect. I lit a cigarette and exhaled slowly as I considered my next move. I was in my usual spot at the head of the table. Fergal sat opposite me, nursing a half-drunk pint of Guinness.

'Bennett walked into that wake to send a message. I didn't expect him to show up, not like that. Taunting the widow and kid,' I said.

'The bastard's got no soul,' Fergal muttered.

'Reggie crossed a line doing that,' Aidan agreed. He was leaning against the fireplace, staring into the flames as though they held all the answers.

'We can't ignore it,' I replied, flicking ash into the overflowing tray.

'But this isn't our war. We'd be stupid to get involved,' Fergal added.

'Sean kept Kilburn under control because people respected him. They feared him at times, but they trusted him. That kind of power has to be earned. We need to strike now and claim O'Connor's turf before Reggie makes a move.'

'What if Sean's men don't want to switch sides?' Fergal asked.

'You saw the look on Josie's face when we turned up at the cemetery. Do you really think she's going to roll over and let you take what's rightfully hers? I think you're underestimating her. She might be small and slight, but she's colder than Sean ever was,' Aidan said before I had a chance to reply.

'He's got a point, Dec. She's grieving. She's vulnerable. And that combination makes her unpredictable,' Fergal continued.

I couldn't get a word in, so I took a long drag. The

end of my cigarette glowed as I inhaled the smoke, mulling over what they'd just said.

'Then we'll make her an offer she can't refuse. Offer to keep her safe. Keep the girl safe. Reggie's not finished with them. Not by a long shot, and Niall's going to be no use to her. He's a waste of space. If we position ourselves as protectors, she'll have no option but to accept our help.' I stubbed out my cigarette and stood up. 'No more waiting. Tomorrow, we'll bring Paddy in and find out which men are still loyal to the O'Connors.'

'Why not bring him in tonight?' Fergal suggested.

He was right. There was no point delaying. Reggie turning up at the wake had shaken the balance. There'd been a shift in power. He was sending a warning. If I didn't get there first, Reggie would. I also needed to move in on Sean's empire before the O'-Connors had time to regroup and find their feet.

* * *

Aidan, Fergal and myself sat around the table deep in thought as we waited for Paddy to arrive. My cigarette smoke curled towards the rafters like ghostly forms. Patience wasn't Aidan's strong suit. He leapt out of his chair and started pacing, but his eyes never left the door.

'You took your own sweet time,' I said when two of my guys manhandled Paddy through the heavy oak door.

They stood like shadows in front of me. Paddy's slight frame was sandwiched between the big lumps.

'Sorry, boss. We got here as quickly as we could, but it's a fair distance to Kilburn High Road from here,' one of my men replied.

I knew it would take them the best part of an hour each way, and that didn't include rousing a pissed-up Paddy from his bed above the betting shop, but that didn't stop me from commenting. Nobody liked being kept waiting.

'Take a seat,' I said, gesturing to the empty chair beside me.

Paddy didn't sit down. He eyed me suspiciously as he swayed slightly back and forth. He looked the worse for wear. His blue eyes were bloodshot and his grey hair was dishevelled. I'd say he'd drunk the pub dry before he'd staggered home from Sean's wake.

'As you're Sean's highest-ranking man, I wanted to discuss some business with you,' I began, going in softly.

'If you're asking me to turn on Josie and Niall, I

can tell you now that's not going to happen,' Paddy slurred.

He might have been drunk, but he still had his wits about him. He wasn't going to be a pushover.

'I'm taking control of the smuggling routes. If I don't step in, Sean's business will go down the pan now that he's not around to run it. It's time the O'Connors took a back seat anyway. There's only room for one family in this game,' I said, leaning into Paddy's wrinkled face.

'Josie will never let you take anything that belonged to Sean.' Paddy's voice rose.

I let out a laugh, then inhaled a long drag from my cigarette before blowing the smoke into Paddy's face. He started coughing and spluttering. His lungs clearly weren't what they used to be when he was in the prime of his life.

'Is that right? Well, let me tell you something. Josie's no match for the likes of us. Is she, lads?'

My eyes scanned the room and rested on each of my crew in turn. All of them were wearing amused expressions.

'As you can see, none of us are exactly quaking in our boots at the thought of the grieving widow being on the war path armed with her wooden spoon,' I scoffed.

Paddy took offence and seemed to sober up instantly.

'Sean never bowed to scum like you and neither will Josie.' Paddy's expression darkened as he jabbed a gnarled finger in my face.

He was either buoyed up by the alcohol flooding his system, or he was on a death wish. Either way, I wasn't going to let him speak to me like that!

I slammed my fist into Paddy's face, sending him staggering backwards as blood spurted from his nose.

'Watch that tongue of yours, old man. Your loyalty will be your downfall if you're not careful,' I hissed.

Paddy stared at me with eyes like saucers. Then he pushed himself up to his full standing height of five foot six and squared up to me with a defiant look on his face.

'So be it. I'd rather that than sell my soul.' Paddy's words were coated in venom.

I rolled up my sleeves, exposing my forearms that were knotted with tension, before I turned to Fergal and Aidan. It was time to unleash some of my pent-up anger.

'Strap him down,' I said.

Paddy made a break for the door, but the pip-squeak didn't get far before he was dragged back and bound to a chair. He glared at me as I lit another cigarette and took a long pull on it to make sure the tip was glowing. He started bucking like a mule and screaming in agony when I ground it out on the side of his neck. The smell of burning flesh wafted into the room.

'You fucking bastard,' Paddy yelled before he spat at me.

I put the cigarette down in the ashtray and unfastened my belt. I ran my fingers over the heavy metal buckle as I paced the room in slow, deliberate steps. Then I walked over to where Paddy sat tied to a chair with blood dripping onto his shirt from his injured nose.

'So I'm a bastard, am I?'

I waited a beat, but Paddy didn't reply, so I swung back my arm and hit him around the side of the head with the buckle. The sound of crunching, teeth or bone, or maybe both, filled the air. Paddy didn't protest. His breathing had become laboured, and his left eye had swollen up.

'You shouldn't have been so quick to pick sides,' I said. My voice was ice-cold.

Paddy spat blood and something white onto the floor, which looked very much like a couple of broken teeth.

'You can beat me until I'm black and blue, but I'm not turning on Josie. Not for you. Not for anyone.'

'That's a shame. I think it's time you had a lesson in what happens to traitors.'

Paddy was brave, I'd give him that, but he was also foolish if he thought I wouldn't take things further. I was just getting started. I stared at him. My jaw was flexing. Then I gave Fergal a small nod. He walked over to a table by the door and picked up a length of pipe. Paddy's eyes widened when he saw it.

'String him up, lads,' I ordered the two guys who'd brought him here.

They untied Paddy, pulled him out of the chair and dragged him towards the far wall as he wriggled like an eel. But he was small and slight, so he was no match for my guys. They secured his arms to a hook in the corner of the room reserved for this purpose, ensuring the tips of his boots barely touched the floor.

The room echoed with the clang of steel and the low whimper of pain as Fergal got to work on him. The first swing cracked against Paddy's ribs. A muffled grunt escaped from his throat. Fergal didn't stop. He struck him with another blow, lower this time, and caught him straight in the gut. Paddy jerked on the chain and tried to curl in on himself.

'It didn't need to come to this,' I said. My voice was

low. Threatening. 'You brought this hiding on yourself.'

Fergal circled behind Paddy and brought the pipe down hard across his back. A loud thud echoed through the room, and the old man cried out in pain.

I stood a few feet back, calm and composed, watching Paddy's face contort.

'How's the loyalty now? Still unwavering?' I goaded.

'F-fuck you...' Paddy's voice trailed off.

His shirt was torn into slivers. Through the gaps, I could see that patches of his skin were already showing bruises. Blood trickled from a cut on his lip and a gash above his eyebrow. I put my hand up to stop the beating.

'Are you sure I can't tempt you to join the Kellys?' I asked with a smile on my face.

'I'd rather die than agree to that,' Paddy croaked.

'Be careful what you wish for.'

I narrowed my eyes and glared at him. He was a defiant bastard. Proper old school, made of grit and steel. Young lads could learn a thing or two from him. I admired his fighting spirit and would love to have him join my crew. But if I couldn't have him, nobody would. By the time I'd finished with him, he'd be no good to the O'Connors either. Being stubborn would get him nowhere.

'Carry on,' I instructed.

Fergal stepped in front of Paddy, brought the pipe up level with his shoulder and slammed it into Paddy's knee. Sean's man let out a blood-curdling scream. Fergal's expression didn't flicker when he obliterated the second knee. After the other blow, more screaming followed. Paddy collapsed in the restraints. Broken. Sobbing. His legs hung below him, useless, both of them shattered beyond repair.

I stepped in close and gripped Paddy's chin with my fingers.

'Now be a good boy and deliver a message, yeah? You tell Josie this is what happens to anyone who tries to stand in my way.'

Paddy was never going to turn. He was too close to Sean. Too close to Josie. He'd made his choice, so I'd made mine. At best, he'd be left with a limp, but he was lucky I'd spared his life after the cheek he'd given me.

The assault on him had been savage. It had needed to be. It had to send shock waves through O'-Connor's crew. Brutality and instilling fear were tools I used to control. After word got around, anyone still loyal to Sean would wish they'd been buried with him.

47

JOSIE

I couldn't sleep. The bed felt too empty without Sean, and I'd been tossing and turning for hours. My mind whirred as I tormented myself, wondering if I could have done something to change the course of events and prevent his death. I was worried that my nagging had caused this situation, even though my concern had come from a good place. Had I driven him away? Had I driven him to stay out late and be reckless? Had I driven him into the arms of other women?

Every time I'd tried to drift off, waves of guilt washed over me. I couldn't stand lying awake any longer, so I went down to the kitchen and made myself a cup of tea. I was staring out at the deserted street, wishing things hadn't turned out this way, when a sob escaped from my lips. I shook the thought from my head and took a sip of my lukewarm brew. I heard faint sirens howling in the distance, so I instinctively pulled back the net curtain. The emergency services were a long way from here. I wasn't going to be able to see what they were responding to, but I did it anyway. I got the shock of my life when a Ford Capri stopped outside my house. I let the curtain drop and jumped back from the window, relieved that I'd been sitting in the dark. A moment later, the rear passenger door opened, and a man was shoved out. He hit the pavement like a sack of spuds.

My breath caught in my chest when Declan Kelly got out of the driver's seat. He stood next to the man, looking up at my house. I hoped to God he couldn't see me lurking in the shadows. With any luck, he'd presume I was asleep. Most people would be in bed at this unearthly hour of the morning. He casually lit a cigarette as the man lay in the gutter, groaning at his feet. He was in no hurry to leave the scene. It was as though he wanted to be seen. Eventually, he got back behind the wheel, revved the engine loudly for what felt like an eternity, no doubt hoping to disturb half the street, and then drove off, tyres skidding on the wet tarmac.

I only plucked up the courage to lift the curtain

once I was sure the Capri had gone. I peered outside, scanning left and right. There wasn't a soul around apart from the injured man. I knew I had to help him even though I was scared to open the door.

I muttered a silent prayer, then pulled my dressing gown tightly around myself as I crept along the hall, being careful not to make a noise. The last thing I wanted to do was to wake Orla. She'd seen enough violence lately to last her a lifetime and it was obvious the person who'd collapsed at the side of the road was in a bad way.

My fingers hovered over the latch as my hesitance got the better of me, but then I plucked up the courage to open the front door. The chill of the night hit me, and I froze on the doorstep for several seconds until I finally managed to force my slippered feet to walk down my path.

'Oh, dear God,' I gasped.

I covered my mouth with my hand when I realised the injured man was Paddy. His face was barely recognisable. It was bloodied and bruised, and his legs were mangled. They were twisted beneath his body in an unnatural position, bent in ways that shouldn't be possible. I'd never seen anything like it. They had to be broken. I fell to my knees beside him. He had a note pinned to his chest. My heart was hammering and my hands were shaking as I reached forward and gently removed it. I placed it in the pocket of my dressing gown for safekeeping.

'Paddy? Paddy? It's Josie...'

He let out a laboured cough, but when he tried to speak, only blood came out. Tears stabbed my eyes. Poor Paddy. How could Declan do this to an old man? He'd beaten him to a pulp and dumped him like rubbish. His moans were weak, but the fact that he was able to make them gave me a small glimmer of hope.

I sat down on the ground behind Paddy and gently guided his head to my lap. My hands trembled as I cradled him, trying to bring him some comfort.

'You're going to be all right. I'll get help,' I said.

My voice had an undeniable tremor, even though I'd been trying to put on a brave face. I didn't know what to do for the best. If I left Paddy alone in the gutter, he might take his last breath while I was away, but if I didn't call for help soon, it might be too late. He was bleeding heavily. Time wasn't on his side.

A flash of pink drew my eyes towards the house. Orla was standing in the doorway dressed in her Bagpuss nightdress with her teddy tucked under her arm. She stayed silent but stared at me wide-eyed.

'Orla, love, what are you doing up?'

I tried to keep my tone light, but inside I was panicking. My daughter had known Paddy her whole life. He was like a grandfather to her. I didn't want her to see him like this after what happened to Sean. It would be too much for her. She'd already been through enough.

'A noisy car woke me up,' she said, rubbing her eyes with her fist.

That was no big surprise. Orla's room was at the front of the house, and Declan had deliberately made a racket when he'd deposited Paddy outside my door. If the sound of the Capri had woken my daughter, I could guarantee half a dozen of my neighbours had heard it too. And friendly as they were under normal circumstances, they didn't want to get involved, so they'd kept a safe distance, watching from their windows, their net curtains twitching like frightened eyes. I didn't blame them for staying away. They were scared of the repercussions.

'Paddy's had an accident and he needs to go to the hospital. Can you go inside and phone for an ambulance? Do you remember how to do that?'

Orla yawned and then nodded.

'I dial nine, nine, nine...'

When Sean had installed the landline, I'd thought it was a luxury we didn't need. Now I was glad he'd ignored my protests.

'That's right. Good girl. Do you know our address?'

'Yes,' Orla replied over her shoulder.

She'd already turned away and was halfway down the hall. A sense of pride welled up inside me. She was just a little girl, but she was as bright as a button.

* * *

After the ambulance left, I sat at the table with Orla on my lap. She was snuggled into me, jaded, but too traumatised to go back to bed. Her eyes were hollow from not enough sleep. She'd retreated into herself and become very clingy since Sean's death, and this business with Paddy had rattled her further.

It was still dark outside when Niall walked into the kitchen, having let himself in. I'd phoned him once Paddy was on his way to hospital. I'd felt bad waking my brother-in-law, but Declan hadn't just sent a message. He'd declared war when he'd broken an old man's legs and beaten him half to death.

'I came as quickly as I could,' Niall puffed.

His chest was heaving. It was clear he was out of breath and had dressed in a hurry. His dark hair was messy, and his shirt buttons were skewed and only half done up. He seemed shocked to see Orla was up.

'How's my favourite niece?' he asked, flashing her a bright smile.

Orla loved Niall; she'd usually run into his arms, chattering ten to the dozen, but she didn't reply. She turned away from him, hunched her shoulders and burrowed her face into my chest.

'Is she OK?' Niall mouthed.

I shook my head.

Niall pulled out a chair and sank into it. He ran his hand through his mop of dark hair before he pulled a cigarette from the packet Sean had left in the centre of the table and lit it.

'We need to get you both out of here.'

I shook my head. 'No way.'

'Josie?'

'Be a good girl and go back to bed. It's too early for you to be up,' I said, kissing the top of Orla's head.

'But I'm not tired, Mummy.'

'Well, you look exhausted, so I want you to do as you're told. I'll be up in a minute to tuck you in. I just need to talk to Uncle Niall about something important first,' I continued.

Orla knew by the tone of my voice that the matter wasn't up for discussion. She climbed off my lap and headed out of the kitchen without saying another word. When she was halfway up the stairs, I walked over to the door and closed it. I didn't want her to overhear our conversation. I took the note out of my pocket and opened it with trembling fingers as I sat down in the chair.

'This was pinned to Paddy's chest,' I said, waving the dog-eared piece of paper at Niall.

'What does it say?'

'"Kilburn belongs to me. This is the price of loyalty..."'

'Declan's not playing games. What he did to Paddy was meant to crush our resolve and terrify the rest of our men into submission. Kelly made an example of him. Once word gets around, people will be scared, Josie. Really scared. None of our crew will want to be next. You and Orla need to get away from here before it all kicks off,' Niall warned.

'We're not going anywhere. This is our home. It was Sean's home. Declan's trying to scare me, but I won't give him the satisfaction of making me run.'

Sean's murder had left me with two options. Either I walked away from everything my husband built, or I seized control of his empire. But stepping into his shoes, into a world dominated by violence, wouldn't be easy. Sean had been a force to be reckoned with although he could also be charming and persuasive. He had been charismatic, able to command loyalty effortlessly. I was a housewife. A mother. A widow.

'There's no shame in being cautious. Why don't you and Orla go back to Ireland just for a while until things have settled down?'

Sean's death had been a major blow. His loss had hit me hard and forced me to confront my vulnerability. I was torn between the instinct to fight back and the urge to run. The uncertainty of what lay ahead had brought me to the brink, and I'd thought long and hard about doing what Niall had just suggested. But packing up and going back to Kerry wasn't the answer.

Something deep within me had begun to harden. Something was shifting behind my grief. Something Declan hadn't counted on. I was finding my strength. Finding my footing. I was determined to channel my pain into vengeance and justice. I felt compelled to seek retribution against those who were responsible for Sean's death and for Paddy's beating. I wouldn't back down from this. I couldn't. Even though I'd seriously questioned if it was worth continuing a battle that had already cost so much. The desire to fight came from the Irish blood pumping through my veins. I had a warrior's spirit that wasn't easily broken.

I stood up, straightening my posture, and walked

over to the window. I peered out at the deserted street as daylight started to break through, and my eyes settled on the bloodstained tarmac. My breath caught in my chest, so I turned away and went back to my seat, slumping down on it. Silence had settled thick in the room, making the atmosphere between myself and Niall feel tense. I knew he had my best interests at heart, but I wasn't going to be forced into going away. I was a survivor, not a pushover. It was about time the men in this city realised that.

'So what do you think, Josie? Do you want me to make the arrangements for you and Orla?'

'No. Running away won't keep her safe. I'm taking the reins. I won't let everything Sean worked so hard to build up be taken away from us.'

'I can run things, Josie. You don't need to get involved—'

I put my hand up, cutting Niall off mid-flow. 'That won't be necessary.'

Niall leaned forward and kept his voice low. 'If you're hell bent on staying in London and heading the firm, we'll need to prepare. Declan's not our only problem. Reggie's going to make his presence felt, too. He's lost his pride and joy, and he's going to make sure we pay for that. These are dangerous men we're talking about.'

'I know that!' I snapped.

Niall didn't look impressed that I'd been so abrupt, but people stating the obvious and treating me as though I was clueless was grating on my nerves. My brother-in-law suddenly pushed his chair back from the table and stood up. Then he rolled his shoulders and cricked his neck from side to side like a man preparing for a fight.

'I'm sorry you felt the lash of my tongue, but I'm fed up of being underestimated.'

'I get that, but if you want to be taken seriously, you'll have to prove that you're more than just Sean's widow.'

'I fully intend to.' I flashed Niall a look.

Anger bubbled inside me, but it would take more than pent-up rage to face what lay ahead and survive the threats closing in on me.

'There was due to be a handover of whiskey at Down Street station tonight. Paddy was organising it, but he won't be able to now. What do you want me to do? Reschedule it?'

I felt my spirits lift that Niall was letting me take control.

'Why do you always do the handovers in the tunnels? Can't we collect the whiskey from the docks instead?' That seemed the logical thing to do to me.

Niall shook his head.

'Every time we've tried to do that, Hargrove seizes the shipment. He's got eyes everywhere, so some fucker always tips him off and he swoops before we can complete the job. Since Paddy's been loading up the van in dribs and drabs over the course of a few days, we've had no issues. Well, not with the cops anyway. Declan's another story.'

He didn't need to tell me that. His crew tried to ambush the last shipment of whiskey at Down Street while Paddy was handing over the consignment. I didn't know what to do for the best, but it seemed risky to use a location Declan knew about.

'Can't we use a different station? Sean told me there's a labyrinth of underground tunnels beneath London's streets, not just the disused Tube stations. There's the mail rail and the sewer systems as well as utility and maintenance tunnels...'

'Organising a different drop off would take time we don't have, and anyway, a lot of the spaces you're talking about are narrow, dimly lit, and rarely accessed. Sean looked into it at length, Josie, and Down Street was the best fit for our operation. If Declan's got eyes on the cargo, it won't matter where the handover takes place, he'll show up. If you're worried, we can postpone it.'

Worried? I was terrified, but what Niall had said made sense. This was the nature of the work. Another firm let you do all the hard graft getting the whiskey to England, and then they tried to steal it at the last moment.

'So what are you thinking? Should I tell the guys the move's off?' Niall asked when I didn't reply.

'No. We'll go ahead as planned. That will send a message to Declan and Reggie loud and clear that Sean might be gone, but it's business as usual in the O'Connor camp,' I replied, and the corners of my lips lifted into a smile. My life suddenly had purpose, which made me feel alive again.

48

JOSIE

The air was thick with tension in the backroom of Sean's speakeasy. I stood behind the worn oak table with my arms folded tightly across my chest. Niall sat at an angle beside me. One of his boots was resting on the chair rung to the left of him as his eyes scanned the room.

Three of Sean's men were at the opposite end, huddled side by side like the wise monkeys. They were looking at me like I had two heads. It clearly bothered them that a woman had not just joined the ranks, but was giving the orders. I wasn't overjoyed, either, to find myself thrust into the male-dominated world of organised crime, but I wasn't going anywhere, so they'd better get used to me being around.

'Let's get down to business. You all know why you're here. The Down Street run's still going ahead tonight. As you know, Paddy won't be joining us. He's going to be out of action for...' I didn't finish my sentence. I didn't have to.

Silence hung in the room until Niall leaned forward and began to speak.

'While Paddy's recovering, we need someone to step into his shoes and lead the men from the docks to the handover in the tunnels. It needs to be someone tough. Someone smart. Someone Sean trusted.'

Niall looked at each of them in turn, appraising them for the vacancy, but none of them would meet his eye. They were practically squirming in their seats with their heads bowed, hoping not to be picked. They should have been honoured to have been in the running for the prestigious position, not shying away from the opportunity.

Paddy's run-in with Declan had rattled the men, which was understandable; that was the purpose of the beating, but I needed them to show me some loyalty. If they deserted their ranks, the business would crumble. My heart was pounding and my pulse raced. I didn't know how to handle the situation. My thoughts drifted to Sean. He always kept a calm demeanour, even when under pressure. Picturing him in my place helped to steady me momentarily. I'd have to become more ruthless in my approach. I couldn't afford to come across as a soft touch, or they'd walk all over me in their size ten boots. I had to step up to the plate and take charge. Appoint one of them rather than waiting for them to volunteer when it was clear none of them were forthcoming.

My eyes settled on one of the men, Brendan. He was in his mid-thirties. He had a strong jaw and broad shoulders and was a man of few words, but he was steady. Reliable. He'd worked for Sean for years and never once stepped out of line.

'You know the tunnels like the back of your hand,' I said in a determined tone. 'Sean used to say you could walk the rails blindfolded.'

Brendan's eyes darted between myself and Niall as he fidgeted in his seat. He looked uncertain.

'It's not the tunnels I'm worried about, Josie. Things have changed...'

'So what are you saying? Are you in or are you out?' I kept my voice level.

'Talk about putting me on the spot,' he replied, shaking his head from side to side without answering my questions.

'Come on, Brendan. We haven't got all night. Time waits for no man,' Niall threw in.

'Jesus, Niall. I've got a wife and kids. I can't afford to end up like Paddy.'

Brendan's eyes were wide. I could almost smell the terror on his breath. But fear was contagious, and it would spread around the room faster than a virus if I didn't stop it in its tracks and stamp it out.

'That won't happen if we put on a united front. We have to stand together and show Declan we're not scared of him or he'll take over our patch and then you'll all be out of a job,' I warned as my eyes scanned over the three worried faces staring back at me. 'I know you're frightened, but I'm asking you not to sink into the shadows. Otherwise, Paddy's sacrifice will have been in vain. He remained loyal to my family. I'd like to think you'll follow his example and do Sean proud...'

I let my sentence trail off as my emotions started to build. If I broke down in front of the men, any progress I'd made getting through to them would be wasted.

Brendan let out a long sigh. 'OK, I'll do it,' he said, but the reluctance in his voice was as plain as the nose on his face.

'And what about you?' I asked the other two men, glancing at them in turn. A long pause stretched out between us.

'For fuck's sake, lads, we haven't got all night. We've got whiskey that needs shifting,' Niall said to hurry them along.

'I'm disappointed you thought so little of my husband. He was always good to you,' I added, piling on the pressure. I'd chosen my words, hoping to appeal to their better nature. I was glad I'd resorted to the guilt trip when they both agreed to stay on board. I hadn't won the men over with a landslide victory. But it was a start. Josephine O'Connor was the new head of the operation, whether they liked it or not.

'So here's what's going to happen. There'll be two lookouts at the docks and a backup vehicle tailing the three of you. Keep your wits about you. If anything smells off, abandon the move. No heroics,' Niall said, running through the plan without wasting another second.

'Any questions?' I asked.

The three men shook their heads, and I gave them the faintest smile.

'You can go now. We'll see you tonight at Down Street station.'

My voice was calm and poised, but my insides were churning like a washing machine.

49

JOSIE

The tunnels beneath Down Street station were colder and damper than I'd expected. The dim emergency lights cast eerie shadows along the platform as Niall and I waited for Brendan and the others to arrive. The constant drip of water from a leaking pipe was making me unsettled. Agitated. Although I was trying my best to mask my fear.

The cracked tiles on the walls were covered in graffiti. It was hard to believe the swanky streets of Mayfair were above this gloomy place. There was nothing posh about the underbelly of the abandoned station. The air was dank, and dirt and grime covered everything.

I shuddered when I spotted a huge rat scampering along the tracks. I turned my back on it and faced Niall, who was standing beside me at the mouth of the tunnel. The bricks at the entrance were blackened. The dull gleam of his torch bounced off the old archway and the length of rusted rail as he kept lookout. My heart was galloping in my chest. I was struggling to keep a calm exterior, but I didn't want Niall to think I wasn't up to the job.

'They're late,' I whispered.

I readjusted my grip on Sean's pistol. The weight of it was making my hand throb.

'They'll come,' Niall replied, scanning the shadows. 'Keep your wits about you. If Declan follows them, he won't be empty-handed. Let's get into position.'

My heart beat like a drum, and perspiration broke out above my top lip despite the chill in the air. Niall knelt beside me, holding his revolver tight against his chest. When a low moan of wind swept through the tunnel carrying the scent of decay and something sinister, I almost jumped out of my skin.

I was way out of my comfort zone. Every creak, every rustle, made my senses heighten. The air around us buzzed with static tension. I tensed when the breeze curled around my ankles and lifted the hem of my coat. Niall leaned in front of me and peered into the darkness. His teeth were gritted.

'Did you feel that?'

I nodded. It wasn't just cold. It was more than that. I could tell Niall sensed it too. It was foreboding, like our past troubles were breathing down our necks. Ahead of us, somewhere in the miles of abandoned track and brickwork, a groan echoed like the bones of the station knew what was coming, and it didn't approve. I couldn't help feeling superstitious. I was spooked. And the longer we waited, the worse I was getting. I was on the verge of giving up. I wasn't sure I was cut out for this.

I hunched my shoulders when the wind whipped through the tunnel again, whistling through the old brickwork as dust danced in the torchlight. Niall glanced at me when we heard the echo of footsteps and muffled voices in the distance. It was unsettling knowing we had company.

The disused track stretched for miles, and it was pitch black, so I couldn't see who was approaching, but as the sound drew closer, I could make out the rattle of the wheels. Then I spotted a lantern bobbing, and Brendan came into view. His breath misted in the dark as he pushed the crate-laden trolley through the narrow passage, panting from the weight of the whiskey. Rats scattered from the shadows as the iron wheels squeaked closer.

Just as Brendan was reaching the mouth of the tunnel, a sudden flare of movement from the sidings caught our attention. Moments later, the first shots rang out. Declan came charging towards us, firing wildly, making me flinch. My ears were ringing. One of the bullets sparked off the tunnel wall beside me, sending chunks of brick, mortar and dust flying through the air. I could taste it in my mouth, so I shielded my face in the crook of my arm.

'You should've walked away, Josie!' Declan's voice echoed from the shadows, which sent a shiver down my spine.

I didn't answer him. If I'd have responded, I'd have given away my hiding place, so I stayed quiet while I tried to slow my breathing. Then I uncovered my face and fired twice into the dark. My heart was slamming against my chest, but my hands were steady. One shot struck the wall. The other produced a sharp cry, so it must have hit flesh. Whose flesh the bullet penetrated was a mystery, but it was definitely one of Kelly's crew.

The echoes of barked orders amplified in the narrow chamber. Then the wind howled again, swirling the gunpowder and dust into a choking fog, which clung to my skin and clothes.

'Get down!' Niall bellowed as more shots cracked through the tunnel.

He returned fire. Bursts of orange flashed ahead of us, briefly lighting up a small section of the track. One of Declan's boys screamed and went down, his leg gushing red.

Figures burst from the shadows of the side tunnel with their weapons drawn. Aidan was leading two other men. My heart pounded as I grappled with a mix of fear and adrenaline while trying to suppress my instinct to run. Before the reality of the ambush had time to properly sink in, the darkness exploded with noise. The thunder of gunshots was deafening in the tight space.

Niall fired off rounds next to me, while Brendan tried to run for cover, but he didn't have time to make it to safety. Aidan raised his shotgun and fired repeatedly without hesitation. The blasts struck Brendan in the chest, blowing him backwards. He dropped to the ground and lay motionless as blood flowed out of the gaping holes in his body.

Guilt slapped me around the face and forced me into action. It was time to prove I was more than just a grieving widow. I rose from where I was crouched behind a piece of abandoned machinery like a ghost from the dark and squeezed the trigger of Sean's weapon. My hands were trembling, but my aim was precise. Aidan's head snapped back when the bullet hit him in the throat. It wasn't a clean kill, but a mortal wound. He dropped his shotgun as his legs buckled and he fell to his knees. Blood poured from his mouth and pumped through his fingers as he stared at me in disbelief. I stepped closer and shot him again to end his suffering. I was cold and unflinching as I aimed multiple times at his chest and head. I'd crossed over a line. I was no longer a housewife. I'd just proved myself to be a formidable force.

Declan's distant roar echoed around us. A guttural sound of rage or grief. Probably both. It didn't matter. All that mattered was that his brother was dead, and I was the one who'd pulled the trigger. I dragged myself away from the corpse and went back to my hiding place to reload my weapon.

As I ducked down, I saw Niall aiming at one of Kelly's men, but when he pulled the trigger, nothing happened. He was out of ammo, so he tackled the man to the ground. The two of them grappled in the dirt, grunting and swearing. Niall smashed his pistol across the man's temple, knocking him out cold before scrambling for cover on the opposite side of the tunnel.

I crawled forward in the darkness with one hand

stretched out in front of me, hoping to find my brother-in-law. My fingers trembled when they landed on the cold steel barrel of a shotgun. Declan loomed out of the shadows seconds later, so I squeezed the trigger of Sean's revolver before he had a chance to fire. As he staggered backwards, I shot him again. This time, I hit him square in the chest. He dropped like a stone. His gun skidded down a slope and disappeared onto the tracks. He was still alive; his eyes were wild as I approached him, stepping over Aidan's body.

'You're not taking our whiskey or our business,' I said, with my gun still raised. 'Not now. Not ever.'

Two of Sean's men grabbed Declan's arms and dragged him to his feet.

'And you're not cut out for this,' he growled, spitting at my feet in a show of defiance.

He was being disrespectful and trying to intimidate me, so I stepped closer to him. I wasn't going to let him scare me off. This was war, so there couldn't be any half-measures.

'We'll see about that!' I replied.

Silence descended in the tunnels, broken only by the moaning of the wounded.

50

JOSIE

The abandoned slaughterhouse at the edge of King's Cross reeked of decay and mildew. Iron hooks still dangled from the steel rafters. They swayed slightly in the draught wafting through the broken skylights. The place was eerie with echoes of violence and death, but it was the perfect setting for me to stage my next move. I'd been forced to step into Sean's world and face the dangerous power vacuum his death had created. Declan needed to know I wasn't afraid to strike back.

I stood in the centre of the bloodstained floor with my arms folded across my body and my coat pulled tightly around myself. Declan was slumped in a steel chair, a broken man. His wrists were tied behind his back, his lip was split and one eye was swelling shut. A strip of dried blood traced his temple where Niall had pistol-whipped him.

I inhaled a deep breath to steady my nerves. Then I stepped forward and crouched in front of him, looking him dead in his good eye.

'If I spare your life, there'll be no more talk of taking over my business. Do I make myself clear?'

My voice was low and razor-sharp. He'd wanted to rule Kilburn with fear and have everyone whispering his name. They would, but not in the way he'd imagined.

Declan spat blood at my feet in another show of disrespect, then a smirk tugged at his mouth.

'You wouldn't have the guts to finish me off, Josie.'

Arrogance leaked out of every one of his wounds, which made me bristle. Where was the bravado coming from? The fate of his life lay in my hands, and yet he was still giving me cheek. I was the one in the power seat. I could have ended him right now if I chose to.

'Killing you would be too easy,' I replied, maintaining my composure.

I walked over to where I'd left my bag and pulled out the Polaroid camera. Sean had given it to me last Christmas.

'I think it's time we had a little photoshoot. I want everyone to know exactly what I've put you through.'

I snapped picture after picture of Declan, battered and bruised, showing his hands bound and his blood on the floor.

'Now I want you to really go to town on him, so if he ever feels like torturing an old man again, he'll know what to expect in return,' I said to Sean's men.

I walked out of the slaughterhouse with my head held high, having got justice for Paddy, before I handed the photos to a young runner from the neighbourhood.

'Drop one at every pub in the area. Take the others to what's left of his crew. Make sure it's known he's still breathing, but only because I've let him.'

The runner nodded and disappeared up the alley, his silhouette cutting through the grey. This wasn't just a message. It was a declaration to anyone who might have underestimated me. I wasn't going anywhere. I had no intention of giving up the empire my husband had built from the ground. I wasn't bluffing. The balance of power had tipped. Declan's ambush had failed. He hadn't been able to assert his dominance over me. I'd secured the upper hand through a combination of strategic ruthlessness and calculated public humiliation.

I fully intended to use Declan as leverage. Rather than killing him, I'd keep him alive and let the whispers spread. While he was in my custody, his crew would stew. The absence of the man who gave the orders would bring instability and feed fear and uncertainty. Loyalties would soon drift. Turf lines would crumble. He'd do well to remember that. Rather than the Kellys taking over the O'Connors' business, the tables could easily turn.

Capturing Declan left me in complete control, not just of him, but of the supply routes, the money and the men. I was going to dismantle everything he'd built, bit by bit, unless he agreed to fall into line. This wasn't a victory. This was survival.

51

DECLAN

After beating me to within an inch of my life, Josie's men had dumped me like rubbish outside my pub in Southwark, mirroring what I'd done to Paddy. They'd turfed me out of a car and left me in the gutter, powerless and humiliated, in front of The Black Harp. I'd drifted in and out of consciousness until Fergal and a couple of my guys had discovered me in the early hours of the morning. I must have been there for hours as I was chilled to the bone from the cold and loss of blood. I was lucky to be alive.

'Declan, Declan, can you hear me?' Fergal called, rushing over to where I lay.

I tried to lift my head when I heard his voice, but I was too weak to reply.

'Jesus Christ, he's in a bad way. Help me get him inside the pub, and then one of you go and get the doctor,' Fergal said, taking charge of the situation.

A fresh wave of pain crashed through me when my men hauled me onto my feet and half-carried, half-dragged me inside the pub. They helped me to the nearest chair, and then Fergal went over to the bar. He brought back a bottle of whiskey and a tumbler, filling it as he walked. He lifted it up to my split lips and held it steady so I could gulp down the contents. The liquor burned and soothed at the same time, quickly taking the edge of my agony.

'Josie really did a number on you. But shooting you in the chest wasn't enough for her. She had to take things further. When we saw the photos, we were expecting the worst. I'm surprised she let you go...' Fergal said.

My mouth twitched. I wanted to give him a mouthful for making me feel like a fool, but I couldn't form any words. Rage was welling inside me, and it was sapping all of my strength.

'Don't try to speak,' Fergal instructed, then he poured another whiskey and offered it up to me.

As I held the single malt in my mouth, I considered spitting it in his face, but it was too good to waste, so I swallowed it down and let it numb my senses.

Word would spread like wildfire that Declan Kelly had been shot by Josephine O'Connor and then beaten to a pulp on her orders. That woman had made a laughing stock of me. I never thought the grieving widow had it in her. I'd underestimated her, been fooled by her frailty, but there was nothing weak about the way she'd stepped up to the plate and led her troops into battle.

We'd expected a landslide victory when we'd ambushed the O'Connors at Down Street station. But that wasn't how things had panned out. Now my brother was dead, and my outfit had suffered huge casualties. It was severely fractured and would take time to rebuild, which left the door wide open for Josie to make her mark.

I was going to be out of the game for the foreseeable future. But this story was far from over. If it took me until my dying day, I'd make her pay for what she'd done to my family.

52

REGGIE

The Thames was black and still. Its surface was streaked with oily patches that glinted in the moonlight. Fog clung to the waterline like breath on glass, swallowing the distant lights of the city. Somewhere upriver, a freighter let out a mournful horn that echoed through the night as the water lapped lazily against the pier.

I stood alone beneath the skeletal arm of a rusted crane at the edge of the loading yard with a cigar gripped in my fingers. I'd pulled the wide collar of my camel-coloured coat up against the cold wind as I watched from the shadows.

My shoulders were sagging beneath the weight of stress. I had no muscle with me tonight. No car waiting. I was broke. I didn't trust the banks. I'd kept my fortune hidden inside The Velvet Ace, and all my hard-earned cash had gone up in smoke. I couldn't afford to pay my men's wages now, so their loyalty had evaporated into thin air.

Shipping containers loomed out of the ground, steel giants standing beside me as we waited for Sean's widow to appear. I'd summoned Josie to a meeting. She was late. I was beginning to think she wasn't coming when I heard footsteps approaching, self-assured and unafraid.

Josephine O'Connor stepped out of the fog, flanked by Niall and two of Sean's men. She was wearing a black wool coat with wide lapels that was cinched at her tiny waist. She was expressionless. Her face was set like carved stone.

'I'm surprised you're here. I didn't think you'd have the guts to come yourself,' I said.

'You asked to see me, didn't you?' Josie replied.

The icy wind swept through the yard, dragging the fog with it, so I decided to get straight to the point.

'Declan's a broken man, and my boys are gone. They want their wages, and I've got nothing to give them...' I didn't tell her that half of them were probably already sniffing around her door, looking for a new boss.

Josie's jaw tightened. 'Is that meant to be an apology?'

'No.' I shook my head. Cheeky bitch. Hell would freeze over before she got one of those from me.

'So what are you trying to say?' Josie asked, narrowing her eyes.

'I'm saying you've won, Josie. I've got no fight left in me. I came to offer a truce...'

She stared at me, unmoved, so I looked out across the water, but the fog had blurred everything.

'A truce? How can we have a truce when I haven't got justice for Sean yet? You put him in the ground, Reggie.' Josie's words were laced with venom.

'Now, Josie, you know I wasn't the one who pulled the trigger,' I replied.

'Maybe not, but you gave the order,' she snapped.

Silence stretched out between us, tense and suffocating. I'd taken a risk coming here alone. But I'd had to do something before Josie came for me. I'd had high hopes of taking Kilburn and everything the O'-Connors owned, but I hadn't expected my men to be so fickle and leave me high and dry the minute I had cash flow problems. They knew they'd get what they were owed once I got back on my feet, but that hadn't stopped them from whining about loyalty not paying the bills. Fucking traitors, the lot of them.

'So tell me, do you really want to end the war, or do you just want to buy yourself some time so you can sort yourself out?' Josie laughed bitterly.

She'd hit the nail on the head. I'd thought I was being clever, but she'd seen my plan for what it was. Desperation.

'I should finish you off now. Leave you face down in the river,' Josie said. Her eyes were full of hatred as she glared at me.

'I suppose you could do that. But you're too smart to play dirty. You're in control now. People are watching you. Admiring you. If I suddenly disappear off the face of the earth, they'll start wondering who's next on your list. You'll make people twitchy.'

Another silence stretched out between us. I could see Josie was mulling over what I'd just said.

'You've got one chance, Reggie. You stay away from Kilburn and keep out of my business. If you step out of line, I won't send a warning.' Josie's words were as cold as the tide.

'Understood,' I replied.

I had to stop my lips from stretching into a smile. I couldn't believe she thought I intended to stick to those terms.

'Oh, and one more thing. If you ever come near

my daughter again, you're going to die screaming. I'll personally make sure of that.'

Josie didn't wait for a reply before she disappeared into the fog as silently as she'd come.

I stood alone, staring out at the inky water. Sean's actions had stripped me of everything, and now Josie was the one holding all the cards. But vengeance wasn't just about pulling a trigger. It was also about timing. And I was going to make sure Josie regretted giving me a second chance if it was the last thing I did.

53

JOSIE

London, December 1975

Christmas was just around the corner. But there was no sign of it in our house. There was no tree. No decorations. No excitement. Even Orla wasn't looking forward to her favourite time of year. The only thing on her list, I couldn't give her. She wanted her daddy back. There wasn't a present in the world that would take her suffering away. She barely spoke any more. She woke screaming some nights as her small hands clutched the bedsheets in terror. Her childhood had been stolen from her, and there was nothing I could do about it.

The cost of the tragedy was carved into my face,

my heart, my soul. I caught sight of my reflection in the hall mirror when I came down the stairs from putting Orla to bed and saw a woman I hardly recognised. I was stronger, tougher, but lonelier than I'd ever been, even though Niall was living with us for the time being.

'Is she asleep?' he asked.

He was leaning against the front room doorframe, a bottle of whiskey swinging loosely in one hand.

'Yes.'

Orla was at peace for now. How long that would last was anyone's guess.

I followed my brother-in-law into the room and went to sit on the sofa while Niall walked over to the teak sideboard and took out a couple of crystal tumblers reserved for special occasions. I glanced at the framed photograph of Sean resting on the polished wood. He was so young. So full of life. It was hard to believe he was dead and buried. His blue eyes looked out at me, fixed and frozen. I wondered what he'd think about the way I'd handled things in his absence.

Niall came to sit next to me and poured us both a drink. Then he placed the bottle between us on the coffee table. He sipped away on his whiskey in silence. I left mine on the table. The air was thick with unspoken words. We were both lost in our thoughts. My conscience was drifting through me, haunting me like a ghost. The weight of my sins rested heavily on my shoulders.

'You should've killed them while you had the chance,' Niall said, his voice flat.

Deep down, I knew that I'd probably made a mistake letting Reggie and Declan walk away. But I'd trusted my faith in God and shown some compassion. I'd had every reason to destroy the two of them, but I'd chosen not to.

'You wouldn't let a rat crawl back to the sewer to heal, would you? You'd crush it under your foot. Declan's injured. Reggie's bankrupt. But you let them both go. That's not a strategy. That's sentiment. It's the kind of foolhardy approach that gets men killed.'

Niall's words stung, and I felt tears stab my eyes, so I reached for my drink and gulped half of it down. Then I slowly turned the glass in my hand, watching the light ripple through the amber liquid.

'I couldn't bring myself to do it. They looked broken. They were already suffering. Killing them wouldn't change anything. It wouldn't take the fear out of Orla's eyes. It wouldn't undo what's been done. And more importantly, it wouldn't bring Sean back.'

Niall scoffed and then knocked back the contents of his glass in one swallow.

'Reggie's humiliated, but that won't stop him from plotting his revenge. He's the kind of man who'll come back when you least expect it. Declan too.'

'And I'll be ready for them if that day ever comes, but in the meantime, let's focus on getting Orla through this. She's traumatised, Niall. She needs us to be there for her. To shower her with love and attention. To prioritise her,' I said.

My daughter's welfare was more important than the threat Reggie and Declan posed. We all needed some breathing space from the bloodshed so that we could adjust to life without Sean.

'Kilburn's quiet now. It's the kind of quiet that's unstable and never lasts long. You think you're in control, but trust me, you've got a lot to learn. There's no victory without sacrifice. The fight isn't truly over. Power like this doesn't just sit still. Sooner or later, the wolves will come sniffing around again.'

Niall issued his warning without bothering to respond to what I'd said about Orla.

He didn't need to keep ramming the message home. I knew better than to believe that the truce I'd made with Reggie meant things would stay peaceful. He'd lost his men. His livelihood. He'd want revenge. And Declan's wounds would heal. When they did, there was no doubt in my mind that he'd seek retribution. I'd killed his brother Aidan, but he'd taken Rory's life, so if you asked me, we were even.

'My mother used to say forgiveness isn't weakness. It's power. Real power. Because it allows you to rise above the people who've tried to hurt you.'

'There'll be no talk of forgiveness. Not now two of my brothers are lying in the ground,' Niall said, and his eyes flashed with anger. 'You're too soft sometimes, Josie. People will take advantage of that.'

'I won't let anyone take advantage of me,' I replied with steel in my voice.

A long pause stretched out between us. Then Niall poured us another drink and raised his tumbler in front of me.

'To the ones who've gone before us, and to the ones still standing.'

I clinked my glass against his.

I'd lost my husband, my rock, but through the hardship, I'd gained something else – people's respect. I'd had to transition from housewife to leader in the blink of an eye. But I'd shown the doubters I wasn't just a woman in a man's world. I was the one running it. I wouldn't let Sean's name fade into nothing.

Niall and I had a different approach to running the firm. In time, I was determined to prove myself to him by protecting my family and ruling with a quiet strength that nobody would ever underestimate again. I was no longer a bystander. I'd slain my first monster. But in doing so, I'd become one myself. May God forgive me.

* * *

MORE FROM STEPHANIE HARTE

The next instalment in the O'Connors series is available to order now here:
    https://mybook.to/DublinRogue2BackAd

ACKNOWLEDGEMENTS

Thank you for all your help and suggestions, Emily Ruston. I've thoroughly enjoyed working with you again.

A big thank you to everyone involved in the production of this book, especially Jenna Houston, Wendy Neale, Jennifer Davies, Helen Woodhouse, Colin Thomas, Ben Wilson, Caroline Lennon and Gerard Logan.

Last but by no means least, I'd like to say a special thanks to the readers, reviewers and bloggers. Without you, none of this would be possible. I hope you enjoy the book!

ABOUT THE AUTHOR

Stephanie Harte is the bestselling gang-lit author of crime novels set in London's East End. Stephanie taught beauty workshops at a specialist residential clinic for children with severe eating disorders for ten years. She also previously worked as a Pharmaceutical Buyer for the NHS and an international medical export company. She lives in North West London.

Download your exclusive bonus content from Stephanie Harte here:

Visit Stephanie's website: www.stephanieharte.com

Follow Stephanie on social media here:

facebook.com/stephanieharteauthor

x.com/@StephanieHarte3

instagram.com/stephanieharteauthor

ALSO BY STEPHANIE HARTE

The Kennedy Twins

Double Trouble

Double Dealings

Double Cross

The O'Connors

Dublin Rogue

Boldwood

Boldwood Books is an award-winning fiction publishing company seeking out the best stories from around the world.

Find out more at www.boldwoodbooks.com

Join our reader community for brilliant books, competitions and offers!

Follow us
@BoldwoodBooks
@TheBoldBookClub

Sign up to our weekly deals newsletter

https://bit.ly/BoldwoodBNewsletter